Intoxication

She felt nothing of the cold, under the potent compulsion of the vampire's stare. The murderer turned her face, then bent to her neck and drank. Her head lolled; crescents of white showed beneath her half-lowered lids. After a long moment the vampire lifted his head, his mouth crimsoned, supporting the girl with one arm. The taste of the blood had dizzied him. Never such a maddening flavor, such a surge of heady ecstasy.

He could not help but drink again, and soon ecstasy became a red, raw need, a primitive exultation. It was as if a hole had opened in his mind, a tunnel from which poured a flood of debased, animal desires. The girl fell and he fell atop her, a black humped shape leeched to her spasming body. He tore at her belly, her cheek; he bit and snapped without aim or comprehension of anatomy, ripping away at the fleshy walls imprisoning the bloody narcotic juice. And . . .

Books by Lucius Shepard

Novels
THE GOLDEN
LIFE DURING WARTIME
GREEN EYES

Short Fiction
THE JAGUAR HUNTER
THE ENDS OF THE EARTH

The
GOLDEN

Lucius Shepard

BANTAM BOOKS
NEW YORK • TORONTO • LONDON • SYDNEY • AUCKLAND

THE GOLDEN

A Bantam Book / August 1993

ISBN 0-553-56303-3

Published simultaneously in the United States and Canada

Bantam Books are published by Bantam Books, a division of Bantam Doubleday
Dell Publishing Group, Inc. Its trademark, consisting of the words "Bantam Books"
and the portrayal of a rooster, is Registered in U.S. Patent and Trademark Office
and in other countries. Marca Registrada. Bantam Books, 1540 Broadway, New
York, New York 10036.

PRINTED IN THE UNITED STATES OF AMERICA

OPM   0 9 8 7 6 5 4 3 2 1

For Michael and Mary Rita

I'm very grateful to the following people for their assistance during the making of this book: Jim Turner, Ralph Vicinanza, Chris Lotts, Robert Frazier, Mark and Cindy Ziesing, Arne Fenner, and Jennifer Hershey.

The
GOLDEN

Chapter ONE

The gathering at Castle Banat on the evening of Friday, October 16, 186-, had been more than three centuries in the planning, though only a marginal effort had been directed toward the ceremonial essentials of the affair, its pomp and splendor. No, most of that time and energy had been devoted to the nurturing and blending of certain mortal bloodlines so as to produce that rarest of essences, a vintage of unsurpassing flavor and bouquet: the Golden. Members of the Family had come from every corner of Europe to participate in the Decanting, traveling at night by carriage or train and stopping at country inns during the day. Now, clad in their finest gowns and evening dress, some accompanied by mortal servants, who—though beautiful and well dressed in their own right—seemed by contrast like those drab ponies chosen to lead Thoroughbreds onto a race course, they mingled in the ballroom, a cavernous vault of mossy stones supported by flying buttresses, lit by dozens of silver candelabra, and dominated by a fireplace large enough to roast a bear. Among the gathering were representatives of the de Czege and Valea branches, who were currently em-

1

broiled in a territorial dispute; yet tonight this and other similar disagreements had been set aside and an uneasy truce installed. There was laughter, there was clever conversation, there was dancing, and it looked for all the world as if it were the kings and queens of a hundred nations who had assembled to celebrate some splendid royal function, and not a convocation of vampires.

Yet despite the gaiety of the assemblage, not every conversation was free from bitterness. Standing by a corner of the fireplace, their faces ruddied by the light, two men and a woman were discussing a topic of some controversy: the proposal that the Family bow to the pressures currently being applied by its enemies and relocate to the Far East, where their activities would be more difficult to detect due to the primitive conditions and the forbidding, often unexplored terrain. Championing the proposal was the elder of the men, Roland Agenor, the Founder of the Agenor branch, whose position as the chronicler and historian of the Family gave added weight to his opinions. Tall, patrician, with a luxuriant growth of white hair, he had the bearing of a retired officer or an accomplished athlete come to a graceful maturity. Opposing him in the discussion was the Lady Dolores Cascarin y Ribera, a dark-skinned beauty with waist-length black hair and a predatory voluptuousness of feature. She had become the de facto spokesman for the more reactionary elements of the Family, those who maintained that no quarter be asked or given in the struggle, an attitude that embodied the Family's traditional disdain toward all mortals. The third member of the group, Michel Beheim, was a lean young man, taller even than Agenor, with curly brown hair and remarkable large dark eyes that lent his face an almost feminine delicacy and ardor and supported the impression that he was always on the verge of bursting forth with some heated opinion . . . though at the moment he felt entirely at sea. As Agenor's protégé he was compelled to lend his support to the historian, yet being among the newest—and thus the weakest—of the Family's initiates, having received his blood judgment less than two years previously, he could not help but be swayed by Lady Dolores's beauty and passion, by the flamboyant and seductive potency of the tradition whose spirit she expressed. He found himself nodding by reflex at her telling points and staring at the dusky swell of her breasts, at the cruel, ripe curves of her mouth, and imagined the two of them together in a variety of erotic postures. So distracted was he by her physical presence that when Agenor extorted him to respond to one of the lady's assertions, he was forced to admit that he had lost track of her argument.

Agenor regarded him with disfavor, and Lady Dolores laughed contemptuously. "I doubt he would have anything of consequence to offer, Roland," she said.

"Your pardon—" Beheim began, but Agenor cut him off.

"My young friend may be new to us," he said, "but let me assure you, he is most astute. Did you know that prior to his judgment he achieved the position of chief of detectives in the Paris police? The youngest, I believe, ever to reach such heights."

Lady Dolores made a deferential gesture. "Nothing in a policeman's experience can have the least bearing upon the subject of our debate."

This time it was Beheim who cut off Agenor when he began to speak.

"With respect, my lady, it demands neither a wealth of experience nor any great art of reason to deduce that changes are in the offing. For the world . . . *and* for the Family. To espouse a doctrine of death before dishonor is scarcely wise, especially when one considers that by doing so one forfeits all further opportunities for honorable accomplishment."

"You do not yet hear the song of your blood," said Lady Dolores. "That much is apparent."

"Oh, but I do!" Beheim returned, though uncertain whether she was referring to something actual or merely waxing metaphorical. "And your arguments have gone far in enlisting my pride, my sense of honor. But pride and honor, too, must confront the realities or else they become mere conceits. As you well know, certain medicines have been developed that allow us to forgo the dark sleep and other of the colorful hindrances long attendant upon our condition, and thus we may pass the daylight hours in whatever occupation we favor . . . so long as we keep from the light. And the time draws near when our men of science, perhaps one who even now labors in my lord's service"—he nodded to Agenor—"will devise a means by which we may walk abroad in the day. This is an inevitability. And with that change, must not everything about us change? I think so. We will be forced to redefine our role in the affairs of the world. I suspect we will someday redefine as well our stance toward mortal men and join with them in great enterprises. Perhaps never wholeheartedly, perhaps never openly as regards who and what we are. But at least to some degree."

"The idea of walking about in the daylight does not entice me," said Lady Dolores. "As for joining with mortals in any enterprise other than feeding, I can find no words to express my distaste. Next you will suggest that we seek counsel from the cattle in the fields. That is no less odious a prospect."

"We were all mortal once, lady."

"Spoken like Agenor's man."

"I am my own man," Beheim said sharply. "Should you require proof of this, I will be delighted to supply it."

First anger, then bemusement washed across Lady Dolores's face. "Insolence can be an entertaining quality," she said. "But beware. It will not always find so kindly a reception."

Her eyes, slightly widened and fixed upon Beheim, went a shade darker, a degree more lustrous, seeming both to menace and to offer sexual promise. A thrill passed across the muscles of Beheim's shoulders, and it was as if he had grown suddenly small and feeble, diminished by the focus of a vast disapproving majority; yet he recognized this to be merely a consequence of Lady Dolores's stare. He could feel in it all the weight of her years—two hundred and ninety, so it was said—and the chill potential of her accumulated power. He was helpless before her, like a bird mesmerized by a serpent. Terrified by fate, yet at the same time seduced by it. Her face and form seemed warped, as it might in a watery reflection, and the ballroom itself also looked distorted, areas of darkness expanded, candle flames drawn into flickering, fiery daggers, the entire perspective become that of a fever dream, shadowy avenues leading away between groups of elongated, elegant phantoms who appeared to have stepped out of a nightmare by El Greco. And then, as swiftly as he had been overwhelmed by this feeling, he was free of it, so completely free that he felt for a moment bereft, unsupported, like a child who wakes in the middle of the night to find that he has

kicked off the blankets that have been overheating him
and causing bad dreams.

"What your scenario fails to take into account,"
Lady Dolores said, continuing as if nothing had happened, "is the lustful imprint of our natures, our need
to possess and dominate."

Beheim, still disoriented, had difficulty in marshaling his thoughts, but the goad of Lady Dolores's
haughty expression inspired him to recover.

"I discount nothing," he said. "Nor will I deny my
nature. I am of the Family now and would not wish
this to change. However, I choose to interpret our essential condition in a different light than do you.
Whereas you insist we have been given a license to exert our will howsoever we desire, a license granted by
some anonymous evil pantheon, I submit that we are
afflicted with a disease whose most significant symptoms are a craving for human blood and an extended
life span. We already have some evidence that this is
the case. I'm speaking, of course, of the substance discovered by the Valeas that is manufactured now and
again in mortal blood and appears to be a factor in
permitting a fortunate few to survive a killing bite and
so join with the Family."

"Extended life span," she repeated. "Now there's
a meager term with which to describe immortality."

"You know far more of the Mysteries than I, lady.
Yet even you must admit there are doubts regarding
the character of this so-called immortality. And therein
lies the importance of modifying your view of our condition. If we are to succeed in achieving true immortality and avoiding the grotesque metamorphoses that
the centuries bring, we must treat the disease in hopes
of ameliorating its long-term effects. If we continue to
think of ourselves as grand, erratic masters of the

night, volatile lords and ladies who, for all their power and dramatic fever, are tragic, doomed, then we will remain exactly that. While this may satisfy a theatrical urge for self-destruction, it serves nothing else. In my opinion we are, in our excesses of violence and cruelty, less enacting the dictates of our natures than we are indulging the emotions attendant upon an aberrant mentality. We are no longer mortal—this is true. And I have no desire to regain my mortality. Like you, like all of us, I am in love with this fever. Yet I doubt a slight modification of our behaviors would rob us of our natures."

"You are an infant in these matters," Lady Dolores said. "Though you speak with passion, it's clear you are puppet to your master's thoughts. You may feel something of what I do, but you cannot know the poignancy of those feelings. You have not yet learned the names of the shadows that haunt us."

"Perhaps not. But it might be said that this is because the symptoms of the disease, the perceptual eccentricities and so forth, are not so well developed in me as they are in you." Beheim held up a hand to forestall her response. "We could argue this endlessly, lady. Logic is a facile tool, and we can both contrive of it an architecture of deceit. But such is not my aim. This is a matter of interpretation, and I'm only suggesting that you attempt to understand my point of view for the sake of improving our lot. Certainly you'll agree that holding to traditional views has not won us many battles of late. What harm, then, will it do to consider that there may be another and more promising avenue of possibility?"

Lady Dolores laughed with—Beheim thought— genuine good humor. "With what logical facility you seek to persuade me against the use of facile logic!"

Beheim inclined his head, acknowledging a touch, and was about to press his argument when Agenor glanced at the stairway at the west end of the ballroom, at the massive doors of blackened oak to which it led, and said in a tremulous voice, "She's here," a split second before the doors swung open to reveal the figure of a blond girl in a diaphanous nightdress. As she descended the stair, lifting the hem of her garment away from the stones, she brought with her the familiar scent of mortal blood . . . familiar, yet with a richer, subtler bouquet than any Beheim had ever known. He turned toward her—they all turned—his hunger roused by the delicate actions of that scent. It was so palpable, he imagined it a kind of terrain in which he might wander, a rose garden with a scarlet stream running through it, and the air a numinous golden haze, set swirling by the rhythm of a languorous heartbeat.

The girl made her way among the gathering, all of whom stood stock-still as if under a spell. For a mortal she was very beautiful. Slender and pale, her cornsilk hair done up into a coiffure as convulsed as the bloom of an orchid. The creamy swells of her breasts figured by faint traceries of bluish veins. Her eyes—Beheim saw as she drew near, easing past a lanky, hawkish man and his servant—had a mineral intricacy, the irises almost turquoise in color, flecked with topaz and gold, and her upper lip was fuller than the lower, lending her mouth a sensual petulance. The face of a willful child not wholly confident of her sexuality, apprehending yet not quite understanding the power of her body. Beheim was entranced by the swell of her belly, the vulnerability of her breasts in their chiffon nests, and most pertinently by the allure of her blood. His mouth watered; his fingers hooked. He was trembling, he realized, barely able to restrain himself, and overborne by her proximity, he lowered his eyes. If the bouquet of the Golden's blood could induce such rapturous hunger, he thought, how would it be to taste it?

Once she had passed, he watched her stroll away, walking with an indolent grace such as she might have displayed while taking the air in a park on a summer's day. The lords and ladies of the Family moved aside, creating a channel that would lead her back to the stairs and thence to the chamber where, under the Patriarch's protection, she would spend the night and the morrow. But as she was about to pass from sight she interrupted her casual processional and turned to look at Beheim. With a faltering step, she came a few paces back toward him. Her clasped hands twisted at her waist, and she displayed symptoms of arousal: her lips parted, cheeks flushed. Her stare spurred his hunger to new heights. Against reason, his restraint crumbling, he started forward. Yet before he could reach the girl, a hand caught his shoulder and yanked him back. Furious at being thwarted, he spun about, prepared to strike, but the sight of Agenor's stony face and the force of those luminous black eyes quelled his anger, and he understood what a gross breach of propriety he had committed. As if to second this view, from those standing nearby there arose a surge of whispers and muted laughter. They had been watching him, he realized. All of them. And on spotting the Lady Dolores among the watchers, on registering her triumphant expression, he suspected that she had somehow orchestrated the girl's arousal—perhaps even his own overwrought reaction—in order to humiliate him. Ablaze with shame, he lunged toward her, but once again Agenor hauled him back, clamping a forearm under his chin and holding him with irresistible strength. The laughter, which had grown briefly uproarious, subsided. The silence that replaced it was freighted with tension.

"Let me go," Beheim said. "I'm all right. Let me go."

Reluctantly, it seemed, Agenor released him.

Beheim adjusted the hang of his evening clothes, rumpled during the struggle, and glared with unalloyed hatred at Lady Dolores. For a second she appeared unequal to his stare, uncertainly clouding her face, but she quickly regained her composure.

"Surely you don't wish to challenge me?" she said in a mocking voice.

"What I wish and what I must do in order to conform to tradition are two different matters," said Beheim. "But I swear to you, lady, you'll regret this night."

Several members of the Cascarin branch moved closer to her, ready to take her part, and behind Beheim, others of the Agenor branch assumed a like posture.

"Consider carefully, cousin," Agenor said to Lady Dolores, "whether it would be wise to seek a feud with the Agenors."

After a moment, with an almost imperceptible gesture, the Lady Dolores signaled her supporters to retreat. She favored Agenor with a curt nod, and her skirt belling with the abruptness of her turn, she stalked off to another quarter of the ballroom.

Beheim made to thank his mentor, but before he could speak, Agenor, keeping his eyes fixed on a point above Beheim's head, said quietly, "Return to your apartments."

"Lord, I only—"

"Are you deaf as well as a fool?" Agenor drew a

deep breath. "I selected you for my protégé because I saw in you qualities of temperateness and calculation that I felt would withstand your passage into the Family. Tonight you've proved me as great a fool as you yourself. Now go!"

Beheim remained standing, flustered and ashamed.

"If you do not leave," Agenor said coldly, "I may not be able to contain myself. Do you understand?"

Beheim fell back a step, muttered a stumbling apology, then fled the ballroom, refusing to meet the eyes that followed his erratic course.

If not for the consoling presence of his servant, Giselle, there is no telling what Beheim might have done that night, for as he hurried along the dimly lit corridor that led away from the ballroom, past niches in which hung antique portraits shrouded in dust and shadow, he grew increasingly angry, his mind fired by a vision of bloody vengeance; by the time he reached his apartment—three vast, high-ceilinged rooms in the west tower of the castle—he was in more of a temper to confront the Lady Dolores than to spend the night haunted by the shade of his humiliation. But the sight of Giselle in her nightdress—her light brown hair and slim figure, her exquisite face with its high cheekbones and pouting lips, all so reminiscent of the Golden—renewed his hunger, and though he had fed only days before, without a word of greeting, he pushed her down upon the black silk coverlet of the canopied bed, brushed back the fall of hair from the vein in her neck, and drank deeply, drank in fury and frustration, sublimating his need for revenge, imagining that it was the Lady Dolores's blood upon which he was supping. Had he been a degree more enraged, he might have lost himself in the act and drunk too deeply, but at last, his hunger sated, still dully aroused, he rolled away from Giselle and lay gazing about the room, absorbed by its funereal atmosphere of candles and black velvet chairs and age-worn tapestries and tall windows with bolted iron covers. Beside him, Giselle gave a plaintive sigh, and suddenly aware of her as a living creature, as something more than a source of food, he felt remorse at having treated her so roughly. Not only did he pride himself on his tolerance for mortals, his liberal recognition of them as more than beasts, he felt an especial fondness for Giselle, a curious mixture of paternal feelings and sexual attraction and romantic love, and he recognized that he had acted toward her with the same contempt and carelessness he had so decried in his conversation with Lady Dolores.

He turned on his side and found her watching him soberly. Her pale gray eyes locked onto his, but she remained silent. There was a smear of blood on the swell of her right breast. She shivered when he wiped it away.

"I thought you would judge me," she said. "You drank so fiercely."

"I'm sorry I frightened you."

"I wasn't frightened." She trailed her fingers across the spot on her breast from which he had wiped away the blood, then inspected the tips. "Why do you withhold your judgment? You know how I long for it."

"I fear losing you."

"Perhaps you won't, perhaps you'll have me forever."

"The odds aren't good."

She propped herself up on an elbow. "You know already, don't you? You know I'll fail judgment?"

"No one can know that. It's just that the odds are never good. I've told you so a hundred times."

She fell back, lay staring up into the canopy. "I don't care. I want my chance. If I were with someone else—one of the de Czeges, for instance—they wouldn't deny me."

"If you were with the de Czeges, likely they would slaughter you, whether or not you passed the judgment."

She started to object, but Beheim, growing annoyed, snapped at her, saying, "You cannot possibly apprehend the dangers of the world you wish to enter. But if you insist, if you truly wish it"—he sat up and leaned over her, with one hand planted beside her pillowed head, shadowing her with his body—"I will judge you this minute."

Her face betrayed surprise, then was flooded with the dreamy slackness of desire, and he thought at first that she would accept his offer; but after a moment she averted her eyes and said in an almost inaudible whisper, "I am not so free of fear as I thought."

"Listen," he said, relieved. "There will come a time when judgment must be given, when no other course is open to us. That is the way of it. It will be a thing of the moment, a moment of surrender and invitation and utter commitment when we will risk much together, when you will take the risk of dying, and I the risk of being left without you. It may be that death is visited upon those who fail to wait until they are consumed by the urge to judge and be judged, that certain enabling chemicals are produced by such an urgency. We have so little knowledge about any of this. But be assured, the time *will* come, and then I will judge you . . . not because you have persuaded me, but out of love."

She turned back to him. "You understand why I'm so impatient, don't you? I want you for all the nights. Forever. Living like this, not knowing what will happen . . ."

"Trust me. And trust yourself."

"I'll try." She put an arm about his waist and brought her mouth close to his, warming his face with her breath. "Tell me . . ." She left the command unfinished.

"What is it?"

She shook her head. "It's nothing."

"Surely not."

"I was going to ask you about death."

"I don't follow."

"When you were judged, you passed through death, did you not?"

"Passed through," he said absently, remembering. "Yes, I suppose that's what happened."

"Tell me about it!"

He looked up at the canopy, like a swollen black abdomen hanging overhead. "There's no consolation for you in my knowledge of death."

"How can you say that? You don't—"

"You're hoping I can tell you that death is not an end, that something exists beyond this life, that some ultimate majesty prevails, that souls swim up from the darkness to circle and sing in the light. Well, I can tell you that something does indeed exist beyond life, but you should derive no comfort from it. There are terrors more profound than that of mere extinction."

"What are they?"

"That I am sworn not to reveal."

"Please! I—"

"I cannot! Someday you may learn the Mysteries

for yourself, but until then, you must accept on faith all I've told you."

She lowered her head so that the mass of her hair shrouded his face, her brow resting against his chest, and murmured an endearment. Beheim felt remorse at having used her so, at having removed her from a natural life and seeded in her a desire for things she might never attain.

"I wish you had begged to enter my service," he said. "I wish you had willingly accepted all the attendant risks and hardships."

"I accept them now."

"Yes, but you did not know what would happen in the beginning. If you had, perhaps I could reconcile my affections with the peril in which I have placed you."

"Lord . . ." she began.

"I am not a lord! Far from it."

"You are *my* lord," she said. "I cannot recall who it was fled from you that night in the streets of Montparnasse, but it was not I. That woman hated you, feared you. But she is dead, and I, the living, can only adore you."

These words stung Beheim more painfully than had her entreaties, and he held her tightly, caressing her hair, her waist and flanks. Before long, though this had not been his intent, she responded to his attentions with caresses of her own. She put her lips to his ear and whispered, "I need you tonight, Michel!"

It was neither her eagerness nor the ripeness of her body that inspired him to make love to her, but rather his desire to do the human thing, to keep alive that measure of humanity remaining to him. And once she was naked, once his own clothes had been tossed to the floor, the old compulsions came into play.

Braced above her, looking down at her lovely face, serene with expectancy, at perfect breasts with areola
the color of dried blood, he knew a man's desperate
urgency, and on sinking into her, feeling her hips tilt
and lift in sweet compliance, he knew as well a lover's
portion of mastery and fulfillment. Her lips shaped a
breathless vowel as he went deep, her hands fluttered
about his shoulders. All this familiar, redolent of human loves and dynasties of lust. But as they rocked
and tangled in the black silk bottom of desire, another
sensibility claimed him. His eyes, until that instant
squeezed shut with pleasure, blinked open with the
abruptness of the reanimated. With her sweaty breasts,
her fevered tossing, she appeared now of a lower and
indelicate order, a convulsed thing into which he had
poked a hot stick, a steamy girl-shaped muscle clever
in its movements, yet witless and dull in all else. He
stared at her, trying to penetrate her as palpably with
that stare as he had with his member. Her eyelids fluttered open, her eyes widened, and her lips drew back
from her teeth as if she were going to scream, horrified by what she saw in his face. Galvanized by fear,
she thrashed and heaved, trying—it seemed—to unseat him, but succeeded only in bringing his arousal to
a peak. With his left hand, he clutched her throat, still-
ing her, and with the right, he clamped her buttocks,
grinding her against him. Fear did not empty from her
face, but rather mingled with the dazed symptoms of
a gentler emotion, as if love and fear were old friends
who often met inside her. Her gasps came rapidly, and
her movements, though yet abandoned, grew less desperate, less involved with escape. Completion and terror glazed her eyes. Her legs locked about his waist,
her fingernails raked his back, and Beheim, himself
driven by a complex of emotions, none of them gentle,

cried out in fulminant rage and joy at being over-whelmed once again by this most poignantly mortal of delights, then went rigid with a molten wattage of pleasure and hung motionless above her, his fangs inches from the pale blue vein in her neck, longing to drain her at the very moment she was draining him, trapped between the pull of two potent hungers.

Their breathing slowed, the flush receded from Giselle's face. Beheim rolled out from between her legs and lay on his back, feeling at once uneasy and triumphant.

"Michel?"

He made a noncommittal noise.

"This is how it'll happen, won't it? My judgment. It'll happen when we're making love."

"Perhaps."

"It almost happened just now, didn't it?" she asked after a pause.

"I'm not sure."

He did not want to turn to her, fearful not of what he might see, but of how he might see her, uncertain as to which half of his soul might then be peering out through his eyes.

Giselle pressed against him, her breasts flattening against his arm, the clammy wetness of her thighs making a sticky patch on his hip and causing him an instant's revulsion. "How wonderful!" she said with what struck him as a kind of prurient exaltation. "To have you inside me and to be so near the Mysteries all at the same time."

He was not sure how to take this, being on the one hand appalled by her lack of innocence and on the other delighted by her comprehension of the sickly sweetness of life, the decaying nuances of the intellect and the blood, by her newly awakened connoisseur's delight in the world of the senses. One second he imagined himself as a powerful man-shaped vileness in a black box with iron closures, and the next, as a kindly soul poisoned by an unholy kiss. Full of contrary urges and opinions, weary of ambivalence, of doubts and demons, wanting only to sleep, he rested his eyes on the tapestry draping the far wall. It depicted a deep wood pillared by gnarled trunks and tangled with vines, where pallid indefinite monsters skulked and a stag was running, its head turned back to search the shadows for pursuers. The coarse material appeared for a moment to ripple, to flow across the wall, as if it were fabricated not of thread but of thousands of insects cunningly interlocked and writhing, making it seem that the room was itself in motion, a slow vessel set on an inexorable course, and that the tapestry was a port opening out onto the turbulent process of a dark and unforgiving world.

Chapter TWO

The next evening Beheim received a visit from Roland Agenor. It was a visit he had been dreading, and as the old man settled into a chair beneath an iron-shuttered window, Beheim made as if to offer an intricate apology and explanation for his previous night's behavior, one he had spent more than an hour in preparing. But before he could fully develop the points over which he had labored, Agenor gave a wave of dismissal and said, "A problem has arisen." His eyes were bloodshot, the normally serene planes of his face haggard, and the tiered lines upon his brow were etched more deeply than before.

He smoothed down his shock of white hair, leaned back, crossing his legs, and favored Beheim with a look of concern. "I have done something, my young friend," he said, then dropped his eyes and thereafter was silent for quite some time, as if overborne by recriminations. Finally he went on, saying, "Something that may afford you an opportunity for great influence, but that will place you in equally great peril."

Beheim was perturbed by his mentor's uncharac-

teristic distraction. Looking at him, recalling the night
they had met, his terror at the revelation of Agenor's
true character, succumbing to the bite, the years of
service prior to judgment, how terror had been transformed into respect and love, all this put Giselle's di-
lemma into a nice perspective and, for the moment,
caused Beheim to soften his attitudes toward her . . .
and toward himself. "I have always trusted in your
guidance," he said to Agenor, seeking to encourage
him.

Agenor let out a rueful laugh. "I pray you'll continue to hold to that opinion." He shot his cuffs, drew
a deep breath, and released it forcefully. "I've just
come from an interview with the Patriarch. As I've
said, a problem has arisen, one with which we are ill-
equipped to deal. Or rather, one with which most of us
are ill-equipped to deal. You, however, are qualified in
the extreme to resolve it, and I have suggested as
much to the Patriarch. He has chosen you to direct the
investigation."

"What sort of investigation?" said Beheim, intrigued.

"There's been a murder."

"The devil you say! One of the Family?"

"The Golden."

Beheim was incredulous. "How could this have
happened?"

"That, dear young friend, is the question you
must answer for us all." Agenor stood and walked to
the window, gazed up at the iron shutter as if contemplating a work of art. "There was no guard set on her
room. Such a crime was considered unthinkable. She
did have a companion, of course. An old servant
woman. But there's no sign of her. The Golden was
found two hours ago by the Patriarch's servants. Com-

pletely drained. Mutilated." He gave a sniff—of disgust, Beheim assumed—and said, "I imagine the culprits, whoever they are, had themselves a rare time in the imbibing."

"Why do you say 'culprits'?"

"Simply an assumption. There would be more than enough blood to go around. Especially in the case of such an intoxicating vintage."

"I don't understand."

"The Decanting, for all its surrounding pomp, is not the Holy of Holies it's made out to be. In reality, it's little more than an old-fashioned drunk . . . for those few permitted to drink. Or so I've been told. It might as well be straight whiskey. A chemical agent acts as an intoxicant. Now if you listen to those who've participated in the rite, they'll claim that a mere sip imbues one with powerful insights, just as though it were an Illumination."

"The Golden . . . it, too, induces clairvoyance?"

"No, no! Death by Illumination is our only avenue to the future. Their claim concerning the Golden is simply a justification for debauchery. I admit I have no experience in any of this, but I know the truth of the matter."

"You've never taken part in a Decanting?" Beheim asked in surprise.

"I have enemies who've sought to deny me the honor." Agenor turned from the window. "Now"—his voice broke, and this show of emotion startled Beheim—"I no longer wish to participate. It's a barbarous practice, though there's no real harm done. One virtue of the blood is that the Golden never fails to pass judgment and so becomes part of the Family. However, in this instance, drained as she was, well . . ."

He let the sentence lapse, and then, in a dispirited tone, added, "There's no returning from that."

"Perhaps there is more to the Decanting than you realize," Beheim said. "I don't mean to seem impertinent, but as you've had no experience of it, perhaps . . ."

"I've seen them after they've tasted the Golden," Agenor said. "Believe me, there's nothing transcendent about the experience. On the other hand, I have witnessed numerous Illuminations, and despite the fact that those who undergo the ritual have been condemned for crimes against the Family, there is an inherent nobility to the act. In the surrender of one's life so as to answer questions concerning the future. I believe that the condemned understand this, that they must gain some profound joy from their sacrifice."

While he spoke these words, a distant, almost beatific look came over Agenor's face, as if he were contemplating his own saintly immolation. Once again Beheim was unsettled by the old man's erratic behavior, but he chose to ignore this and concentrate upon the more imminent problem. He took a seat on the edge of the bed, placed his hands flat on his knees, and studied the pattern on the patch of carpet between his feet.

"What are you thinking?" Agenor asked.

"I was wondering why anyone would risk such a crime."

"You of all people should understand the Golden's allure."

Beheim ignored this reminder of his intemperate behavior. "I refuse to believe that anyone would have done this merely for a taste of blood."

"You may be overestimating some of our number. The de Czeges, for example."

"I doubt even the de Czeges are capable of committing a crime with so uncomplicated a motive. Perhaps to make a statement of some sort, perhaps as an act of rebellion. But not for blood alone."

"Well, I won't argue. After all, it's your job to decide the issue." The older man crossed to the bed and rested a hand on Beheim's shoulder. "And you'd best set to it at once. The Patriarch will not be able to hold everyone here for more than a few days."

Beheim nodded, yet felt no enthusiasm for the work, his fascination with the crime dimmed by an intimation of the difficulty of the task before him.

"Perhaps I should not have volunteered you," Agenor said.

"No, no," said Beheim, hastening to reassure him. "I'm—"

Agenor commanded him to silence by holding up a hand. "For the sake of our friendship I should not have volunteered you. It may eventuate that by doing so I have sacrificed you, for you will meet with great danger, and though you have the Patriarch's support, many will perceive your investigation as a gross indignity. And should you unmask the culprits, they will doubtless defend themselves to the death rather than undergo an Illumination. But there is far more at stake here than friendship." He went a few paces into the center of the room and stood facing away from Beheim, hands clasped behind his back. "Should you succeed, you will gain tremendous influence with the Patriarch and those who have his ear. More influence than I could ever bring to bear. It's possible this may be the event that turns the tide of opinion in our favor, that adds the one necessary voice to the chorus of reason so we will be able to guide the Family, to guarantee that it will thrive and consolidate its power.

So"—he wheeled about—"I have done what I have done. But let me assure you, my friend. You do not stand alone. If you fall, I fall with you. I would not put your eternity in jeopardy without sharing the risk."

Beheim felt awkward and enfeebled, fully apprehending now the potential for disaster attaching to the case. "I will try to justify your confidence," he said, but the words sounded empty to his own ears; then, in a shaky voice: "I scarcely know where to begin." He came to his feet and rubbed a finger along his cheek. "With so many suspects, it will be impossible to interview them all in a few days."

"As to that," Agenor said, "it's possible to narrow the field. For one thing, I've formed an alliance only this evening that may bear fruit before long. And further I've taken the liberty of sending servants to every Family member, requesting they supply you with information concerning their movements. Some may refuse to comply out of arrogance, and some will lie rather than compromise a rendezvous or some other intimate matter. But for all our power, we are the most predictable of creatures, and I believe that certain of my cousins will surprise me with their candor. We may be able to eliminate a majority of our suspects in one fell swoop."

"Even so," Beheim said, "even if we eliminate all but ten, say, it will be a monumental chore to discover which of them is guilty. Our best hope is that the body will provide a telling clue."

"Then let me take you there at once."

"With all due respect, lord, while I greatly appreciate your assistance and will doubtless ask you to aid me during the course of the investigation, I would prefer to operate without anyone looking over my shoulder. I will be less distracted as a result."

Agenor inclined his head. "Very well. But I insist on being apprised of your progress . . . for your protection and my own."

"I'll do my best to—"

"No, you *will* keep me apprised, Michel. I demand it."

Though the old man's instruction had been merely stern, Beheim could have sworn he detected desperation and a hint of pleading in the set of his face, and that perplexed him—never before had he seen Agenor so unsteady, even when under personal attack.

"If there is more to this than you have told me," Beheim said, "it is my right to hear it now."

Agenor's patrician features tightened with anger, but only for an instant; then his flesh seemed to sag away from his skull, the long years of his unnatural life becoming suddenly apparent. He stared hollow-eyed at Beheim as if confused by what had been asked of him. At last he said once again, "I have done something."

Beheim waited for a disclosure, but none was forthcoming.

"Yes?" he said. "You have done something?"

Agenor's head twitched, he blinked at Beheim, as if just awakened to his presence. "The alliance I spoke of . . . I felt I had to make it in order to give you some advantage, yet I cannot be sure whether it will in the end help or hinder you." He let out an exhausted sigh. "We will have to wait and see."

"And the nature of this alliance?"

"I would rather not reveal it at this time."

Beheim knew the hopelessness of pressing the issue. "I would ask that a number of servants be put at my personal disposal," he said after a bit. "I will, of

course, employ Giselle as my agent, but because of the
scope of the investigation, I'll need more help than
she can supply."

"Whatever you wish."

Beheim came to his feet, still a bit weak in the
knees, but beginning to feel something of the old eagerness for the chase that he had known during his
days in Paris.

"Remember what is at stake," Agenor said. "No
matter what you find, no matter how highly connected
you discover the culprits to be, you must not falter in
your resolve to bring the truth before the Patriarch."

"I'll do everything in my power not to fail you."

"You cannot fail *me*," said Agenor, clasping
Beheim's right hand with both of his and fixing him
with a searching look. "I have already failed, I have
lost the Patriarch's ear. He considers me an old fool, a
scribe with the delusions of a Cassandra. But you can
compensate for my failures, Michel. It's in your grasp
to kindle victory from the ashes of my defeat. Do not
fail yourself. That is my charge to you."

The body of the Golden lay naked and pitiful atop
the eastern turret of Castle Banat. The girl's eyes were
iced shut, and a cracked red glaze covered the black-
ish stones beside her. Mutilated, Agenor had said, but
that word had not prepared Beheim for the savagery
of the wounds. There was a ragged hole in the side of
her neck large enough in which to insert a fist, and
there was a similar wound in her belly. Lesser yet no
less grievous wounds marred her face, breasts, and
thighs. Though the body was frozen, Beheim could detect signs of lividity and rigor, which meant that she
must have been killed during the waning hours of the
previous night, a time during which it had been suffi-

ciently warm to permit the inception of decay. Still, he was surprised that these processes were not further advanced. There must, he concluded, have been a cold snap during the day that had retarded them. Yet even if this was the case, it did not seem sufficient to explain the relative lack of decomposition. Perhaps there had only been a brief warming period just before dawn, and then the freezing cold had set in at first light. That would pass for a theory, but it likely could not be proved, as it was probable that none of the servants had ventured outside in daylight, all keeping close watch over their masters, guarding against treachery.

The girl's waxen hands were posed in clawlike attitudes, her mouth open in a silent scream. No hint of her freshness and beauty remained, apart from the sheen of her blond hair and the faint tantalizing scent of blood that arose from the stains painting the turret stones. Whoever had done this, Beheim thought, would have been bathed in blood. And despite Agenor's conjecture that several people had been involved, in Beheim's opinion there could have been only one murderer. This sort of violent excess demanded the intimate circumstance of the sexual act, it spoke to an ultimately private sinfulness. He had never known killers acting in concert—vulnerable to the shame of witness, even that of an accomplice—to be so uninhibited in their slaughter.

Closing his eyes, calling into play the mental skills that had been in part responsible for his meteoric rise with the Paris police, he merged with the past, using all the telltales, all the tiny bits of evidence and atmospheric constants, to empathize with the murderer, to intuit his state of mind and how it had been to kill, to return to the moment of the crime, to the turret the way it had been the previous morning. A bloated yellow moon hung in the east above the mounded hills that surrounded the castle, illuminating impenetrable thickets and short, squat oaks with dwarfish branches, creating deep bays of shadow in the folds of the earth. Winded silence. Then the turret door creaking open, and a dark figure, a man—or perhaps it had not been a man! Beheim thought for an instant that he sensed the male shape of the murderer's hunger, the muscularity of his madness, but then a hint of something, a delicacy of movement, a hesitancy, made him think otherwise. Yet for the sake of conjecture, he dubbed the murderer a man. Tall. A tall man leading the girl out into the chilly air. Her pale hair feathered in the breeze. Her filmy nightdress molded to breasts and abdomen and columned thighs. Her expression was dazed, her movements somnambulistic. She felt nothing of the cold, under the potent compulsion of the vampire's stare. The murderer turned her to face him, then bent to her neck and drank. Her head lolled; crescents of white showed beneath her half-lowered lids. After a long moment the vampire lifted his head, his mouth crimsoned, supporting the girl with one arm. The taste of the blood had dizzied him. Never such a maddening flavor, such a surge of heady ecstasy. He could not help but drink again, and soon ecstasy became a red, raw need, a primitive exultation. It was as if a hole had opened in his mind, a tunnel from which poured a flood of debased, animal desires. Soon he was no longer drinking, he was tearing at the frail tissues with his fangs, seeking to mine the source of the fiery pleasure that was consuming his intellect, his soul, wanting only to dig and claw and rend until he could kiss the open artery and drain it of its perfect yield. The girl fell, and he fell atop her, a black humped shape leeched to her spasming body. He tore at her belly, her cheek, he bit and snapped without aim or comprehension of anatomy, ripping away at the fleshy walls imprisoning the bloody narcotic juice. And . . .

Something was wrong.

A bright terror pervaded his thoughts. He glanced up. The moon was burning, burning, a blazing monstrosity that appeared faceted one second, then rippling as if seen through a film of heat haze. The sky had gone a poisoned color, and the entire world glowed as if irradiated by an unearthly force. The blood affecting his vision, he decided. It must be the blood, the drunkenness. Or could it be something else? He thought it might be something more than the blood, but he couldn't remember. Then he saw what he had done to the girl.

Revulsion warred with a sense of pride in his power, his feral rule. He felt dizzy . . . not the exhilarating dizziness of moments before, but sick and vague and besotted. Everything was too bright. Blood glistening like a slick flow of lava across the stones, light steaming up from the spills, the puddles, from cracks between the stones. A wave of nausea overwhelmed him, and he staggered to his feet. It was all wrong somehow, what he had done, what he felt and saw, everything was wrong. Too much light, light exploding in his skull, streaming from his eyes, from the girl's wounds, from the slashed meat of her breasts, bloody light piercing upward to stain him with guilt, to taint all his life. A hot fluid rose in his gorge, and he gagged. His stomach emptied redly. There was a weird singing in his head, a screeching like fingernails raked across slate. He tried to stop his ears, but could not muffle the sound, and, disoriented, frightened—of what, he did not know—dripping reddened bile from his chin, his heart hammering, he fled into the darkness of the castle. . . .

Beheim came alert to discover that he was gripping the turret wall, gazing out at the Carpathian hills, at—to his considerable surprise—a smallish silvery moon quite different from the bloated yellow monstrosity he had imagined. He had an apprehension of someone standing behind him, but on wheeling about, he found only the body of the Golden . . . though the air remained thick with presence. He savored that presence, hoping to isolate its particulars, certain it was a mental track left by the murderer, a clue as tangible as a bloodstain or a boot mark; but it faded quickly, and he was unable to gain any further knowledge. He tried to assemble his various impressions of the murderer into a portrait, but the figure in his mind's eye remained as featureless as a silhouette cut from black paper. Likely a man. An arrogant sort, yet with a fair degree of conscience. Drunk to the point of hallucination on the blood of the Golden. Driven to murder, then shamed to nausea and flight. That was all.

He knelt to examine the body. A fragment of black thread caught beneath a broken fingernail was the only evidence it yielded. Hardly telling. What man among the gathering had not been wearing black? Steeling himself, Beheim shifted the body. The flesh had frozen to the stones and made a horrid sucking noise as it was lifted away. There was very little of interest hidden beneath it. More blood, and scraps of the ripped nightdress. He inspected the scraps, but having no microscope, he was unable to learn anything from them. Feeling helpless, frustrated, he got to his feet and began moving cautiously about, peering at the moonlit stones. Once he had thoroughly explored the illuminated portion of the turret, he got down onto his hands and knees and searched the shadows alongside the wall, probing the cracks with his fingernails. He had covered nearly half of the area when he spotted a shard of broken glass. Not far away lay more splinters and pieces of glass, among them the neck of a small bottle to which a silver cap was affixed. It was, he realized on closer inspection, an extremely old bottle, likely an antique, and judging from the size, it had probably held perfume. A fanciful capital letter was engraved upon the cap, but time had worn it almost completely away, leaving only a flourish intact, and Beheim could not determine what the letter had been. *U* or *N*, perhaps. Possibly a *V*. He turned the cap over and over in his hand, then pocketed it and continued his search. But there were no further discoveries.

Three clues. The bottle cap, the blood—somewhere in the castle would be hidden blood-stained evening clothes—and the fact that the culprit had been a man. Not much of a basis upon which to begin an investigation. Beheim knew he would need luck . . . luck and a great deal of hard work, most of that to be accomplished by the Family's servants. He would set them to searching for the bloody clothing at once, and to seeking the owner of the bottle cap; he would study the results of Agenor's initiative concerning the whereabouts of Family members during the early hours of the morning.

But what could he set himself to do?

There was something troubling about his re-creation of the crime . . . something about the hallucination in particular. The way the moon had looked. Now that he thought about it, he recalled that the moon on the previous morning had resembled this evening's moon: small, silvery, and just past full. And yet to the murderer it had appeared bloated and huge. Perhaps he suffered from an affliction of the eye. Or perhaps he had been drunk before tasting the Golden, and thus already subject to perceptual distortions.

Both possibilities, he decided, were worth looking into.

Once again he examined the silver bottle cap. It was unlikely that the girl had been carrying it—there were no pockets in her nightdress. But what would the murderer have been doing with a bottle of perfume? Beheim sniffed the cap. A scent clung to it, though not of perfume. A harsh acidic odor. Medicine of some sort? A drug with which he had overcome the Golden's companion? Yet why would he have bothered to use drugs when he possessed a natural aptitude for swaying mortals to his will? And where was the companion? Likely crumpled in some crevice below the castle, flung there from a high window. More servants would be needed to search the hillsides; with all the sheer drops and ravines hard by, the body might have come to rest some distance from the castle walls. But the bottle, now. What could it have contained? Beheim rubbed the ball of his thumb across the remnants of the engraved letter, coming more and more to feel that the answer to this question would illuminate all other questions. Of course it was possible the bottle had nothing to do with the murder, that it had been lying there for some time before the Golden and the murderer had put in their appearance . . . though not for long, otherwise there would have been no odor. But he did not believe this to be so. The silver cap seemed to hold a vibration, a residual tremor of the violence that had occurred upon the turret.

He glanced down at the body. Until that moment

he had given little thought to the Golden's personal tragedy, relating to the case as a breach of honor and tradition; but now he recalled her beauty, her gracefulness, and wondered what she had made of all the passion surrounding her and what sort of woman she had been. Had she known the particulars of the ritual? Had she been greedy for immortality? So close. Almost a queen and undying. His mind turned to Giselle, equally beautiful and informed by the same imperatives. He considered her childhood in Quercy, her genteel education, her debut in Paris. None of that could have prepared her for the life she now led. How she must tremble to live among these dandified, morose lords and ladies, these blazing-eyed killers with their blood full of dreams and strange weathers, and thoughts like black spidery stars shriveling in their brains. How deeply her fear must flow! Fear that in an instant could be transformed into love, like an underground river bursting out into the light of day. He considered her eventual fate. Either dead by his hand or immortal. How would he react to that first and most probable result? He would be desolate, surely. Distraught. He would weep. Yet he knew he would find a means not only of placing her death in perspective, but also of exulting in it, and that sickened him—this ability to justify every horror in the name of dark arcana and mystic passions. Agenor was right: the Family must change . . . and not simply because it would be the wise thing, the safe and pragmatic thing. And if by bringing the murderer down, he, Beheim, could be an agent of that change, that would go a long way toward effecting redemption for what he had done to Giselle.

He stepped back from the body, looking out over the worn hills, yet he retained an image of the Golden's sprawled limbs and clawed hands, a featureless image resembling a golden root that seemed to settle in his mind and melt like butter into the dark matter of his brain, infusing him with new resolve. Insoluble though the problem appeared, he was determined to ferret out the guilty party. This was, after all, only a murder, no matter how unusual its perpetrator. In Paris he had solved crimes of violence that had initially offered even less hope of solution. Full of resolve, he turned toward the turret door, but as he moved back into the darkness of the castle, his confidence was dispelled by the irrational fear that behind him the silver and proper moon had waned, and hanging in its place, like a cancer in the sky, was a bloated, disfigured sphere of sickly yellow, an emblem of derangement and unholy fever, of a new fire in the blood, of mysteries and terrors yet undiscovered, whose dread particulars he could not presuppose.

Chapter THREE

The interior design of Castle Banat had been contrived not with practical considerations of fortification or habitation in mind, but according to a series of peculiar architectural fantasies created by an Italian artist who had been one of the Patriarch's lovers some six hundred years before, and its insane enormity reflected the scope and complexity of the problem that confronted Beheim. Vast chambers as large as entire castles themselves were spanned by bridges—some of them drawbridges—that led to doorless walls; hundred-foot-wide stairways ended in midair, and there were chambers that opened onto gulfs in whose murky depths stranger edifices yet could be glimpsed. Windowed towers sprouted from the most unexpected places and rose toward dim vaulted roofs, and here and there were enormous wheels such as those used to raise and lower a portcullis, only the majority of these had no purpose whatsoever. At any point one could look up to see—in the light of the wrought-iron lanterns that hung everywhere—seemingly infinite perspectives of arches and stairways, with thick loops of chain hanging down like vines, and pulleys and ropes with no apparent function, and lofty stone porches embellished with nymphs in bas relief and bearded faces with great iron rings depending from their mouths. On one level a body of black water spread from a shore of bolted iron plate, horrid statuary rising from its depths, showing frilled heads and taloned hands. Pigeons that had never flown under the sun nested in crannies and on ledges, and soared through the heights, fouling the surfaces beneath with their droppings, and there were other beasts aside from the sculpted gargoyles and dragons that stood guard over the supreme emptinesses of the bridges; rats, centipedes, serpents, and, most notably, degenerate men and women who had once served the Patriarch but had in the end been loath to accept the risks of blood judgment and now, still too much in love with the possibility of eternity to leave, lived like vermin in the depths of the castle, fleeing at shadows, stealing garbage, traveling—it was rumored—along secret ways that permitted them access to even the most sacrosanct areas of the castle, and performing brutish ceremonies that were gross imitations of those practiced by the Family. The size of the place was such that it had its own weather. Clouds could form in the heights; rain fell from time to time. A man standing athwart one of the bridges would appear no more than a speck to someone below. This insane scale, along with the bizarre design and ornamentation, seemed redolent of a monumental conceit and folly. Indeed, certain of the internal structures had been designed as ruins: crumbling stone piers with ferns sprouting from their cracks; shattered fountains in the shape of griffons' heads and gigantic infants and various other creatures, from which water spilled into ponds or gutters or mere crevices in the floor; a spiral staircase with a holed railing; faceless statues and iron beams protruding from a gapped wall. Throughout could be felt the chill, brooding presence of the Patriarch. It was as if he had built an immense skull of grayish black stone to contain the bleak materials of his personality, and while Beheim found the wealth of baroque invention oppressive, he could not help but admire the grandiose conception that underlay it.

Yet as the first unrewarding results of the investigation became apparent, his admiration was replaced by a profound frustration, and he wished he could raze the enormous building, hammer it down into its constituent stones, because, he thought, only by doing so, only by eliminating the profusion of formal inessentials and blind alleys it emblemized, would he ever unearth the vital fact necessary to a solution. Not one of the Family had failed to account for their whereabouts during the time of the murder, and though a number of their alibis were certainly fraudulent, it would be impossible to discredit them in the time available. No bloodstained clothing had been found, nor was there evidence that any of the guests suffered from an affliction of the eye. He had wasted most of an entire night, and he was near the end of his rope, unable to think how to proceed, when Lady Alexandra Conforti, perhaps the most powerful woman of the Valea branch, burst into his quarters, followed by a breathless and agitated Giselle.

"This *thing* of yours," said Lady Alexandra coldly, indicating Giselle with a toss of her long auburn hair, "has had the gall to invade my rooms."

Giselle flushed, and her cheekbones appeared to sharpen; but she kept silent.

"I apologize for whatever inconvenience you may have suffered, but you must be aware of the exceptional circumstances," said Beheim, crossing the bedroom toward Lady Alexandra. "And I would be grateful if you would refer to my servant either by her position or by her name—Giselle."

Lady Alexandra turned a deaf ear to this. She looked away from Beheim, offering him a view of her graceful neck and stunning profile. She was so extreme in proportion, it was impossible to deem her beautiful in any ordinary sense of the word. Though her suitors tended to describe her as "willowy," as far as Beheim was concerned she gave new and eccentric meaning to the word, being freakishly tall, nearly four inches over six feet. Her limbs, particularly her legs, had an alien elongation. Her heart-shaped face, with its porcelain skin and lustrous, widely set green eyes, arched eyebrows, and full crimson mouth, verged upon an erotic caricature. Yet due to the cautious grace with which her every movement was invested, making a balletic act out of even the simplest gesture—likely a conscious compensation for a fear of clumsiness resulting from her unusual height—and because of the sexual confidence that rose from her like steam, she nonetheless conveyed an impression of great beauty. Giselle had apparently caught the lady at her toilette, for she was wearing a robe of pale blue silk worked with gilt thread, its loose fit allowing Beheim a glimpse of the freckled upper slopes of her breasts, cupped in shells of white lace. But from what he knew of the Valeas, and of Alexandra in particular, who had flirted with him on several previous occasions, he understood that no matter how compelling her anger, she would never have visited him dressed in this fashion unless she had desired her appearance to have an effect, and this caused him to doubt the depth of her mood, and to wonder toward what end she wanted to manipulate him.

"I take it as an insult that you would send a thing to question me," she said, showing him her back. "Send it from the room."

Beheim made silent speech with his eyes to Giselle, at once offering an apology and asking her to do the lady's bidding. After she had gone, he stepped to the lady's shoulder, an intimate proximity from which she did not withdraw, and asked in what way he could assist her.

With a languid gesture, keeping her back to him, she held up her right hand, showing him the antique silver bottle cap that he had discovered on the turret.

"I believe it is *I* who can help you."

"Ah!" said Beheim, touching the cap with his forefinger. "Then can you tell me who owns this?"

Her long fingers closed over the cap, making him think of the petals of a carnivorous flower folding about its prey. She moved away and glanced at him over her shoulder.

"Perhaps."

"Lady," he said, "the Patriarch has charged me to catch a murderer, and I'm afraid I must forgo the amenities in seeking information. I have no time for coyness. If you have something for me, you must tell me now. Otherwise I'll be . . ."

"Otherwise you'll do nothing." She moved farther away, peering down at the carpet, placing her feet carefully as if fitting them into old tracks. "You have no promising line of inquiry. All you do have at the moment is the hope that I may help you. And without my help, you will continue to sit here and contemplate your failure. Do you know why that is?"

"I'm certain you're bursting to enlighten me."

"Don't take that tone," she said, facing him. "You have no power over me, except to ask questions that I may or may not choose to answer. Of course you are beautiful, and that is a characteristic that lends one a certain kind of power, it is true. But my power over you is unqualified. Undeniable."

"So you say."

"Yes, so I say." She sauntered back toward him, brushing against his sleeve, sending a static charge across the skin of his arm.

Beheim repressed an urge to catch up her hand, partly because he was not sure what he might do once he had hold of her, whether he would attack or attempt to seduce. Like all women of the Family, she was infuriating in the manner in which she employed her sex. Though she did not accord with his ideal image of feminine beauty, he could not deny that he was attracted to her; but the nature of the attraction was perverse, an anticipation of shivery delights, the sort of fascination one might have for a serpent with breasts. He imagined that should they ever lie down together, a tangle of limbs far more complicated than that achieved by any ordinary coupling would result—a Gordian knot of living white ropes whose contorted heaving would resemble the writhing of a nest of worms.

"The Patriarch did not appoint you to investigate the murder because of your skill at detection," she went on. "He is wiser than that. Surely even you must understand that given the time allotted for a solution and the character of those you must investigate, you have little hope of success. The Patriarch understands this, too. Yet he also knows what a marvelous pawn you make, weak and new as you are. And he is aware of what an excellent game your investigation offers. He knows how dearly we love intrigues, how deeply our passions run. And he knows, too, that various of our number will be unable to resist the temptation to turn the game to our own purposes. Whether for gain, revenge, or some more obscure motive; that is irrelevant to the Patriarch's scheme. It is his belief that by taking part in the game, *we* will solve the crime, or else inadvertently set you upon a course that will lead to a solution."

Despite the fact that her summary of the situation was so at odds with Agenor's, Beheim heard a ring of truth in her words and absorbed them with a minimum of resentment. It might be, he thought, that Lady Alexandra's intervention was the product of the mysterious alliance of which Agenor had spoken.

"So," Beheim said, "you have come to make the first move."

She returned a deferential shrug and strolled across the room to the tapestry and made a show of examining it; then she leaned against it, gazing at Beheim with undisguised amusement. Her white face and reddish hair stood out sharply against the black tangle of the evil forest, looking as if one of the mysterious denizens hiding among the branches had been recently retouched. She held up the bottle cap between thumb and forefinger. "This belongs to one of my cousins." She paused—for dramatic effect, or so Beheim assumed. "To Felipe Aruzzi de Valea."

Beheim seized upon the name. Felipe Aruzzi de Valea: the patriarch of the Valeas; a colleague and ally of Roland Agenor's; a blood scientist of the highest reputation; considered a moderate in the debates now raging. And yet of late he had become the lover of Lady Dolores Cascarin y Ribera. It was rumored that the Lady Alexandra was no longer Felipe's supporter, that she had aligned herself with Lady Dolores and other reactionaries against Agenor and his friends, and

that she sought to unseat Felipe as the head of the
Valeas. He was not sure he believed that Alexandra
had become a reactionary; it was more likely she was
pretending to be one in order to consolidate her
power and effect some ambition, be it the unseating of
Felipe or something else. He did not doubt that she
was telling the truth about the ownership of the bottle
cap—a lie would be too easily detected. But when he
considered the complexities of the situation, the variety of plots that might be at work, plots of political significance to both the Valeas and the Family as a whole,
he was visited by a new depth of understanding concerning the murder, elevated to a height from which
he could see clearly and with great detail the maze of
potential intrigues surrounding the crime. What if Alexandra was attempting to ruin Felipe by supplying
false evidence that appeared to incriminate him? And
had she or one of her lovers done the murder? Or had
Felipe actually been the perpetrator? Or could this be
another blind alley, another waste of precious time? In
their statements, Felipe and Dolores had used one another to establish their whereabouts during the time of
the murder. Might not this mean that they had both
been present on the turret? Or was their affair an element of a larger scheme, a tactic on the part of Lady
Dolores to neutralize a potent adversary? Or was
Agenor himself playing a game? More and more
Beheim began to discern Agenor's fine hand at work
in all this dubious matter, and this caused him to believe that the answers to his questions would be of little moment. Knowing the identity of the owner of the
bottle cap might serve no more to illuminate the black
field of the crime than did Lady Alexandra's head illuminate the murky foreground of the tapestry against
which she was leaning. It was a beginning, true

enough. Yet by supplying a single answer, she had only increased the number of questions he would be forced to ask; thus, in essence, he was at a greater loss than before.

He glanced up at Lady Alexandra, who was smiling broadly.

"Now do you see?" she said, and laughed—a melodic trill as precise as a piano exercise. "You have no choice but to allow yourself to be moved from square to square, to hope that our passionate errors will direct you to a successful end." She walked slowly toward him, as graceful in her approach as a wend in a river channeling bright water; the eerie formality of her white face seemed both artful and vital, like a face painted on a flower come to life. "One more thing. Felipe and Dolores are creatures of habit. Several hours before dawn, they will lock themselves away in Felipe's bedchamber, and there they will remain for the day. His servants are among those currently assisting your investigation. It will not be difficult to make sure that they are kept busy. If you intend to search his apartments, you may do so at that time. It will not be so great a risk. The bedchamber is separated from the other rooms, and Felipe will not hear you so long as Dolores occupies him." Another delicate laugh, a springtime laugh of lacy dew on cobwebs and joyous green energies. The Lady Alexandra, Beheim realized, was enjoying herself immensely. "That, and not my revelation, is the first move," she continued. "Once you take it, you will be inextricably mired in the game, without control or direction. And you must take the move or else give up the charade of this investigation." She stopped beside him and rested a hand on his forearm. "I know you cannot trust me, and I will not claim to have other than my own interests at heart. But I am your ally in this. However, to begin with, you must learn to trust yourself, and to do that you must enter the game. Only in the game will you discover who exactly it is that you can trust."

"Are you suggesting that I do not know myself?"

"Is that not a concern of yours? It was one of mine when I was new to the Family."

She released his arm, but it seemed to Beheim that the connection between them remained constant, the warm charge of her blood encircling his wrist.

"You cannot pretend with me," she said. "I have lived through the turbulent time, the time of metamorphosis that you are now entering. I know the conflicts within you, the storms that will beset you, the decisions you will have to make."

"Well, then," said Beheim, irritated by her pose of superiority, "perhaps you'll be kind enough to enlighten me as to how these conflicts will be resolved."

"You will understand soon enough, and in your own way. It's not my place to influence you." A wry smile. "Not in such intimate questions, at any rate." Suddenly brisk, she moved toward the door. "I must go now. But I will give you all the help I can. And . . . Ah! I nearly forgot." She came back to him and pressed something into his hand. "A key to Felipe's apartment."

"Why should I bother to search Felipe's rooms. They've already been searched."

"By servants," she replied. "Surely you consider yourself a more reliable functionary than they. What choice do you have? I suppose you could retire from the case. Of course, then not only will you be subject to Agenor's displeasure, but also to that of the Patriarch. Scarcely an enviable position."

Beheim turned the key between his fingers. "You seem very sure of how I'll act."

"It's as I said, you have little choice. And not because it's your only hope of solving the murder. The risks of the game will compel you. You are in some ways cautious, as are we all, yet it is also in your nature to hazard everything on a single throw of the dice."

Beheim's annoyance swelled into anger. "I've become rather weary of people claiming to understand me better than I do myself."

"Then you must grow in understanding, mustn't you?"

"Perhaps you expect me to change my mind concerning Lord Agenor's proposals."

She made a gesture of dismissal. "You will be who you must, cousin. I expect nothing of you . . . at least nothing you would now be able to comprehend. Truly, I would be a fool to have expectations of you, for it is not yet clear whether you will survive your own investigation. You are quite out of your depth. And yet . . ." Her voice dropped in pitch, becoming heatedly familiar. "Listen, Michel. Perhaps I am being overbold in saying this, but I have seen in you the promise of great substance and great heart. I pray you will be able to avoid certain of the difficulties that I encountered when I was new. You are laboring under a number of misconceptions, many of which are likely to lead you into folly. One in particular is dangerous in that it may retard your development, and that is your affection for the thing you sent to my apartments. I'll wager that before this investigation is through, if all goes well, you'll discover how different is the character of your relationship from what you now believe to be true. And perhaps you will also discover uncommon worth where now you see only menace."

With a quick step forward, she drew him into an embrace, her hands pressing against the small of his back, and kissed him—a forceful kiss upon the lips that stimulated him hardly at all, seeming more an attempt to seal a bargain than to arouse; but just as he was about to make a comment to this effect, he was overcome by a spell of vertigo and a sudden dimming of his vision. Against a backdrop of undulating green, as of some watery deep—the same color as her eyes— there he saw the naked person of Lady Alexandra swaying with the gentle grace of kelp in an ebb tide, her arms and hands inscribing hypnotic figures, easing closer and closer, like a dream taking form before a drowning man. He tried to fight off the vertigo, but his mind was entangled in a soft, warm net, his thoughts cluttered and helpless like silver fish in fine mesh, and instead of reacting in fear, he marveled at the exotic character of her beauty and wondered how he could ever have thought her other than beautiful. With her pear-sized breasts and lovely legs, the long thighs delicately flexing, stems supporting the bloom of her belly, she was a miracle to his eyes, tinder to the fire of his senses. With every passing second, her sensuality became more affecting. He could smell her sex. Her blood. Her face was so near, he could no longer make out its shape. Her crimson mouth opening, her pink tongue licking forth slowly like sea life. And then it ended. All sensation, all feelings of intimacy and wild blood sheared away. Stunned, unsteady, he found that she had disengaged from the embrace and was standing several feet away, watching him with an expression that while not devoid of calculation, seemed also to embody a measure of both fondness and confusion.

"What now?" she said in a small voice, appearing to be speaking less to him than to her inner self. Then her features were tightened by a resolute look, and she said in a firmer tone, "I believe I will stay with you awhile. To assist you. But you must send that—" She broke off, paused a second. "You must send your servant away. This Giselle. Put her to some other use. I will not tolerate her company."

Beheim, still wobbly, muttered something to the effect that he needed no assistance.

"That may be," Alexandra said. "But you do need to be convinced that the key I have given you is your best hope in all this. I will stay with you until you have matured in that conviction. At the very least, my presence will afford you added protection while you continue your interviews."

He could not deny that, but was troubled by this sudden shift in her intentions. "Why do you want to help me?"

"As I told you, it is in my interests."

"And there's nothing more?"

"Oh, cousin!" she said, giving a lilt to the words that made them seem to have the resonance of a quiet, wistful laugh. "There is always something more."

Chapter FOUR

The brooding quiet of the Castle Banat had been overborne to some extent by an atmosphere of emotional turbulence. Most of the Family were keeping to their rooms, but a fair number had taken to prowling about the upper levels and engaging in arguments, even brief scuffles; their shouts and clatter echoed throughout, faint as the cries of birds and the scuttlings of squirrels, but nonetheless startling to hear in all that funereal hush. Among them were several men and women whom Beheim intended to interview personally. He came to wonder if their agitated movements might not disguise a desire to avoid being interviewed, for had Alexandra not been with him, he would have had the devil's own time in tracking them, and when he finally did manage to beard them, they were none of them cooperative, but presented either snarling or stony faces. Elaine Vandelore, whom they found reading by candlelight in the servants' pantry, hurled her book at him and answered his questions in icy monosyllables. Hermann Kuhl they discovered seated in an armchair in an abandoned quarter of the castle; he responded to Beheim with haughty indifference, inter-

48

rupting his answers to give erotic instruction to the female servant who knelt between his legs all the while. Georg Mautner, occupied in a game room with Lupita Cascarin y Miron, half sister to the Lady Dolores, amused himself by skewering a mouse with a dart and then favoring Beheim with a glance of hostile significance. The only one whose behavior might be characterized as in any way responsive was Ernst Kostolec, a political ally of Agenor's, though scarcely his friend, and an elusive sort whose wizardly reputation caused even the most powerful of the Family to tread lightly around him. They located him in the Patriarch's library, less a room than a great circular stair sunk through the center of the castle, more than a mile in depth, its walls lined with books, many so ancient that to open any one of them would be to transform it into hundreds of scraps of yellow paper that would then flutter down into that dark well like the brittle ghosts of a swarm of butterflies. It was one of the few rooms in the castle, at least of those in common use, where lanterns, not torches, provided the illumination—it seemed the Patriarch cared more for his books than he did for the safety of his children.

Kostolec, a man of Agenor's apparent age, but far more decrepit in aspect, stooped and wrinkled and vulpine, with tufted eyebrows and a few strands of fine white hair floating above his mottled scalp like wispy clouds above the surface of a dead planet, was standing on one of the landings, an octagonal space some twenty-five feet wide, hunched over a lectern, peering through a magnifying glass at a large leatherbound book open to a page covered in florid script. Rays of orange light sprayed out into the center of the well from a lantern with five panes suspended above the lectern, but they did not illumine the opposite wall. A look of annoyance crossed his face when he saw them on the landing directly above him, and he slammed his book shut, expelling a puff of dust from between the covers; the gilt inscription on the front of the volume was in Portuguese and beneath that lay the ornament of a gilt palm surmounted by a crescent, and on the spine was the symbol of a crown and a leaf. Beheim noticed that the front of Kostolec's gray silk shirt was thick with dust, evidence—perhaps—that he had slammed shut other books not so long before. A sign of frustration, possibly. But as they approached he smiled in a pleasant manner. Pleasant, at least, in contrast to the general run of smiles with which Beheim had met. And so, for all his anxiety over questioning so formidable a figure, Beheim was put somewhat at his ease.

"Ah, excellent! Our little policeman," said Kostolec, wiping his hands on his trousers, which were also gray; the emptiness around them caused his voice to carry a slight reverberation, and his words seemed to stir a little something in the central darkness of the well. "How droll! I feel I've been transported into the midst of a traveling theatrical company." He cast an arch glance toward Alexandra. "And what part are you playing this day, my dear? Not the fluttering ingenue, I trust."

"For purpose of this scene," she said dryly, "you'd do best to consider me a spear carrier."

"Such nice menace. I approve." Then, to Beheim, who was shuffling through the loose pieces of paper on which he had made his notes: "Be wary of her, Mister Policeman. She has a talent for self-delusion which serves all the better to obscure her actual motives."

Beheim ignored this. "Your servant Jules," he said, "has stated that he was with you in the library on the night of the murder. You were both here the entire night?"

"Did not Jules so state?"

"Yes, but I—"

"Then I would not doubt him. He is a gentleman of exceptional character." Kostolec leaned against the lectern, not the stiff movement of an old man, but giving an impression of supple strength. "He hunts books for me. It saves time to have him run them down."

"And why is he not assisting you now?"

Kostolec laughed. "Something more important has come up. He is at present scurrying about Banat, asking questions and running fool's errands. On behalf of some policeman, I believe."

"For that, my apologies," Beheim said, and again shuffled through his notes. "Jules has also indicated that you are embarked upon a lengthy study. Might I ask what is the subject of your researches?"

"That is irrelevant to your investigation."

"It may well be," Beheim said. "But I'm afraid I must be the judge of that."

"Your imperatives are not mine," said Kostolec, anger edging into his voice.

"True, I cannot force you to answer. I can only note that you do not. However, it's possible that your researches have some relevance of which you are unaware. And even if they are irrelevant, why not settle the matter?"

Kostolec was silent for a long moment; nothing about his posture or expression gave a clue to his mood. Beheim gazed down over the railing at the corkscrewing stairway beneath. Beams of light struck into the center of the well from a number of lower landings, given distinct form by the dust suspended in the air; bindings gleamed in the shadows like seams of

ore. Far below, a glowing orange dot bobbled like a
firefly in the grainy darkness. Probably another scholar
ascending with a lantern. A faint creaking noise came
from the landing above, but Beheim saw no one there.
The structure settling, he supposed.

Finally Kostolec said, "I'm certain you have taken
into account the insult implicit in your questioning."

"Obviously I regret the necessity—" Beheim began, but Kostolec cut him off.

"On the other hand," he went on, "*I* must take
into account your inexperience and the impossible position in which you have been placed. Therefore I will
answer your question."

A bland smile etched the lines deeper on his
withered face, and Beheim, shocked by this display of
rationality, murmured his thanks.

"I am studying the future," Kostolec said.

Beheim waited for a further explanation, but none
was forthcoming. He glanced at Alexandra; she lifted
one shoulder in an almost imperceptible shrug. Kostolec continued to smile.

"Would you care to be more specific?" Beheim
asked.

"No, I would not."

"Very well." Beheim paced to the edge of the
landing, glanced down again into the well. Another
faint creaking noise came to his ears. "It seems that
the future, at least your conception of it, is somehow
related to the records of the Royal Portuguese Botan-
ical Society. The book you were examining appears to
contain some of their colonial journals. The palm tree
on the cover indicates to me that the work concerns a
tropical land. The crescent"—he spread his hands—
"perhaps refers to Islam. A tropical Portuguese colony
with an Islamic population? I am not familiar with the

history of the Portuguese expansion. However, certain sections of Africa spring to mind. Or perhaps a colony farther east. What do you think? Since the Orient is the focus of a discussion that has recently occupied our attention, I would hazard a guess that you may be searching for a site in the Far East that would be suitable for our relocation."

"I once had a dog who could stand on his hind legs and bark," Kostolec said. "A clever little fellow. Most entertaining."

"I'm pleased to have awakened your nostalgia," said Beheim.

"But mere cleverness can achieve nothing, and that is precisely what you have achieved by discerning the subject of my study. What relation could there be between my bookish pursuits and the murder of the Golden?"

"None that I can see," said Beheim. "And yet this question of our migration is a color that tints the entire investigation. At least I have a sense that it does. Few of our interrelations are simple affairs. Whatever the sequence of events, whatever the superficial justification for those events, the actions we take seem to resonate on many levels, to draw together a variety of concerns into the mechanisms of a single passion. I believe it would be foolish to take a simplistic view of the crime, to attempt to separate it, in my consideration, from its backdrop. Thus your political involvement intrigues me. As far as I can determine, you have until lately held yourself apart from this sort of issue. Certainly there has never been any love lost between you and Agenor, and yet now you are his ally. A political alliance founded on mutual self-interest? Perhaps. However, I would be a fool if I did not examine the possibility that there is more to it than that."

"I cannot think how this leads you to suspect me of murder."

" 'Suspect' is too strong a word. I have no real suspects. Because of limitations imposed upon me by time and circumstance, I must concentrate my energies on those who display what strikes me as uncharacteristic behavior. As yours strikes me. It may appear that I am grasping at straws, and indeed I am. But investigations of this sort rarely proceed along logical lines. A slip is made, a secret is whispered, an accident of fate occurs. And suddenly the whole thing is revealed. As for my part in things, I'm casting my net in murky waters, hoping that a shark will see my legs and seek to take a bite, thinking I am merely clever."

Alexandra gave a soft, pleased laugh, and Kostolec's eyes cut toward her; for an instant his features were concentrated into a venomous mask. Then he, too, laughed. He nodded to Beheim. A civil nod. "Will you pardon me?" he said, and with a prodigious leap that carried him to the foot of the stairs, he raced up to the landing directly above them. Beheim heard a cry, sounds of a brief struggle. Seconds later Kostolec reappeared, dragging behind him a terrified young man dressed all in black, with ragged brown hair and a thin, long-jawed face; a fresh crop of pimples straggled across his forehead.

"Who is this?" Alexandra asked, and Kostolec said, "A creature of the Vandelores. Aren't you?" He lifted the man up by the collar, holding his head close to the lantern, and swung him so that his knees smacked against the railing. "This disgusting wretch is the third spy they've set on me since my arrival."

"My lord, have pity!" said the man, clutching at Kostolec's wrist to prevent himself from swaying back and forth. "I meant you no harm."

"Thank God!" said Kostolec mockingly. "I was afraid for my life." His stare was as unwavering and black as that of an old reptile. "Who sent you?"

The man wet his lips; his eyes darted to Alexandra, then to Beheim. "Marko," he said. "It was Marko. Lord, I did not willingly—"

"Be silent!" said Kostolec; he glanced at Beheim. "Do you understand now why I react with such enmity to your questions? Day and night, I am beset by the Vandelores. How can I tolerate this constant interference in my affairs?"

"What could the Vandelores want of you?" Beheim asked, watching the man trying to swallow, half-choked by his tightened collar.

"They want," Kostolec said, enunciating each word with studied precision, as if aiming and firing them at Beheim, "to know my secrets."

He forced the man's face close to his and kissed him on the lips. The sight of the two faces pressed together, the smooth skin of one being nuzzled and sucked by a pale, wrinkled beast in a fan of ruddy light in the midst of an immense darkness, bred a strange distance in Beheim, as if he were peering into a dimension in which every constant had been rearranged, where animals walked about in men's forms, and true men were handled like sheep, where the physical world was a cave filled with gilded symbols and dust, and life was a sinister, wasted value, death an exalted goal.

Kostolec broke off the kiss, studied the man dangling limply from his hand. "Tell Marko that if this ever happens again, I will pay him a visit." He appeared to be mulling something over; his owlish eyebrows hinged in the middle, his lips pursed. "On second thought," he said, "I'll tell him myself." And looking straight at Beheim, with a casual flick of his wrist he tossed the man over the railing.

He seemed to twist at the center of the well for an instant, his mouth agape, eyes white with fear, as if held aloft by the rays of lantern light that touched him redly, then—as Beheim made a futile lunge toward the railing—he tumbled down head over heels into the darkness, trailing an abandoned, throat-tearing scream. Beheim watched him fall, watched him vanish, the sight conjuring a queasy chill in his belly. He whirled about, ready with a violent question, but his outrage was quelled by the sight of Alexandra and Kostolec standing face-to-face, tense and furious, the tall, beautiful woman in her nightdress and the predatory old man—like otherworldly raptors. He expected them to run at each other, to tear and punch and bite. But instead they relaxed from their aggressive poses, and Alexandra, in a calm voice, said, "That was badly done!"

"Badly done!" Beheim brought his fist down against the railing, cracking it. "You might just as well call it a faux pas! What's next? Will you call genocide a discourtesy? Infanticide an act of mischief?"

She did not look at him, continuing to address herself to Kostolec. "If you must teach a lesson," she said, "there are more effective ways."

"Is that what it was?" said Beheim. "A lesson? And what should I have learned from it? Respect for my elders?"

"Caution, I should hope," Kostolec said. "Without it, you will not be long among us."

When Beheim started to respond, Kostolec shouted, "No more! Try me no more!"

He turned away, facing outward into the well, the lantern light firing his wisps of white hair, painting a shine along the back panel of his silk shirt. "I've done no murder," he said in a steely voice. "Tipsy pleasures of the blood hold no attraction for me. I am in every way the Patriarch's man and would never violate his traditions. But believe as you will."

There was a trilling vibration newly in the air, the sort of disturbance that might derive from the far-off operation of a mighty engine, and Beheim could not rid himself of the notion, however irrational, that Kostolec was the source of this vibration. He thought that if Kostolec were to turn, he would be much changed, his eyes aflame, his wrinkled face transformed into a barbarous mask of bronze, his tongue a black adder. Yet when he spoke, it was in a ruminative and not a threatening tone.

"These are difficult times," he said. "We each must play our part in them as best we can. However, you would do well to remember that my part in all this has nothing to do with the world as you know it. I bear you no ill will, but I will not permit further distractions." He heaved a sigh. "Do not trouble me again."

Alexandra put a hand on Beheim's shoulder; she nodded toward the entrance several levels above, and Beheim, his temper cooled by a sudden anxiety, let himself be drawn away. But as they ascended the stair leading to the next level, moved by some sense of wrongness, he paused and stooped and peered back down through the railing.

The rays of lantern light had grown sharply defined, blades of radiance that spread to touch the ranks of books and folios on the opposite wall, and as they brightened further Kostolec himself began to darken, his flesh and his clothing losing detail and color as if he had fallen under a deep shadow, until at last the light dimmed to its normal brilliance, and what stood

by the railing beneath it had itself become no more
than a shadow, a figure of absolute, unfractionated
black. This absence of a man stood without moving,
but within a matter of seconds the figure flew apart
into papery-looking scraps of black vitality, like bats
and ashes, and these remnants fluttered off into the
darkness; then, like a seam of gleaming anthracite exposed in midair, a shiny surface manifested at the center of the well, seeming to pour both upward and
downward, to be measuring in reflection the passage
of a light in motion. Beheim felt a shiver in his flesh,
as if some just-less-than-physical thing had passed
through him. And with that the gleam faded and everything was as before, except that Kostolec was gone
and in his stead were only a few dust motes eddying
slowly in the orange glow of the lantern, glittering like
the ghosts of nebulae and stars.

As they proceeded along the corridor that led
away from the Patriarch's library, Beheim began to
consider Alexandra in a new light. It did not seem reasonable that she would stand ready to defend him
against someone of Kostolec's power simply to achieve
a political goal, and yet it appeared that she had. He
recalled her moment of confusion after their embrace.
Was it possible, he asked himself, that she had developed some infant attraction for him? He did not think
this likely, but neither would he have thought it likely
that his attraction for her would have grown as partic-
ularized and consuming as it had. He found himself
watching her on the sly, noticing her ways. Her habit
of gnawing on the edge of the nail of a forefinger
when she was perplexed. How shadows appeared to
shift about in her green eyes whenever she grew dis-
content. Her walk, so careful, almost somnambulistic

in its cautious energy, contained to the point of repression, except when she became excited, and then she would twist to look at him while she walked, put half skips into her stride and go bouncing along like a gawky schoolgirl. The solemnity she displayed when listening to him, head down, eyes lidded, all her features in repose, like a nun at prayer. She laughed easily, but when she did, it was as if she were not laughing with her whole being, as if the place inside her where vivid responses were manufactured remained blank and gray and dull, and this gave her an eerily inconsistent vitality, like someone under a spell. He wondered how he could ever have thought her extreme height grotesque, for now her body struck him as elegantly slim, exquisitely formed, a miracle of aesthetic proportion, and when he pictured them together, it was not, as previously, in some weird Gordian entanglement, but joined in a sleek and perfectly coordinated union. To entertain such thoughts was ridiculous, he told himself; they were accomplices in some as yet undetermined political action, nothing more. Yet he could not keep from entertaining them, nor could he keep from interpreting her sidelong glances as being other than the articles of a freshly waked affection. He believed that she was affording him glimpses of her true self, now and then dropping the glibly aggressive style that she had affected when she came to his apartments, and letting him see the personality behind the facade, one capable of anger and joy, petulance and sadness, all the usual components, yet tempered by an underlying seriousness and charged by a kind of ardent composure. He still suspected her, he still doubted the character of her intentions; but he felt that he was not entirely deluded in thinking that she had changed toward him, that what-

ever she had wanted from him in the beginning, she
wanted more now.

They turned into a side corridor, long and
lantern-lit, roofed with whitewashed stones, broken by
arches that led off into tunnels, open spaces, other corridors, and at a moment when they caught one another
staring, Alexandra looked quickly away and asked what
he was thinking.

"Not an easy question to answer," Beheim said.

"I disagree," she said. "It's the easiest of all questions to answer, unless one has something to hide."

"I don't wish to appear foolish," he said, after
walking a few paces in silence.

"I believe we have come far enough along this
path to be gentle in our judgments."

"Very well, then. I was thinking about you."

They were just passing a lantern mounted in a
niche, and her shadow, which had been trailing behind
her on the floor, suddenly leaped up onto the wall and
stalked along at her side, a leaner, sharper self, as if
the huntress within her had been put on the alert.

"Oh?" she said, and laughed nervously. "And how
am I?"

"Fascinating. Troubling." He tried to catch her
eye. "Beautiful."

"And how exactly am I troubling?" Another laugh.
"You see, I accept without complaint the unconditional
virtues."

"Perhaps it's not you that troubles me," he said.
"Perhaps it's a lack of faith in my own discrimination."

"That's only a kind way of saying you're not sure
of me."

"I suppose."

They came to an arch that opened onto a large
unfurnished chamber, where three men and a

woman—Family members by their rich clothing—
were standing a hundred feet away or more in an ob-
long island of light cast by two lanterns. The woman
was half-naked, the bodice of her gown down about
her waist, and the men were all partially disrobed.
There was an air of ominous stasis to the tableau,
Beheim thought, as if it had been contrived for their
benefit and was not a sexual incident that they had interrupted. It made him very uneasy. The woman beckoned to them, but he was not in the least tempted to
accept the invitation.

"Do you recognize anyone?" he asked Alexandra.

She studied them a moment longer. "Not at this
distance. The man in the red tunic, though. That
might be—" She broke off, peered at them again. "I
can't tell."

Once again the woman beckoned.

"Come on. Let's leave them to it," said Beheim.

"Don't you want to interview them?" Alexandra
asked.

"A group this large, they'd only support one another's lies."

His sense of uneasiness grew stronger. He took
Alexandra's hand and began trotting along the corridor,
half dragging her along, glancing back over his shoulder.

Alexandra looked startled, but she did not try to
pull free, nor did she object when Beheim began to
run, leading them on a crooked course through a maze
of corridors; but once they had stopped running, she
asked him what was wrong.

"I had a premonition," he told her. "A feeling that
they might be . . . I don't know. That they posed a trap
of some sort."

They had emerged from a corridor into a cavern,

a place carved from marble to resemble a cave, whose nether end was submerged beneath a smallish lake, with roughly hewn blocks of marble scattered about its shoreline; a bleached, bluish-white light was provided by the cavern walls, or more particularly, by the luminescent moss that embroidered almost every square inch of stone and floated in crusts upon the black water like miniature glowing islands. One of the walls was pierced by a sizable round hole, large enough to permit a man to walk through without stooping; it offered a view of some complex iron machinery, enormous gears and driving rods and other unfamiliar parts; through gaps in the machinery could be seen sections of a marble plain that sloped steeply upward, thus giving the appearance of an intricate puzzle laid out on a white backdrop with several pieces missing. Overall, the place had a look of fey enchantment, and when Alexandra perched on a marble block, drawing up her knees, resting her chin thereon, she seemed to acquire an aura of unreality, to become a creature of that place, a nymph or one of the Lorelei.

"A premonition," she said thoughtfully. "In other words, a feeling in which you placed your trust."

"I would have been a fool not to trust it."

"Yet you apparently don't trust certain other of your feelings. Or have you had a premonition concerning me?"

"Hardly. It's just I don't feel on solid ground with you." He sat next to her; deeper in the cavern, where the ceiling came down low and the walls narrowed, something big and quick was swimming just beneath the surface, making a rippling bulge in the shining black water, but showing no portion of itself. "In any case, it doesn't matter."

"What doesn't?"

She tried to conceal a coy smile by lowering her head.

"You're playing with me," he said.

She shrugged. "I'm trying to persuade you to tell me what you were thinking, but I'm not having a great deal of success."

"I'm certain you know what I was thinking," he said impatiently. "I was thinking about you and me. I was wondering how it might be with us."

"That's candid enough," she said.

"Of course," Beheim went on, put off by her neutral tone, "as I said before, it doesn't really matter, one way or another."

"And why is that?"

"Among other reasons, in a few days we will be leaving Banat. I will be returning to Paris, you to your home."

"I don't understand."

"What's the point of initiating a relationship when there's so little time to explore it?"

She shot him a searching glance, then gazed off toward the hole in the wall, twisting a strand of her auburn hair about a finger. "A relationship," she said. "What a strange thing to want. I want whatever I want without condition. I don't worry what will happen after I have it." She glanced at him again. "Usually, anyway."

His dignity wounded, he said, "It's probably just a symptom of my, uh ... What did you call it? My 'time of metamorphosis.'"

"No, I don't think so," she said, refitting her gaze to the hole in the wall and the mechanical puzzle beyond. "Agenor said you might be remarkable. It may be that he was right."

She seemed truly confounded by him, or by

something she felt that was somehow related to him. He had the sense that he could influence her now, so long as he did not overstate his case. "I can't believe it's remarkable to want something good to last," he said.

"I don't expect it is. But I haven't thought in those terms for a long time."

There was a silence during which he heard the lapping of water and saw something small and black moving rapidly on the marble plain that lay beyond the hole in the wall, coursing back and forth, becoming visible now and again through the gaps in the machinery. He closed his eyes and could feel her beside him, feel her warmth, the rhythms of her breath and heart. The scents of orange water, her natural musk, and sweet, hot blood mingled in a heady perfume.

"I'd like to ask you a question," he said. "One that may anger you."

"I'll try not to be angry."

"The man Kostolec killed. How do you reconcile something like that, the acceptance of that sort of callousness and cruelty, with the sensitivity—or should I say the humanity—you're displaying now?"

He could not see her face; she had turned her head a bit, and her hair fell across her cheek, obscuring her profile; but he could see the question strike her—the ligature of her neck cabling, a general tightness affecting her posture. But when she answered him, there was no anger in her voice, just a touch of hesitancy.

"Naturally I find it difficult," she said. "You have killed to feed. You understand the hypocrisy involved in considering those upon whom we feed in an emotional frame. And yet many of us do exactly that. I have done so myself. The guilt that eventually results from these futile associations, I believe, influences us to treat all mortals as animals, to reject them so that they cannot grow close to us." She brushed back her hair from her face and looked soberly at Beheim. "When I came to visit you earlier tonight, my treatment of your servant was, I would suppose, to some extent a defensive reaction. And, too"—she darted her eyes toward him—"I suppose I was a bit jealous of her. I've been attracted to you for quite a while. But at the same time she disgusted me. Perhaps my disgust was compensatory. Perhaps we only learn to despise them because we must. Or it may be that we change too drastically to respect them in any fashion. Yet sometimes I think we are not so different from mortals, that the one true difference between us is that we are stronger, and our cruelties are but vivid exaggerations of their cruelties. Even the worst of us has his rival in evil among humankind. So"—she clasped her hands, held them to her breast—"when you ask me about Kostolec, I am forced to say, we do what we must to live. What he did may seem evil or a waste, however you wish to characterize it. But he is old, of another generation. He has forgotten what once he was, and he lives only partially in the world that you and I inhabit." She made a plaintive noise. "That's all I know to say. That's . . ." She shook her head ruefully. "That's all."

He had expected to argue with her, to attempt some proof, but her answer was so succinct and clear, so poignant in its honesty, so free of the bombast with which most of his questions had been greeted, that he was utterly persuaded by it and could think of nothing to say. What she had said roused a feeling of sadness in him, and he tended to equate truth and sadness. Like most good Frenchmen, he thought, he did not believe in happiness, or rather he believed that nothing happy could be truly profound.

"What's that? I wonder," she said, pointing toward the hole in the wall, at the black, swiftly moving thing that appeared now and again on the marble plain.

"I've no idea."

"I want to see."

She hopped down from the block of marble and set out around the lake toward the hole in the wall. Reluctantly he followed. He had, he realized, been hoping to kiss her, and now that eventuality seemed remote.

The machinery that lay without the cavern was functionless, loose gears and frameworks, cogs and rods, much of it tumbled about like the discarded toys of a gigantic child, but some pieces joined by bolts with heads the size of serving platters, thus creating simple mechanical sculptures. Overhead, an immense, slanted mirror reflected silvery light downward from some invisible source. Like moonlight, Beheim thought, and he wondered if there might not be a system of mirrors channeling moonlight down from the battlements of the castle. Beyond the machinery, the plain of white marble sloped up for several hundred feet toward a wall pierced by a dozen arched doorways, and clattering across it, lowering its head and charging at some imaginary playmate, then cantering off, stopping to stare at Alexandra and Beheim as they approached, was a black stallion. A two-year-old, perhaps. Fully mature, but still coltish in its behavior.

"It's beautiful!" Alexandra said as the stallion trotted away, rolling its eyes at them. Its skin looked oiled. Gleams outlined the play of its muscles. It was perfect in its energy and sexual power, a living engine of blood and satiny skin and bone. At a distance, standing stock-still with the slope behind it, it might have been an emblem stamped into the white marble.

"What could it be doing here?" Alexandra asked.

Beheim said, "Maybe it's not really a horse."

"What else could it be?"

"Old Kostolec, perhaps. Or an enemy on whom he's cast a spell. In this place, it might be anything."

But the horse was exactly what it appeared to be, for—like a true horse—it refused to allow them to come close and touch it, sensing their strangeness, displaying extreme fear each time they tried, whinnying and moving farther away. Beheim considered the possibility that it might be, as had been the death of the young man at Kostolec's hands, a kind of lesson, set here to remind them of their unnatural life, of their predator's natures, and so ruin any illusion of normalcy they might wish to inhabit. That, at least, seemed the measure of its effect on Alexandra. She grew morose, silent, and when Beheim tried to kiss her, when he put his hands on her waist and fitted his mouth to hers, she responded to him for a split second, but then slipped from his grasp and told him that she was no longer sure of what she wanted.

Chapter FIVE

O ther rooms of the up-
per levels, like the
cavern and the marble
plain, came complete with occupants whose presence
seemed a function of design, or who at least appeared
to be on display. In one of these they encountered a
pitiful old man chained to a wall, surrounded by
scraps of gristly meat and piles of feces, who would
break into a merry nonsense song whenever they
came within ten feet of him, and would abruptly cease
his singing when they moved farther away than ten
feet, as if an internal alarm were triggered by this exact proximity. In another they found a black mastiff
with a medallion of red gold about its neck who stared
at them and panted; in another a lion slept beneath a
rose tree whose petals were green glass and whose
blooms were carved of carnelian. In a room with a
long rectangular pool filled with bright water and murals on the walls depicting pale violet skies and distant
snow peaks and graceful buildings with Doric columns
and peristyles, there were three beautiful women so
involved in a sapphic tryst that not even Beheim's
shouts could gain their attention. In a small chapel, its
ceiling decorated with frescoes in the style—if not by

68

the hand—of Michelangelo, a bearded man lashed to a cross spoke in a lectoral tone in a language that Alexandra identified as archaic Hebrew; now and then he would burst out laughing. In what had once been an aviary, a room littered with broken screens and rusted cages and birdlime, thousands of carrion beetles were feasting on the carcass of a huge and unidentifiable animal. In a room whose walls and ceiling were tented with black silk, a grossly fat woman lay naked on a canopied black bed, playing a game whose counters were tiny bones with ornate silver inlays; her opponent was a swarthy, emaciated man no more than eighteen inches tall, who sat on the edge of the bed, for the most part gazing in horror at the pack of little yapping white dogs that stood on their hind legs and pawed at the coverlet, trying to get at him.

There were, Alexandra said, dozens of such rooms, perhaps hundreds. Beheim would have liked to investigate them all, for he thought they might yield clues that would illuminate hitherto uncataloged facets of the Patriarch's character and thus serve to increase his comprehension of the Family; however, time was short, and they proceeded on past these rooms toward one in which Alexandra believed they would find Mikolas de Czege, the younger brother of Buka de Czege, who was patriarch of that branch. As the Valeas and the de Czeges were feuding, she was leery of confronting Mikolas, not because she feared him—she claimed she did not—but because she did not want to exacerbate the feud. "Don't let him bait you into anger," she cautioned him. "You'll never learn anything that way." Given the reputation of the de Czeges, Beheim himself was none too eager to interview Mikolas; but once he had passed this test, he thought, the worst would be behind him, and so he went forward with, if not confidence, then something of a hopeful frame of mind.

One wall of the long, narrow room where they found Mikolas was gray, with strips of peeling wallpaper hanging down and set with tall, narrow windows; behind the glass of each were powerful lanterns from which chutes of chalky counterfeit sunlight spilled onto the rough wooden floor. Like winter light, it pointed up the general disrepair and made the space it lit seem emptier, more desolate. Three children, two boys and a girl dressed in rags, all with dirty blond hair, listless and pale, all approximately eleven or twelve years old, were sitting beneath the window farthest from the door, staring into nowhere; beside them was a solitary straight-backed chair upon which some clothing and a towel were heaped. The other walls, also peeling and gray, were windowless, and from pegs thereon were suspended a variety of weapons: swords, whips, maces, spears, daggers. At the center of the room was a black pole with two buttons mounted on it that ran up into a box of white metal on the ceiling, and a man-sized dummy of pale, heavily grained wood with a saber bolted to its hand. Its head was a long faceless oval, pointed at each end, something insectile about the shape, and it attached to a thinnish neck; its body was scarred and nicked; a red heart was painted on its chest, and wires ran from its limbs to a complex arrangement of cables and tracks that converged upon the box on the ceiling and permitted the dummy to move about the room, even into its farthest corners. Whenever Mikolas attacked, the dummy would parry and then make a rickety-looking yet effective counterattack. After watching from the doorway for a while, studying the box and the wires, Beheim could not determine how the mechanism worked. There must be, he concluded, a device within the metal box that translated Mikolas's thrusts and parries into appropriate reactions on the dummy's part, but such a device would needs be of unheard-of sophistication, and he could not begin to imagine its essentials.

Mikolas was a short, burly man, apparently in his middle twenties, with blacksmith's arms and a brutish, heavy-jawed face; thick stubble shadowed his cheeks. His black hair, which was cut like a monk's, was for the moment hidden beneath a studded metal cap, and he wore a padded tunic and leggings. Each time he swung his sword, he emitted a piggish grunt. Sweat poured down his reddened face. As he circled the dummy it seemed he must have spotted Beheim and Alexandra standing in the doorway, but his concentration was so fierce as to admit no other sight apart from his mindless opponent, for he did not notice them until Alexandra, growing impatient, called out his name. He looked toward them, startled, then ducked away from the dummy's slash, receiving a glancing blow on the side of his metal cap that sent him reeling. He leaped to the pole, pressed the top button, and the dummy came all disjointed and hung limply.

"Trying to kill me, Alexandra?" Mikolas laughed and walked a few swaggering paces toward them; he removed his helmet, sailed it across the room in the general direction of the three children, none of whom stirred or in any way reacted to the noise. "You'll have to do better than that."

She gave no reply.

"Who's that with you?" Mikolas asked, peering at Beheim; he began unbuttoning his padded tunic.

"My name is Beheim. I've been sent—"

"Oh, right! I've got no time for this shit!" Mikolas shrugged out of the tunic, revealing a massive chest as thickly furred as a bear's; he started to unsnap his leggings. "I didn't do it, all right? Not that I wouldn't have enjoyed a drink or two from the blond bitch. But I never had the chance. Maybe next time." He shucked off the leggings and stood naked before them, grinning apishly at Alexandra. "What do you think, cousin? A hell of a man, aren't I? Come on home with me, and I'll give you a fuck you won't forget."

Alexandra regarded him with unalloyed malice. "You'd best put your toy away," she said. "It appears all that exercise has made it shrivel."

"Oh-ho!" Mikolas shook his head as if in an excess of mirth. "Damn if I don't wish things were different between Felipe and Buka! I'd be knocking on Felipe's door, trying to arrange a marriage." He winked at Beheim. "She's got a pretty pair of tits, doesn't she?"

"I'm afraid I have to ask you some questions," Beheim said.

Mikolas scowled at him; then, in mocking imitation, said, " 'I'm afraid I have to ask you some questions.' " He snorted in amusement. "I'll just bet you're afraid. Maybe if you stopped hiding behind the Giraffe's skirts, you'd learn to act like a man."

Beheim restrained himself, examined his notes. "You claim to have gone hunting with your brother the night of the murder. Exactly where did you hunt?"

Mikolas's scowl deepened; but after a moment he made a petulant noise and said, "Hell, I'll answer your questions. I've got nothing to hide. Come on." He led the way toward the chair and the seated children, his hairy buttocks jiggling. "We went hunting in the depths of the castle. That's where I picked up these three." He gestured at the children with his sword. "Make a nice set, don't they?" He propped his sword against the wall and began toweling himself dry. "I like

them so much, I've given them names. This one"—he
indicated the smaller of the boys, who looked to be
asleep—"is Breakfast. This one here"—he tapped the
second boy on the top of the head, causing it to loll to
the side—"is Lunch. And this one"—he lifted the
girl's chin; she gazed at him dully—"is my favorite."
He smacked his lips in a parody of appetite. "Supper."

They were, despite their slackness of expression,
pretty children; their necks all bore dried bloodstains.
Beheim's revulsion was overwhelming, but he forced
himself to disregard the children and kept his eyes on
Mikolas. The man's face was the image of unhealthy
excess. His skin was blotchy. A red line was indented
on his brow from the pressure of the metal cap. Mad
black eyes tucked into fleshy folds. The thick, cruel
lips of a sensualist. A web of broken capillaries spread
across his boxer's broad, flattened nose, and the lobe
of his left ear was ragged and discolored; it appeared
to have been bitten off.

"Is there anyone else who can testify to your
whereabouts?" Beheim asked.

"Certainly." Again Mikolas pointed to the children. "Question them if you wish."

"I scarcely think they will make credible witnesses."

"Well, you can ask anyone if these three were
with me before that night. And then you can ask the
children what happened and how long we took in having our fun. We had a wonderful time." Mikolas pulled
on his trousers and leaned close to Beheim, envelop-
ing him in an aura of acidic sweat. "Ever taste a virgin's blood? Quite a treat. I'd offer you some now, but
sad to say, she's no longer a virgin. Active little bitch,
she was. Flipped about like a fish out of water."

"You incredible pig!" said Alexandra.

"Now look what I've done! I've made the Giraffe jealous." Mikolas slipped into a red wool shirt, beaming at them.

"You know," Beheim said to Alexandra, his control faltering, "I've just had a splendid idea. There's no point in continuing the investigation. We'll probably never be able to unmask the actual culprit, but we don't have to. We have the perfect candidate right here."

Mikolas said, "What in hell's name do you mean by that?"

"You've no real proof of your whereabouts," said Beheim. "There's not a soul who wouldn't believe you capable of such an obscene act. All I have to do is dredge up one or two of your enemies who'd be willing to testify against you. Manufacture a few pieces of evidence. I believe the Patriarch would be delighted to have all this resolved so tidily."

Mikolas's expression was a cipher; he finished buttoning his shirt. "Bear with me a moment," he said. Then with one hand he lifted the taller of the two boys, pushed his head to the side, and drank from the vein in his neck. The boy's eyes showed in crescents of white beneath his drooping lids. His left hand trembled. Breath whistled in his throat. As Mikolas gulped down the blood he stared at Beheim and Alexandra through a fringe of the boy's hair.

Beheim felt Alexandra's hand on his arm, but he needed no restraint. The children were dead already, and whatever compassion he had felt for them had been overborne by his loathing for de Czege. And perhaps, he thought, he had never felt any compassion. Perhaps all he had felt had been regret for feeling nothing.

"There now," said Mikolas, depositing the boy

roughly on the floor. "Much better." He wiped a smear of blood from his mouth and gave a sigh of satisfaction. "I think I'll tell you a story. A de Czege story."

"Spare us," said Alexandra.

"No, really! You must hear this." He settled his pants about his hips, rotated his head to ease some stiffness. "There once was a man, a man very much like myself, as a matter of fact. A rough bastard who took what he wanted and dared the world to spit in his eye. Now, he was no admirable character"—Alexandra laughed at this; Mikolas paid her no mind—"but he'd never aspired to be an admirable character, so that didn't bother him. The only thing he'd ever wanted to be was as brave a man as his brother. And that was uncommonly brave, for his brother was counted among the bravest men in the country. Well"—he picked up his sword and laid the blade flat against his palm—"one day his brother told him that he'd been bitten by a vampire. He'd managed to escape, but he was sick, afraid that the vampire would be able to control him. This was a very long time ago, back in the days when vampires were taken as a matter of course, so the man had no qualms about believing his brother."

Mikolas went half a dozen paces out into the center of the room. "Do you know what the hero of my story did? He decided to kill the vampire." He glanced back at them over his shoulder. "Don't you think that was brave of him?" he asked mildly "Knowing what a vampire was and still having the courage to confront it. You see, he realized he would never be able to find where the vampire slept, at least not before he could pose a further danger to his brother. He would have to visit the vampire's dwelling place that night and kill him while he was awake. He was afraid. Oh, he was terrified! But fear was a goad to him, and so without delay, he went to the vampire's house and hid in a closet, and when the vampire appeared, accompanied by two sickly ladies, he stepped out from his hiding place. He had a sword in his hand. Like this one. A saber. The vampire laughed and laughed. He knew a sword could do him no permanent harm. But instead of attacking, the man drew the edge of the sword across the palm of his own hand, making a deep cut. Like this."

As he had described, Mikolas laid open the palm of his hand. Blood trickled down his wrist.

"Now, this was an extremely stupid vampire," he went on. "Extremely vain. He believed his overpowering charm was responsible for the man's act of courage. And so he did not weaken the man with his eyes before taking blood. He lapped at the man's hand, almost playfully, and then he struck into the man's neck. The man was dizzy with the rapture, but he maintained his resolve, and he pulled out an oak stake that he had secreted in his belt and pierced the vampire's heart while he was feeding. The women attacked him, but they were weak, disoriented by their master's death, and he was able to elude them." He wiped his bloody hand on his trousers, examined it. "A happy ending, you might think. But there's an irony involved. The man rode home to tell his brother, only to find that his brother had died, and that in dying he had gained life immortal. Before he could give him the news, his brother judged him. And thus it was that the de Czege branch was born."

Mikolas stared at them, his face tightening. "Do you really believe that I could fear you?" he said, his voice thick with rage. "That I could fear anything?" He swung his sword in a windy arc. "If it's threats you want to play at, here's one for you. I'm going to cut you into goddamn pieces and see how long it takes for you to grow whole again."

He closed on them in a series of quick steps and slashed at Beheim's head. Beheim darted away, pushing Alexandra ahead of him. He evaded another charge by Mikolas, lunging to the right, then sprinting off past the windows, fetching up against a sidewall, where several dozen weapons hung from pegs. As he turned he saw Alexandra knocked to the floor by a blow from Mikolas's fist. She lay without moving. Beheim snatched down a sword with an ornate guard and unsheathed it.

Mikolas's laugh was exultant. "Ah! A contest!" he said. "I wondered if you were a man, and now it appears you are. Not much of one, perhaps. But enough for the business at hand, eh?" He bowed, made a flourish with his saber. "I accept your challenge."

He stepped forward a pace, wary now, but before he could advance farther, Beheim launched a desperate attack, driving him back into the center of the room, close to the black pole and the fencing dummy. For more than a minute they fought in a fury, exchanging dozens of blows, the ring of steel on steel making a bright counterpoint to their grunts and exclamations. Beheim grew in confidence. The sophistication of his attack was offsetting Mikolas's superior strength. But his confidence soon eroded as Mikolas began to fight defensively, forcing Beheim to spend his energies, seeking to wear him down. Sweat trickled into the corner of his eyes. His breath came shallowly. Through the weave of their swords he saw Mikolas's smirking. The light of the false sun was affecting his vision, flashing on the blades, dazzling him.

"I'm going to cut off your bastard head," Mikolas said, and parried. "I'm going to"—another parry, a

probing attack—"put it in a hatbox. I'll feed it rats."
He lunged, thrust, slashed, then retreated. "I wonder
what will happen. Will it grow a new body? Will the
body grow a new head? What do you think?" His
shoulder brushed against the fencing dummy, and he
shoved the thing aside, sending it into a jittering
dance. Beheim was struck by an idea. He was not at
all certain it would work, but he was absolutely certain
of what would happen were some new element not
added to the equation.

He spent the next minute or so convincing Mikolas that he had grown more fatigued than in actuality
he had, until at the end of that time he was in full retreat, leading Mikolas a chase throughout the room,
passing closer and closer to the pole. At one point he
was almost too convincing in his portrayal of weakness, and the tip of Mikolas's saber drew a hot stripe
of pain across his upper thigh; but he could feel the
wound beginning to heal almost immediately, and it
did not cause him even momentary inconvenience.
Mikolas continued to taunt, to threaten, and by this
gauge, Beheim was able to measure the increase of his
arrogance. Finally, with Beheim's weariness becoming
a real liability, he threw himself toward the pole, hoping that he had chosen the correct angle of approach.
Mikolas followed him, having to shoulder past the
dummy once again, and Beheim punched the top button on the pole.

With an uncanny series of movements, the
dummy seemed to reassemble itself, took on human
posture and lurched into motion; reacting to the push
Mikolas had given it, it slashed him across the back,
then aimed a second slash at his neck, which Mikolas,
in turning, just managed to parry. Beheim seized the
opportunity to thrust his sword into Mikolas's side just

below the ribs; he ripped the blade sideways as
Mikolas howled and twisted, dropping his saber. An
instant later the dummy pierced him through the
belly, thus effectively skewering him from two directions. Mikolas swayed, his eyes rolled back, he vom-
ited blood. Then both the dummy and Beheim yanked
their weapons free, and he collapsed onto the floor,
blood diapering his trousers and soaking his red shirt.
Beheim started toward Alexandra, who was sitting
up, holding a hand to her temple. The dummy came
after him, its saber at the ready and wires singing in
their tracks, its clever feet clacking on the boards.

He had assumed that the dummy would only react to an attack, but now, having offered no attack, staring at that oddly inimical wooden head, at
the scarred body with its faded valentine heart, he
knew that he had been wrong, that some undreamed-
of scientific miracle had invested it with deadly
independence. The dummy struck at him, its weirdly
articulated joints lending a mantislike stiffness to its
movements, but moving far more rapidly than any
crawling thing, the persistent click and clatter of its
limbs adding a sinister value to its violent intent. It
was all Beheim could do to fend off its attack, let alone
mount one of his own, and as he was driven across the
room he thought that the best he could hope for was
that once he had been severely wounded, whatever
regulation governed the dummy would be satisfied
and it would desist. The dummy's saber notched his
shoulder. Sliced his chest. In desperation, he ducked
under the swung blade and grappled with the thing,
his face pressed against the cool, smooth oval of its
head; but it began to shiver and shake, to jerk uncon-
trollably, and he was thrown to the floor. He rolled
away from a downstroke, came to his feet, and

sprinted toward the pole at the center of the room, hoping to reach the buttons and switch the dummy off; but it made an unearthly, ungainly leap, going unbelievably high, that carried it across the room in time to block his path. It turned to him, its limbs coordinating in a horrid mechanical rhythm that caused him to picture a crab stalking along the sea bottom toward some helpless pulpy victim.

As it confronted him, its head tipped to the side as if in perplexed study, saber pointing toward his chest, the grain of the pale brown wood seemed to contrive an eerie, eyeless face. He could have sworn he sensed a faint radiation like the presence of personality from the thing, and he had the feeling it was assessing him in some way, matching his skills with an array of tactical possibilities. "I yield," he said, hoping against all rationality that it would hear him. He glanced over at Mikolas. Still down. Alexandra had not moved. "Stop," he said to the dummy, wondering if it might not respond to a simple command, a magic word.

The dummy took a step forward, holding its saber in an unusual high guard up by its cheek, blade pointing to the ceiling. It stood still a moment, then initiated a whirling attack, wielding the saber in great circles, at times aiming slashes at Beheim while its back was turned, moving at incredible speed. Beheim dove to the floor, tried to cut the wires attached to its legs, but could not penetrate its defense. He regained his feet and backed away, unable to do other than protect himself. He was tiring badly. Each parried blow sent a shock into his elbows. The sword grew heavy, the grip slick with sweat. He closed with the dummy a second time and wrenched at its head, its arms, hop-

ing to tear them off, but was thrown off again before
he could do any real damage.

And then, without warning, it went limp, hanging
from its wires as impotent as a marionette, head down,
sword trailing on the floor. Beheim, who had been in
the process of scrambling to his feet, sagged back. He
saw Alexandra standing by the pole, bashing at the control buttons with a mace. The children were still sitting
in listless poses beneath the window, their blond hair
glowing in a spill of wintry light so clearly defined it
might have been a tilted column of crystal; their eyes
were like smudges in their white faces. Mikolas was
crawling feebly in the direction of the door, leaving a
smeared track of blood as he went. After a bit he
stopped crawling and sat there, his legs tucked beneath him, holding his wounded stomach. With a
mighty effort, Beheim got to his knees. Once he had
managed to catch his breath, he stood, walked over,
and kicked Mikolas in the chest, laying him out flat.
Mikolas gasped and closed his eyes. When he opened
them, Beheim stabbed him in the throat, turning the
blade to widen the wound, and then in the groin. He
felt tremendous joy well up inside him. Blood filmed
over Mikolas's lips. He tried to speak, but the wound
in his throat prevented it; he stared at Beheim with
black intensity, and Beheim looked quickly away.

"Enough!" said Alexandra. "There's no purpose to
this, not unless you intend to kill him."

"Now, there's an idea!"

"No." She closed her long fingers about his wrist;
for an instant there seemed to be a flurry of lights and
darks in her eyes. "This has not helped to ease matters
between the Valeas and the de Czeges. I don't want it
to go any further."

"As you wish, then," he said. "But I refuse to have

him hounding me during the remainder of the investigation. Give me the mace."

"What are you going to do?"

"Break his legs. That should take two or three days to heal."

Mikolas rolled away, trying to reach his sword. Beheim hauled him back by his belt and held him while he thrashed and fumed; a pinkish liquid bubbled from his throat—the wound was healing quickly.

"What of his brother?" Alexandra asked. "And what of the rest of the de Czeges? Their legs will be whole."

"One of them, at least, will no longer pose a threat." Beheim stretched out a hand to her. "Give it to me."

"I don't trust you," she said after a pause. "I'll do it."

"Don't be ridiculous! Go and see to the children."

"What's the use of that? If we take them away from him, they'll only return. You know that."

He continued holding out his hand, and with obvious reluctance, she passed him the mace and walked off toward the window where the children were sitting.

"You know," Beheim said to Mikolas without looking him in the eyes, "I understand you. I used to arrest men like you. Sometimes I had to kill them. I understand you very well."

He tapped the mace lightly against Mikolas's knee, watched the leg stiffen in anticipation. Then he raised the mace high and brought it down on the kneecap with all his strength, shattering bone, smashing the fabric of the trousers down into a mire of blood and cartilage. A high-pitched whining escaped from Mikolas's lips, and he lost consciousness. Beheim crushed the other kneecap with a second blow and sat patiently, waiting for him to wake up. Alexandra, he saw, was kneeling beside the children, ministering in some way to one of them. Finally Mikolas stirred. His eyes fluttered open. Focused on Beheim.

"Now I'm going to tell *you* a story," said Beheim, pushing Mikolas's face to the side with the ball of the mace so that he was unable to use the power of his eyes. "Not so long ago in Paris there was a maniac who had killed four women with his hands. He was, as a matter of fact, a man very much like you. A physical marvel, possessed of inhuman strength. We could see that from the brutal things he'd done to the bodies. He sent us messages, laughing at us, challenging us to find him. He boasted that he would kill anyone who dared come near him. He wrote poems about our stupidity and mailed them to the newspapers. Eventually we discovered who he was, but since he lived on the streets, in the sewers, any dark place that he could dominate with his strength, it was no easy task to bring him to ground. At long last, however, we managed to trap him in Montparnasse one night, and we chased him up onto the rooftops."

Alexandra came up beside him and started to speak, but he held up a hand, urging her to silence. "Just give me a moment," he said. "I'm almost finished here."

Mikolas tried to turn his head, to look at Alexandra, but Beheim gave him another firm push with the ball of the mace.

"The houses in that particular section of Montparnasse are set very close together," he went on. "Many of the streets no more than alleys, the alleys barely wide enough to permit a grown man passage. The rooftops are like a country all their own, a terrain of odd peaks and gables and steep slopes, all tiled and slick underfoot even in dry weather. A dangerous place to hunt so formidable a man as our maniac. We knew he could not escape us. We had cordoned off an area of several blocks. Sooner or later we were bound to catch him, either on the streets or on the rooftops. But we had two concerns. First, we did not want to take many casualties. If we flooded the rooftops with men, the maniac would almost certainly be able to kill several of them. Perhaps more. He would leap upon them from some dark cranny and rip them apart or throw them off the roof. We would have to be very cautious. Yet at the same time speed was of the essence, for we believed that if we did not catch him soon, he would succeed in breaking into one of the apartments and wreak havoc upon those dwelling there. Naturally we were attempting to evacuate the buildings, but at that time of night it was a slow and laborious process. The chances of our completing it before the maniac decided to effect entry were negligible, indeed.

"A compelling problem, don't you agree? Seemingly one without a happy solution." Beheim nudged Mikolas with the mace. "I wonder how you would have solved it. You would have burned the whole damned area down, I'd imagine. You see, men like you are not accustomed to operating under constraints. They believe that such constraints are enfeebling, that men like me who suffer them are witlings, easy prey. But they're wrong to believe that. Those constraints breed a certain type of canny strength that is often the downfall of men like you, men who put their faith in willfulness and brute force."

He noticed Alexandra staring at him and, annoyed, said, "What is it? Where are the children?"

"Both the boys are dead," she said tonelessly.

"The girl . . . perhaps she will live. I've sent her on an errand. She'll be in good hands."

He glanced at the two blond, still forms seated beneath the window. Their deaths seemed almost irrelevant to the loathing he felt for Mikolas, to add no more than a thin wash of color to his emotions, and he thought now that this was because he had long since given up on them. And yet knowing that they were dead changed him in one way, making him less interested in confiding in Mikolas, more eager to get on with things.

"I'm not going to tell you the rest of my story," he said to Mikolas. "Though perhaps I should tell you how it ended. We did not lose a single man, and ten minutes after I went alone onto the rooftops, the maniac took his own life." He bent close to Mikolas, keeping his head still with the mace. "I'm not afraid of you," he whispered. "I want you to come after me. That is, if you're man enough. If you think you can face me without running to your brother for assistance. I'm sure you'll be tempted to turn what is essentially a personal matter into a feud with the Agenors, but consider what that says about the caliber of your manhood. Frankly I don't think it's in you to engage in a conflict that you're not absolutely certain of winning. You're a coward, a bully. And not such a formidable bully at that. You couldn't kill me here, on your own ground, and anywhere else it's going to be easy for me. I'll be waiting."

He pushed himself up to his feet and sent the mace skittering across the floor into a far corner, and with Alexandra in tow, he left Mikolas to his hatred and his pain.

As they walked along a corridor that led away from the gray room, Alexandra kept looking expectantly at him, and finally she said, "Aren't you going to tell me?"

"Tell you what?"

"What happened on the rooftops of Montparnasse. With you and the maniac. I'm curious how you managed it."

In one of the rooms nearby a clock was tolling midnight; from the distance came terrified shouts, wild laughter, then a tinny clangor, and the convergence of these sounds, their hollow resonance and dark specificity, reawakened Beheim to the alien immensity of his environment. Alexandra's face, despite its loveliness, its openness, struck him as being a devious contrivance, as threatening and perplexing as the blank wooden face of the fencing dummy. Secrets flashed and darted in the shifting currents of her green irises. Give nothing away, he thought. Show the world a face empty of everything except that which they want to believe of you. He felt suddenly, disastrously weary, exhausted by the poisons of fatigue and adrenaline. He wanted to rest, to stop his thoughts from spinning in their unstable orbits.

"No," he told her. "Not for now, anyway."

Chapter SIX

Several levels beneath the room where they had fought with Mikolas, they found a large unoccupied chamber with whitewashed walls and plaster angels that flowed from the molding in the corners of the ceiling, their grave, contemplative faces seeming to guarantee the sanctity of the space they overlooked; it was furnished with two overstuffed chairs, a chest of drawers, and the wreck of an ebony bed, one of its legs broken, its tented canopy half-collapsed, that was big enough and sufficiently morbid in design—the frieze on the headboard depicted a crowd of tormented faces—to serve as a funeral barge. Two lanterns hung from the ceiling; when lit, they burned with a pale constant flame. They wedged the chest of drawers beneath the bed, succeeding thereby in placing the mattress on a more or less even keel, and once this was done, Beheim stripped off his bloody shirt, stretched out, and closed his eyes. Alexandra, however, went pacing about the room, and after five minutes or so had passed and she continued to pace, Beheim propped himself up on an elbow and asked what was troubling her.

"I'm not troubled," she said. "Just a little nervous. I'm always a little nervous."

"Are you worried that the de Czeges will come after us tonight?"

"No." She leaned against the wall, hands behind her back. "They'll brood and plot and attempt to devise some ingenious trap, but in the end, if they do anything, which is not a certainty, they'll lose their tempers and charge. That's their way. They're incapable of subtle maneuvers."

"Which makes them excellent suspects."

"In the matter of the Golden?" She shook her head. "I don't believe it. Not that they wouldn't be capable of the violence. But this particular murder doesn't seem the sort of outrage they would commit. It would take some planning at least. And as I said, they tend to act on the spur of the moment."

Beheim examined the sheet beneath him; it bore a delicate raised pattern, white on white, of thorns and roses.

"I've been thinking," he said. "I'm not making any progress like this. I'm going to do as you suggested. The bottle cap is the one consequential piece of evidence I have. You were right. I really don't have a choice."

"I thought you'd see that." Her voice was subdued.

"Will you go with me to Felipe's apartments?"

"I can't," she said. "I can't risk it. If Felipe caught me there, if he discovered I was plotting against him, it would ruin everything. You'll need someone to keep watch, though. Your servant, Giselle. Take her."

Here we are, he thought, here's the part you have to shine a light on. Here's the fundamental discourse upon which all your decisions regarding her must be based. "What exactly would it ruin?" he asked.

A petulant expression came fleetingly to her face. "Everything I want."

"Power."

A hesitation. "Yes, power."

"But there's more."

She nodded.

"You're not going to tell me, are you?"

"It's nothing important. Just some things I want."

"How do you know you'll get them? Are you certain I'll find evidence implicating Felipe?"

"How *could* I be certain?" Anger made her voice shrill, stiffened her shoulders as she paced across the room and stood by the opposite wall. With her back to the whitewashed surface, the red tints in her hair and the blue of her silk nightdress and the vivid coloration of her eyes were all enhanced; it looked as if she were a goddess emerging from a dimension of whiteness, from a featureless white sky.

"You're only hoping that Felipe's involved, then?" Beheim said.

Another nod.

Beheim sat up straight, his back against the frieze of faces. "These things that you want, could one of them be the Lady Dolores?"

Hectic spots of red burned in her cheeks. "No!"

"It's said the two of you have become close."

"Close!" She spat out a laugh. "That's hardly the term I'd choose."

"Which term would you choose?"

Her flushed cheeks reddened further, and he thought she was going to shout at him; but she said nothing.

"My questions seem to be upsetting you."

"It upsets me that you're treating me like a suspect."

"How else should I treat you? You won't volunteer anything."

She appeared to be giving this question more attention than she had the others. After a considerable pause she crossed to the bed, sat on the edge, and trailed her fingers across the sheet.

"Felipe asked me to help him find out what Dolores wanted from him," she said. "He was suspicious of her. He had been ever since they became lovers."

"Why would he ask for your help? You two have been quits for some time, haven't you?"

She shook back a curl from her cheek and gazed up to one of the plaster angels, as if receiving instruction. Beheim's eyes went to her graceful neck, the blue vein that figured it, barely visible beneath the white skin, vanishing in the hollow of her throat.

"I don't know if I could ever explain how it is between the two of us," she said. "There've been times aplenty when he's used me badly, times when I have used him. It's always a struggle with me and Felipe. Always. He's a cruel, perverted bastard. I would not grieve to see him undergo an Illumination, yet at times I feel something akin to love for him. There is something that binds us. Something of the blood, I imagine. Whatever we feel toward one another, it's strong."

"I've been laboring under the impression that you have designs on usurping his power. In assuming the leadership of the Valeas."

"That's no secret. Felipe and I agree on many things, but he's not aggressive enough. He's too involved with his pleasures to be a competent steward of our interests."

"In what way," Beheim asked, "do you believe that he's insufficiently aggressive?"

"In every way. He's let our differences with the de Czeges get out of hand, for instance. There was no need for a feud. He simply didn't exert himself in smoothing things over. And lately, this whole business about the Family moving out of Europe. Ostensibly he sides with Agenor. But he won't commit. Not entirely. He keeps hedging his bets, not because he's having doubts, but because he really hasn't studied the matter."

"How do you stand on the question?"

"I could not support a migration at this juncture," she said. "But I believe a group should be sent to investigate the possibility at once. And if things are as open and unthreatening as Agenor states, we would be fools not to establish a colony. At the very least, a colony."

Her opinion had been delivered with firmness, confidence, and did not seem at all facile. Beheim could detect no trace of duplicity in her speech or manner.

"Does that surprise you?" she asked.

"Given your reputed friendship with Dolores, yes, it does. But you haven't told me about that yet."

The stiffness returned to her shoulders. "Dolores has published the rumor that we are friends, but it's not so." She let out a sigh and leaned against the post at the foot of the bed. "After Felipe asked me for help, I pretended to become her friend. Perhaps she saw through my pretense. Or perhaps friendship has a different value for her than that I place upon it. One evening when I came to visit her, she seduced me. I have been with women before, but always of my own choice. Dolores used her power to enforce my submission. She was too strong for me. She coerced me, she made me do things against my will. It was every bit as much a violation as the most violent of rapes. I hated her for that. I hate her still. I cannot begin to tell you how much. For Felipe's sake, I've continued to play at being her friend, hoping to learn something that would turn him against her, that would drive him to kill her."

"And have you learned anything?"

She plucked at a fold of blue silk, rolled it between her fingers. "I don't know. They're both so damned elusive. I've had hints, but nothing incontrovertible. Lately I've come to believe that although Felipe wanted me to spy on Dolores, he had something else in mind as well. I think he was playing a double game, using me against Dolores and using Dolores against me, informing her that he would set me to spy on her, as if it were not the truth, and pretending that he was doing this in order to let her make me her lover, something she had always desired. But I can't be sure. I have no means of discriminating between what he truly intended and what I fear may be his intent. And as to Dolores's motives ..." She gave a dismayed laugh. "Everywhere I turn I find evidence of some sly possibility. I've begun to fear for my life. If Dolores seeks to control Felipe, mustn't she then view me as an impediment? Or could all this merely be theatrics, a horrible joke? I'm not sure even they know at this point." She put a hand on Beheim's knee. "That is why I involved you. I was afraid. I saw an opportunity to use you against them." Her voice faltered. "I wish now that I—"

"You wish that someone else, not I, had been charged with this weighty responsibility. In the few hours we have been together, it has grown clear that there is a great natural affinity between us, a connection that you value and would not want to risk. But I *have* been charged with this responsibility, and you must let me go forward, hoping that the assistance you have lent will not only serve your ends, but will enable me to bring the matter to a quick and successful resolution so that we may then employ our affection to the fullest and so all our pleasures prove."

He said this in a flat, deferential manner, ending with sheer sarcasm, as if his words were a summation of an obvious and rather dubious state of affairs; he kept his face empty and watched for her reaction. Anger, he had thought, would be the most difficult reaction to interpret, but while a trace of anger—or perhaps, defiance—did show itself in her face, it was swept immediately aside by a dawning look of confusion and alarm, and when he had finished speaking, she turned away, downcast, and said, "Why are you trying to degrade the very feelings you sought to have me confess not an hour ago?"

He could not believe that the injury in her voice was false, but he refrained from answering her, wanting to accumulate more evidence before he arrived at even a partial conclusion.

Alexandra looked at him over her shoulder, her expression as grave and sweetly concerned as the faces of the angels that guarded the corners of the room. "I cannot ease your suspicions. Not completely. Suspicion is in the air of this place, especially now, especially considering the task before you." She lowered her eyes. "But I will do what I can."

She stood, crossed to one of the hanging lamps, and reduced its flame to a tiny white spear point.

"What are you doing?" Beheim asked.

"As I told you," she said. "What I can."

She turned down the second lamp, creating a lovely dusk in the room. Then she slipped one of the straps of her nightdress from her shoulder. The newly exposed flesh glowed in the half-light.

"This is scarcely original of you," he said, feeling a mixture of longing and anxiety. "I'm not a fool. Do you expect this to prove anything?"

"Proof is not what I have to give you." She moved close to the bed and stood with her right hand on the remaining strap. "Well, Michel. Tell me what I should do?"

His tongue was thick, his mouth dry.

"Can you deny that you want me?"

"No," he said. "I cannot."

"Forget the murder for a while, Michel. Forget who we are. And where. We may not win at this. It often happens that what one thinks one feels suffers in the consummation. But if we are to lose, let us do so as man and woman, not because we have let suspicion cloud the issue." She settled on the bed beside him. "I want to make love, Michel. Not sex. Sex is always available. I don't care about it. It's never very good. But making love, that's different. It's been years since I've made love. So many, I can't remember what it's like. With you . . ." She took his hand, ran her thumb across his knuckles. "With you, I have the feeling it will happen. What do you think? Is it possible for us?"

He started to respond, to murmur something, more an encouragement than an answer, but she put a finger to his lips, stopping him.

"I know," she said, her voice falling to a whisper. "I know."

In the false dusk a light seemed to accumulate around Alexandra's body, pale and moon-colored against the sheet. There was so much of her, such incredibly long legs, such an extreme flow of line and volume, Beheim became entranced by the exaggerated perspectives available, gazing up at the equatorial swell of her belly, toward the flattened mounds of her breasts with their dark oases of areola and turreted nipples, or down from her breasts toward the unruly pubic tuft between her thighs, in all reminding him by its smoothness of the sand sculpture of a sleeping giantess he had seen years before on a beach in Spain. When he kissed her, minutelong explorations of kisses, his erection trapped between their bellies, she trembled, trembled in her core, in some unprospected secret adit, and those elusive tremors, their seismic delicacy, made him feel huge and potent. He wanted to braid them together into a glorious upheaval that would send comets streaking across her mental sky and set all her flesh to quaking. He began to kiss his way down her body, past her rib cage, making glistening snail tracks with his tongue. "No," she said weakly, clutching at his head, trying to pull him back. But he was determined, unstoppable. He positioned himself between her legs, his own legs sticking off the end of the bed, and penetrated her with two fingers, working them deep. As he licked and touched, his hand making an erratic round of her breasts, it seemed that in the rich tartness of her taste he detected subtle accents of dismay, of anxiety, and he knew that he should crawl back up, kiss her mouth, reassure her, because she felt alone and lost, uncertain in her responses, of how he wanted her to respond. Then she began to find a rhythm, and not just in her movements, but an internal rhythm, a sly, uncoiling beat that cued the exercise of his lips and tongue. Her hips rocked, shuddered. She caressed his hair, a tacit permission. Her legs angled wider. He was, he thought, plunging through a stratum of pent-up emotions toward that gray place he had sensed within her, threatening to revitalize its deadness. He slipped his hands beneath her buttocks, lifted her, his mouth barnacled to her, like a man drinking from a tureen. A fierce groan shook her, a birth groan, something ripping from her side. Her slicked thighs clamped to his head. Blood sang in his ears. He could hear her babbling. Unintelligible words, skewed whistles of breath, frills of pretty noise, keenings cut short by gasps. He felt the stew of her responses, fragmentary until that moment, a moil of disparate elements, starting to bubble and mix, pervaded by the heat he had kindled. He loved the violence of the release that was building in her, loved creating it. Like a caveman grunting in delight over his flint-struck flame. But then she was plucking at him, saying, "Michel! Michel, please!"; hauling him up, leaving him crouched beside her, sticky-faced and confused, his erection waggling and waning in the suddenly chill air.

"What is it? What's wrong?" he asked, and she said, the words coming in a clumsy rush, "Not the first time, not like that. Is it all right? I'm sorry. I just want you here. With me."

Embarrassed, feeling that he had been failing to please her, he said, "I'm sorry, I thought you'd . . ."

"No," she said, pulling him close, cradling his head to her breasts, "no, it's not you, I just need to see your face, your eyes." And when he started to speak again, she kissed him to stop the clutter of words.

After a moment quiet flowed in to surround them, the way it fills in the ruptured spaces created by an explosion, softening the angles of the room, refining it into an intimate and finite place. They kissed again, and the kiss cured the last of their awkwardness. She lifted her right knee, rested it on his hip, letting his member glide between her legs; if he had shifted a degree, he would have penetrated her, but he held back, a bit unsure of himself now, wanting her to guide him. Her breath quickened. Her kisses grazed his lips, his cheeks; her tongue flicked out. Lamb kisses, serpent kisses. At last she reached behind her, her fingers curling about his member, cool as live marble, and he went deep in one long, sweet plunge, feeling those empty years give way, then close around him, her oiled heat clutching, pressing, all accompanied by a musical exhalation, and then, as he went a fraction deeper, a sharply indrawn breath. Her hips hammered against him, a frantic rhythm, as if she had gone weightless in a flurry of wings.

"You're so wonderful, Michel!" she whispered.

Even submerged beneath the sexual veneer, the luster of intimacy, that childlike phrasing and fairy-tale word sounded with brazen incongruity in his ears. That she could think of him as wonderful in any wise distanced him, made him doubt her once again. And yet bound to her, he could not wholly doubt her, and he was inspired to match her energy, to batter against her, as in some demented contest, breathing fractured endearments into her mouth. But she could not keep up the pace, and when she lapsed, her rhythm becoming sporadic, unguided, he worked her into a slow, lascivious grind, a calm torsion at the heart of their storm, a space in which speech was possible, tenderness expressible. He told her how beautiful she was, and looking up at him, touching his jaw, his cheek, she said, "Michel," soberly, reflectively, as if he were a treasure she had discovered at the bottom of an old chest and now she was giving it a name, deciding to know it by that name. He drew her tongue into his mouth, and at the same time touched the place where they were joined, the gluey mix of sweat and juice that sealed the join, that was smeared across their groins. She caught at his hand, pressed it to her cheek, then licked the taste of their mutuality from his fingers. He began to move furiously in her, but she held him still, her eyes luminous, half-lidded, and said, "Wait! I want to feel you like this for a minute . . . just for a minute." Her head drooped, her brow rested against his. Something was pushing down on him, some dark restraint. He imagined the air was hardening around them, growing warmer as it molded to their shape. Words and emotions crowded together inside him, but he found it impossible to speak. His hands roamed aimlessly over her breasts and waist and flanks, a blind sculptor familiarizing himself with new materials. There was a pulse in every part of her body, rapid as a bird's. He knew she was eager to engage him fully, but for long minutes she lay quiescent, her face dazed with concentration. Finally she hooked an ankle behind his knee, a movement that conveyed an insistent easiness. And strength. Damn, she was strong! There were vast complexities of strength inside her, all focused upon the place where she held him deep, nets of satiny sinew lashed over a saddle of bone, and those connected to great flows of muscle and bridges of tendon over rivers of blood, wired, webbed constructions that carried a thrilling neural traffic, symphonies of roaring anxiety and screaming joy that evoked an entire city of convulsive power, a female world of incomprehensible endurance and resilience. His own strength seemed insubstantial by contrast, a joke, a measly animal virtue, whereas hers was redolent of timeless mystery and tragic tradition, so self-contained and assured it did not require stupid totemic acts of male authority to validate itself, to ratify its measure. It existed; it flowered in secret; it was its own nourishment. Sensing this, he felt oddly innocent and unsophisticated, and that simple action, the hooking of an ankle behind his knee, made him feel that by moving in her, he would satisfy some inborn purpose of her strength. But when she pulled him atop her, fencing him with her long thighs, he lost this sense of submissiveness and felt absolutely with her, equals in their hunt for pleasure. Their cries and whispers seemed part of a cocoon they were weaving of warmth and closeness, extruding happiness like strands of silk. They progressed from a steady, explorative beat to wild variances of rhythm, suffering only minor incompatibilities of pace and accommodation: thrashing, sweaty passages; gentle, almost balletic shifts of position; idling movements during which they gathered their energies, reminded themselves of tactile specifics before accelerating toward some ill-defined intensity. He had assumed that he would finish before her, a genital assumption based on the thickening heat in his groin, but then he felt her body change beneath him, grow slack, then stiffen, then ripple internally as if she were experiencing alternations of gravity. The tidal flex of her hips and buttocks became spasmodic. She thrust at him, rising to meet his thrusts too soon, their flesh smacking together in midair. An ugly groan was dredged from her belly, the cry of someone just regaining consciousness, rolling over, waking to the pain of the blow that has knocked her out. And then another groan, this one a fevered, rattling expulsion. Her heels dug into the backs of his knees; but a second later her legs fell apart, and the tension that had clenched the muscles of her calves and thighs flooded her abdomen. Her hands fluttered about his face; then she flung them out to grip the edges of the mattress, and with a heave, she lifted her head and shoulders, staring wildly at their toiling hips, as if she had wanted to know what was happening down there and was dumbfounded by what she had seen.

He soon came to feel that he was participating in a transformation, or rather a repossession, the liberation of an angel of desire and its struggle with the repressive demon who had inhabited her body for so long. Her head tossed back and forth, and she snatched fistfuls of the sheet, trying to rip it up from the mattress. Her features were stretched, distorted. Her hips shimmied and twisted. One leg stiffened, knocking against his side like a loose board in a gale. Then she went limp, and he felt, actually felt through the join of their flesh, a gliding inside her, a planing away of response, relief in the form of some sensation that was easier to bear, as with rain after lightning. She looked beautiful again, agleam with sweat, past the crisis, and he was once again awed and innocent before her, perceiving her as intrinsically different, alien or angel, one of those characters in fantasy novels who fall to earth from some enchanted sphere and are like us but not like, who hear the heartbeats of insects and smile to display anger and have only love in common with humankind, and who, ensnared in that base and pathetically primitive society, after their own innocent grandeur has been sullied by betrayal, suffer some complicated ecstasy of death . . . or else are transformed into ethereal beings of whom we have even less comprehension.

Alexandra's body began to shake a second time, to

tremble, every nerve involved. Sweat beaded her breasts and neck, shone on her face. Her nails raked his back. Her hands fumbled at his hips, and he braced himself above her as she arched and bucked, thinking that she wanted him to hold still. Her cries seemed bewildered, alarmed. Her fangs scored her lower lip, drawing a drop of blood. It was as if she were being violated, savaged by the electric shocks of some godly yet ungovernable and mutant force set loose within her, and he laid his palm on her breast, speaking her name, trying to soothe her as her moment finally subsided, as she sailed down like a feather sails, in gentle pendulum sweeps, through the final shivers and drifts of feeling.

The shadowy air circulated around them slowly, warmly, pricked by a confusion of pinhole flashes, the way a djinn must circulate in its prison bottle, a murky cloud of genius and magic. Beheim did not want to finish, he wanted to remain inside her, to hold on to the peace and easiness that enveloped them. The things he had been unable to tell her earlier now seemed possible to say, but he was afraid that even something as insignificant as the sound of his voice would infect the atmosphere. He smoothed his hand along her hip, and just that touch, that and her response, a slight shifting beneath him, brought him to the edge. He felt a trickle of pleasure, a trivial unburdening, like a thin, hot gold string being spooled out. He thrust hard into her, trying to enhance the feeling. Thrust again. And recognizing what was happening, she rolled her hips, pulling him deeper, herself climbing one last small peak of intensity, sobbing out bursts of disjointed words, saying, "I'll never . . . never . . . ah, Michel! . . . I'll never . . . never betray you. . . ."

And then, as he lay spent, she locked her hands behind his back, pressed her mouth to his throat and—as if trying to speak the word to his blood, to convince whatever dwelled there of her improbable fealty—she whispered fiercely, "Never!"

Chapter SEVEN

Felipe Aruzzi de Valea's apartments were located, as were those of all the lords of the Family, behind a doorless wall set at asymmetrical points with octagonal windows—like crystals scattered randomly in dark ore—that overlooked an immense drawbridge stretching between two towers with curious boxy bay-windowed enclosures atop them, rather like fortified cottages. An iron lantern half the size of a cottage itself hung high overhead, casting shadows from the statues that lined the bridge; the stonework was crusted with a millennium of pigeon droppings, and on either side, the view from the bridge was daunting: a vertiginous drop into a labyrinth of stairways and archs and flying buttresses and ornate stone piers, all so like one another it seemed the vista must have been contrived from the mirror images of a handful of originals. To gain access to the passages that ran inside the wall, one was forced to cross the bridge and enter a spreading crack that appeared to be the result of an earthquake or some structural flaw, but in reality was an intentional effect, disguising a winding stair; and as he and Giselle hurried across the bridge, fearful of being spotted from

103

above, Beheim—though to some degree preoccupied
with the task ahead—continued to puzzle over all that
had happened to him with Alexandra, the things he
had felt with her, the things she had said, the dangerous path she had set him on.

Though there were other matters that related
more to the business at hand, or that might ultimately
have more significance, Alexandra's declaration that he
was, essentially, an unfinished work came to dominate
his thoughts. It was not that he disagreed with her. He
knew he had much to learn, much to experience. But
he had assumed that his growth would entail a deep-
ening, an enrichment of the qualities and characteris-
tics already integrated into his personality, whereas
she had implied by her use of terms such as *metamorphosis* and *turbulent* and *storms* that the changes he
was to undergo might be far more wrenching. Despite
the ambivalence of his feelings toward a variety of
subjects—the conflicts of which Alexandra had
spoken?—he was comfortable with the man he was,
and her suggestion that he was ignorant of his own nature seemed ludicrous. In large, he thought, he had
remained the man he had always been: quiet and retir-
ing; passionate in his inner life, but shy and somewhat
tentative as regarded his relationships with both men
and women; studious, a bit of a bookworm; methodical
in all things, careful in his diet, temperate in use of al-
cohol. True, since his judgment, brighter colors had
been added to that dreary scheme, and many of the
acts he had committed in his new life repelled him,
even though he delighted in the potency that afforded
him the license to commit them. And he would admit
that at times his personality appeared to consist of two
incompatible halves, one capable of gentleness and
sympathy, the other madly calculating and violent. But

was not this contrariness identical to that which invested the human condition, and would not—as was the case with similar human variances—the disparate halves of his being eventually cease their warring and grow together? On sounding his depths, testing himself for any taint of self-delusion, he found no flaw in this interpretation. He was changed, surely. What man would not be who had tasted blood and seen the prospect of eternity open before him? Yet he was still moved by many of his old reflexes and desires. He must learn, he told himself, not to give so much weight to the words of his new brothers and sisters . . . or at least he would have to learn to balance what they said against what they wanted. Perhaps Alexandra had only been trying to unnerve him, he thought, trying to direct his attention away from some more pertinent matter by drugging him first with words and then with kisses. And perhaps she had succeeded more than she might have intended, for he was unable to forget the desire with which she had infected him. That single encounter put to shame all that he had known with other women, not so much in the clinical aspects of the act as in its emotional richness, the tenderness Alexandra had inspired in him; and for some reason this made him uncomfortable with the conclusions he had reached in his brief self-appraisal.

The supports of the bridge terminated in cubes of black stone, which in turn supported crumbling granite statues some fifteen and twenty feet in height. The figures were grotesque yet startlingly lifelike, all posed in attitudes of exhaustion: there was a potbellied troll with fangs and bugged eyes, its slumped body robed in rumpled folds of sculptured stone, notched sword dangling from one taloned hand; a gargoyle with a grievous slash in its side, head lolling, eyes closed, the claws of its left hand englobing a ravaged human head; an imp with pointed ears, slit-pupiled eyes, and a long-chinned, weasely face, sitting hunched, its entire posture expressive of defeat and dread. Nearly two-score of these grisly eminences lorded it over the bridge, and as they passed beneath each Beheim grew disquieted. The statues possessed a preternatural solidity, as if imprisoned alive within a sphere of powerful gravity, and it was easy to picture them—the survivors of a beaten satanic army—shrugging off some centuries-old enchantment, an evil glow returning to their blind eyes, their granite chests heaving, their rock-thewed thighs bunching, crumbs of stone and falls of dust sifting from their ancient joints as they stepped down from their pedestals to complete some interrupted slaughter.

Giselle, too, cast an anxious eye at these malefic presences. Dressed as was Beheim in loose-fitting cloth trousers and a man's peasant jacket, her hair pinned up, she had the look of a pretty child, and her frailty in the midst of this oppressive and mutant geometry had never been more evident. Though he had not wanted to involve her in the search, he could trust no one else to be his accomplice, and this facile disregard for her well-being caused him to think that Alexandra might have been right, that his concern for Giselle would soon be outweighed by other imperatives. As they slipped through the crack in the wall and began climbing a torchlit stair, he considered sending her back to wait for him, but he could not bring himself to risk entry into Felipe's apartments without having someone to stand watch, and so he led her along the corridor at the top of the stairs, past the locked brass-bound doors behind which the pale hierarchy of the undead were taking their ease.

It was cold and damp in the corridor; licks of torchlight cut the tarry shadows. Walking along the narrow passageway, feeling the worn declivities in the stone beneath his feet, Beheim felt he had left behind the civilized present and entered a barbarous past. Why, he wondered, did the lords of the Family risk naked flames for light when lanterns would have shielded them from the possibility of a mortal accident? Some dread nostalgia, perhaps, or a statement of their disdain for peril, their confidence that they could overcome any menace, even those self-imposed? Beheim himself shrank from the torches. The crackling of the flames seemed to express a language of threat.

Once he had opened Felipe's door, he stood listening a moment. Beyond the alcove was a hallway leading off to the right. From beyond the closed door at its end issued the gasps and cries of strenuous lovemaking. He instructed Giselle to take one of the torches from its iron socket on the wall outside and stand at the entrance to the corridor.

"If anyone comes," he whispered, "flee to Lord Agenor. He will protect you. Use the torch against anyone who seeks to harm you. Do you understand?"

Her chin quivered, but she nodded.

"Don't hesitate if you are threatened," he said, perceiving that she was not concentrating on the matter at hand, but was weakened by sentiment and concern for him. "If anyone tries to harm you, burn him. Then find Agenor. You will be safe with him."

"But you," she said, "what will—"

"Be quiet!" he hissed, angry both at her weakness and at himself for taking advantage of that weakness, for using her so after having betrayed her with another woman . . . though he refused to consider it a true betrayal. If anything, he thought, he might now consider the act of making love to Giselle a betrayal, a show of disrespect for something of greater import and sweeter potential.

She recoiled from his show of anger, biting down on her lower lip, a gesture that again lent her the aspect of a sexually precocious child.

Like Beheim's quarters, Felipe's living room contained heavy, dark furniture and lanterns and ancient, almost indecipherable tapestries; the shadows cast by the dim lighting were mere smudges on a faded Persian carpet with a pattern of indigo and rose and brown. Though he did not know what to look for, though he took pains to make no noise, knowing that Felipe's ears were sharp, he went hurriedly about the search, more exhilarated than afraid, like a boy who has accepted a dare. He fumbled through the contents of a writing desk, a mahogany cabinet, and a small oak chest, but could find no evidence of the Valea leader's complicity in the murder. A search of the servant's bedroom, too, yielded nothing, as did a cursory examination of a third and last room—a study—which did not appear to have been occupied in some time, all the furnishings and the large globe and the book-lined shelves being furred with gray dust. Layers of cobwebs overlaid the hatbox-sized blocks of stone that composed the walls.

Disappointed, Beheim stood in the doorway of this third room, straining his ears. He heard breathless gasps and fey melodic exclamations, punctuated by grunts and the squeaking of bedsprings. Felipe and the Lady Dolores were still at it, but he did not want to press his luck. Yet he was reluctant to abandon his only lead, and he did not believe that Alexandra would have steered him in this direction were there not solid evidence to be had ... unless, of course, by persuading him to folly, by engineering his capture, she hoped to bring dishonor upon Agenor. But if this were the case, would she not have already given the alarm? No, he told himself, her motives would not be so easily graspable. There must be something here.

He let his gaze swing one last time about the dust-covered study. The books had apparently gone untouched for years, and it was odd, he thought, that Felipe, given his scholarly disposition, had not been moved by curiosity to examine at least one or two of them.

More than odd.

And then he noticed something odder yet.

Except for a strip along the walls of the room, there was no dust on the floor, making it apparent that a carpet had recently been removed.

It was possible, Beheim thought, that this had been done for cosmetic reasons prior to Felipe's arrival; but if the carpet had been removed because it was dirty or worn, why then had it not been cleaned or replaced?

He dropped to his hands and knees and, as he had done atop the turret, began a careful inspection of the stones. At the center of the room he discovered a section of five stones whose edges were worn smooth. He pried at them and detected a slight shift. There must be a lever, he thought, some sort of mechanism that would move them. He sprang to his feet, went to the bookshelves, and began feverishly pulling out books one by one, but soon he realized that he might save time by giving the problem calm consideration ... though judging from the noises issuing from the bedchamber, he had no need to rush.

He spent the next few minutes pulling out combinations of books that he selected according to title or color or subject; there was no depression or crack that could hide a switch, and he thought that if, indeed, there was a trapdoor, a secret room, the books must either conceal or themselves be the mechanism that would open it. But no combination he tried had any effect, and finally, angry with himself, with Alexandra, he gave the globe a frustrated slap and set it spinning.

Without a sound, the section of five stones swung downward to reveal a stairway.

Beheim remained frozen in an expectant and fearful attitude, certain that Felipe must have heard the slap he'd given the globe. The noises from the bedroom had ceased. A moment later, however, the lovers started up again with a rustling of sheets, an exchange of soft endearments, with sweet exhalations and profound sighs, all signaling, he assumed, a shift in position, a pianissimo movement in their lustful symphony. His chest began to ache, and he understood that this was because he had been so gripped by tension, he had stopped breathing.

With infinite caution, he descended the stairs—there were no more than a dozen—and entered a dark corridor reeking of dampness and mold, so cramped he was forced to go in a crouch. He went along it for a considerable time, groping his way blindly, feeling the spidery fingers of claustrophobia tickling the back of his neck; at last, on turning a corner, he spied a chute of silvery light illuminating the corridor's far end, the beams as distinct as those cast by a magic lantern. Moonlight. Spilling through a slit window into a tiny room furnished with a rough wooden table and chair. Still wary, he edged forward. The view was of an uninteresting slice of moonlit Carpathia: pale clouds, black hills with a glittering river winding through them. A dead cigar lay on the table—thin and black, a villainous accessory. Felipe, Beheim recalled, was in the habit of smoking an occasional cigar. And there was further evidence that the Valea leader had spent time here. Ashes strewn about the floor. Some papers covered in a bold script, tucked into a leather folder. A penknife with an engraved V on the blade. In addition to the table and chair, an unvarnished cabinet was set flush against one wall. Beheim opened it. On the lower shelf stood a pitcher of water. And to his great surprise, on the uppermost shelf were three flasks and three small perfume bottles with antique silver caps, all filled with liquid—pale yellow, Beheim decided after holding one of the bottles up to the window—and a large tumbler containing perhaps a quart of this same liquid. A scrap of paper was tucked beneath one of the bottles, and on it was scribbled a list of measurements like those appropriate to medicinal dosages.

He sat at the table, sifted through the papers, which proved to be a portion of a travel journal written in both French and Italian, random jottings, how Felipe felt about various of the Family whom he had seen at the Decanting for the first time in years—he was less than kind in his opinions—and so forth. He stopped on spotting the name Agenor and read the pertinent passage:

> . . . Agenor continues to demand that I be swift. I understand his urgency, for his claim that we may be in the last days of our kind does not strike me as wholly unreasonable. Yet I must be certain before I approach the Patriarch. I know Agenor wishes to make a dramatic presentation during the Decanting, but I refuse to be rushed and will

continue to rely on my own judgments. He
will not coerce me into a precipitate disclosure, nor will I allow him—or anyone
else—to take matters into their own hands.
Another few weeks, perhaps, and I will be
prepared.

Prepared for what? Beheim wondered. He read
on, but after skimming through the remainder of the
papers, though his Italian was not expert, he was dis-
posed to think that there was no further mention of
the two men's business.

He removed one of the bottles from the cabinet
and unscrewed the silver cap. A harsh acidic odor. The
same that had clung to the bottle cap he had found
atop the turret. He put a drop to his lips. The taste
was vastly superior to the odor. Similar to overly tart
lemonade. Judging by the partially filled tumbler and
the list of dosages, Felipe had been drinking the liquid, and thus Beheim felt no compunction about trying it himself—what poison, after all, could harm a
vampire? If he could identify it, he thought, he might
be closer to proof positive concerning Felipe's involvement in the murder. He tipped back the bottle and
downed a hefty swallow. Palatable, though too bitter
by half. Medicine of some sort, apparently. He could
discern no immediate effect. Whatever the nature of
the liquid, the bottle cap and the odor made it apparent that someone with access to the secret room had
been on the turret on the night of the murder. This
alone was sufficient to place Felipe at the head of his
list of suspects, but it was scarcely incontrovertible
proof of murder. Still, the evidence was worth bringing before the Patriarch; it might provide a lever with
which Beheim could force the representatives of the

various branches to remain at the castle long enough for him to conduct a proper investigation.

Realizing that he could not depend upon Felipe's sexual prowess for much longer, Beheim pocketed the bottle and headed back along the corridor to the stair, eager to collect Giselle and be gone. But on mounting the stairs, he realized that this might not be so easily achieved. The sounds from the bedchamber had stopped. Cursing his incaution, he eased toward the study door. He held his breath, listened, but heard nothing. Not a whisper, not a hint of Giselle's presence. No telling what had happened to her. There had been too much stone between them for even his sharp ears to pick up her movements. She might already have fled, and Felipe would be waiting for him at the door. Or else the lovers might have fallen asleep.

That must be it, he decided. What he had assumed to be a mere lull in their lovemaking, those sighs and whispers, must have signaled an end to their passion, an exchange of endearments preparatory to sleep.

But as he stepped out into the living room, his heart sank and weakness fettered his limbs, for there, at the entrance to the alcove, dressed only in a pair of trousers, stood Felipe Aruzzi—a blond youthful-seeming man of more than four centuries in age, lean and fit, pale arms and chest banded with muscle, yet with bloodshot eyes and a glabrous complexion, his face warped by an expression of contemptuous rage. Clad in a green robe, her black hair tumbling about her shoulders like smoke made solid, the Lady Dolores stood beside him, lovely in her disarray. She bared her fangs and started toward Beheim, but Felipe caught her arm.

"Welcome, cousin," he said in a dry, somewhat

nasal voice. "Do you bring greetings from Lord Agenor?"

This perplexed Beheim, but he was too frightened to consider what it might mean. Against the gloomy backdrop of an old dark tapestry and worn carpet, the two vampires were aglow with vitality, with a tangible emotional charge, seeming to outshine the lanterns, which cast a smoky yellow light throughout the room.

"Your pardon, my lord," Beheim said. "As you know, the Patriarch has ordered me to investigate the murder of the Golden—"

"And that, of course, is what brings you here."

Felipe spoke these words in a mocking tone, and Beheim, encouraged by the fact that they had not attacked him, said, "Why else?"

"Why else, indeed?"

Dolores shook off Felipe's arm and shrilled, "How can you allow this insult? Kill him now!"

Felipe tipped his head to the side as if considering this. "No," he said calmly. "There's something more interesting."

"Lord," said Beheim, "you misunderstand my motives! I've come here tonight not to humiliate you, but to put to rest all suspicion concerning your guilt."

Beheim broke off his protestations as Felipe came a pace forward and lifted his arms like a priest supplicating a god; then he brought his arms down slowly as if suppressing some invisible resistance. The arcs his fingertips described became visible as black lines, thin slashes in the fabric of reality, creating the outline of an oval at whose center Felipe was standing. The blackness of the lines began to mist, to spread and fill in the oval, making it appear that a doorway was opening into the heart of night, a darkness so palpable, it bulged from its confines as might a volume of black gas restrained by a transparent membrane.

"Do you know the Mysteries, cousin?" Felipe asked, stepping aside so that Beheim's view of the oval was unimpeded. It floated a few feet off the ground, impossible yet undeniable, a horrid black interruption of the real some four feet high, like the maw of a huge disembodied worm that had burst through the wall and the begrimed tapestry into the midst of the room. "I'm sure you are familiar with some, but this one, I'd wager, will be new to you."

"Listen, I beg you!" said Beheim, terrified, his eyes drawn to the black oval. "I was sent here by Lady Alexandra. She offered evidence implicating you in the murder. I had no choice but to investigate."

"Liar!" Lady Dolores's dark face darkened further, suffusing with blood; she turned to Felipe. "How can you permit him to spew such poison?"

"Keep quiet!" He went a few feet toward Beheim, who retreated into the doorway of the study. "Even were I to believe you, it would not lessen your offense. You have entered my apartments without invitation, you have by your own admission made a tacit accusal of murder. I have no qualms about killing; I harvest my food as it pleases me. But I am no slaughterer of tradition. And I care not whose charge you bear, I will not tolerate such dishonorable treatment. I do not credit your tale concerning Alexandra, but because I know who has inspired this breach of trust and common decency, I am moved to be merciful."

"I assure you, lord, I'm telling the truth!"

"No, you are not. You are simply a point in an argument between Lord Agenor and myself. A point ill-taken, I might say."

"I know of no business between you and Lord Agenor."

"What are you talking about?" Lady Dolores asked Felipe. "Are you and Agenor involved?"

"Agenor thinks we are," said Felipe impatiently. "Though I have told him we are not."

Frightened as he was, Beheim nonetheless did not fail to notice the discrepancy between Felipe's journal and his words.

"Then why does he continue to press you?" Lady Dolores insisted.

Felipe shrugged. "Who can say? Perhaps he *has* taken me at my word. Otherwise I doubt he would have sent a thief to steal from me. At any rate, he has always been mad, and now he wishes me to validate his madness with my chemicals."

He pushed Lady Dolores—who appeared bewildered by this response—to one side, and approached to within a foot of Beheim. Beheim was captivated by his cruel, too pink lips, his reddened eyes with their black target pupils, the sickly polish of his skin, the handsome features reduced to a brutish fixity by arrogance and willfulness.

"I want you to comprehend the fate that awaits you, cousin, for it is uncommon both in its essentials and its merciful character." Felipe indicated the black oval with an eloquent gesture, and—the gesture apparently being the agency of a further magic—the blackness was lent depth and form, so it seemed that Beheim was peering into a vacant eye socket that afforded a view of an emptiness figured by pale phantoms, winged entities too vague and fleeting to identify. There was a faint rushing hiss, like a wind driving grit against a windowpane. He felt cold and frail, as if standing upon the edge of a gulf into which one could fall forever.

"Hermeto DiLanza, a convert of my daughter, Alexandra," Felipe said blithely, "she whose reputation you sought to injure, he was the Columbus first to sail the waters you now survey. In passing from life to life upon his night of judgment, he chanced to brush past this particular darkness, and recognizing it to be uncharted territory, sensing an advantage to be had, he told no one of his discovery and set himself thereafter to laying bare its potentials. Sadly for poor Hermeto, his researches did not go unnoticed." He picked up the ceramic figurine of a fancily dressed dancing lord and lady from an end table next to Beheim. "Were I to allow my children to carry out unlicensed research, I would undoubtedly lose their respect. Thus I accosted Hermeto one evening while he was exploring the abyss you see before you by merrily pitching his servants into it. I thought it only fair that he follow them."

He tossed the figurine into the oval. On breaching the surface, it was suspended for an instant, the surrounding blackness displaced, splashing out around the depression it had created with the sluggishness of mercury, of some liquid heavier than water, a few droplets flying into the air, hovering there briefly, like peepholes punched through into an ebon sky, then falling back as the figurine receded, spinning slowly, comic in its stiff gaiety, yet somehow a sad and terrible image, those two painted courtiers with their embroidered silks and rouge-dappled cheeks wheeling down into the absence of everything, into the utter dark. Just before the figurine vanished, one of the pale winged shapes came swooping near.

Death, Beheim thought; he had never before

glimpsed this place, this particular Mystery, but knew it to be part of the black country he had traveled during the time of his judgment, and the prospect of entering it, of enduring even a shadow of the pain and fright he had then endured, made him feel faint and unsteady.

"Intriguing, is it not?" said Felipe, considering the figurine's passage. "I have never gained a satisfactory understanding of it, yet I think of it as a pool on the plain of death in which things are suspended from judgment. Everything it absorbs continues to live after a fashion. If you were as attuned as I to the vibrations of the ether, you might sense the vital signals of Hermeto and his servants . . . and of the creatures that torment them. I am ignorant of their natures, these creatures, though I believe they may be an evolutionary stage of the spirit to which Hermeto and his fellows will one day aspire." He gave Beheim a cheerful grin. "You see, I am not condemning you to death. A new transmogrification awaits you. Or else I may someday discover how to retrieve what I have stored there. In that case, I will reclaim you from the deep. Doubtless you will have an intriguing tale to tell. So!" With another florid gesture, he invited Beheim to enter the black oval. "Come now, cousin. What's the point of delay?"

Beheim, half under the spell of the unearthly sight before him, half-seduced by the sonorous quality of Felipe's voice, suddenly became aware of the immediacy of the danger and sprang toward the alcove, toward the Lady Dolores, who blocked his path. He swung his fist at her, a backhanded blow with all his weight behind it, but she caught his hand, gave it a wrench, knocking him off balance; then, using her grip as would a hammer thrower, she slammed his head against the wall. White light splintered in his eyes, and the top of his skull felt aglow with pain. He tried to shake off the effects of the impact, to struggle to his feet, but Lady Dolores knelt beside him, her hand on his chest, pushing him back. Her dark, predatory beauty had evolved into the animal, eyes dead black, runners of saliva bridging between her fangs and lower teeth. Felipe stood at her shoulder, looking on placidly.

"I don't believe she cares for you," he said. "If you prefer, I'll simply have her tear you apart."

"Don't . . . please," said Beheim, slurring the words, unable to focus. "I . . . I can't . . ."

"Of course you can, cousin." Felipe grabbed his jacket and yanked him to his feet. "There, you see! You only thought you couldn't."

He shoved Beheim across the room, lifted him by the collar and the seat of his pants, and with irresistible strength, swung him toward the oval, stopping his momentum so that Beheim's face was only inches away from the blackness. Beheim felt a cold pressure on his skin, a gentle probing, as if the oval sensed his nearness and was testing him, becoming familiar, the way a blind man touches another's face in order to know its conformation. He thrashed about, desperately trying to escape Felipe's grip, but Felipe only pushed him forward a few inches so that his head entered the blackness. For a moment he could neither see nor breathe, nor could he feel anything of his body other than a freezing numbness that had fitted itself like a mask to his face; but then, either his eyes adjusted to the darkness or by some other unfathomable process the darkness was translated into images in his brain, and he saw a vista of folds like those of an immense curtain, radiant yet black, resembling a negative of the

aurora borealis, and drifting among them, structures
that put him in mind of outcroppings of quartz, geom-
etries of pallid obelisks, crystal cities. He heard a
warped resonant booming, as of a drunken voice heard
through a wall by another drunk; then, from the farthest reaches of his vision, a flash of heat lightning
thinned into a razor's edge of blinding white as wide
as the sky and sliced through the blackness toward
him, setting all the folds to rippling, the crystals to
bobbling, as if a sword had been swung through a medium of black gauze and water. Only it was not a
sword, he realized as it drew near, widening, acquiring
detail, but a swarm of hideous, glowing creatures, all
different, yet having a unity of malformed character,
pig rats and cockroach lions and dog spiders and crab
worms and more, swelling to fill the field of his vision,
thousands upon thousands of them, an infinity of dire
visage and form. As they dove toward him it seemed
he had grown to a great size, the size of the sky itself,
for rather than swarming over him, burying him beneath a crawly tonnage of light, they shrank and struck
into his flesh, driving needles into his cheeks and forehead, points of such searing pain that he imagined
each to be sparkling, delineating a constellation of pain
tattooed across an enormous dark face. And then he
was back in Felipe's rooms, his body convulsing, still
held helplessly aloft.

"What did you see, cousin?" Felipe asked with
mild curiosity.

Beheim was burning with cold, shivering, his
teeth clattering.

"Take your time, dear boy," said Felipe. "I'm in no
hurry."

Still shivering, Beheim tried to collect his impressions, to embroider them with invention, for he would

have employed any deceit in order to delay being thrust back into that freezing alien blackness. But just as he was preparing to tell a totally unfounded tale of his experiences, Lady Dolores screamed and Felipe let him fall to the floor.

"Put it down," said Felipe sternly. "And come here to me."

Though he was not certain who was being addressed, Beheim knew by Felipe's shift in tone that it was not he. He struggled to his knees, fired by the hope that someone had come to his aid. Lord Agenor, perhaps. Or Alexandra. But it was Giselle who had entered the apartment, her bloodless face stamped with fear. She was holding a burning torch close to the hair of the Lady Dolores, who cowered from the flames in a corner of the alcove.

"Come to me," Felipe repeated.

Giselle's hand wavered.

Lady Dolores's stare was full upon her, and Beheim knew it would be a matter of moments before she was overcome by one of them or the other. He came to his feet and, eluding Felipe's grasp, stumbled across the room. He snatched the torch from Giselle's hand, keeping it well away from his body, his mind shriveling with fright at the nearness of the dancing flame, the crackling flower of death, but willing in his desperation to risk burning. He held the torch inches from Lady Dolores's hair, exulting in her terrified gasp.

"I swear to you," Felipe said to him. "I'll hold your heart in my hands."

Beheim waved the torch at Lady Dolores, eliciting a shriek. "Keep back!" he said to Felipe. "Go into the study."

Felipe let out a snarl, but retreated a few steps.

"Quickly!" Beheim said; Giselle pressed against him, clinging to his arm. "Follow him," he told her. "Lock him in."

"First Agenor steals from me, and now he sends a thief," said Felipe, continuing his retreat. "Tell him I'll suffer no more humiliation at his hands. Not for the sake of any cause. I'll hunt him through the light of hell itself if necessary."

"Get into the study!" Beheim locked his fingers in the Lady Dolores's hair, twisted her head so that she faced Felipe, displaying for him the full extent of her fear. "Do what I tell you! At once!"

Felipe continued his retreat. "Do you know what awaits you now, you simple bastard? You—"

"I'll give you another second before I burn her," Beheim told him. "After that you'll have all the time in the world to threaten me."

Felipe stepped back into the study. "The light of hell," he said again, just before Giselle closed the study door after him and shot the bolt. "Make sure you tell Agenor that. Use those exact words. Not even in the light of hell will he find respite."

Lady Dolores had fallen to her knees; her head was lowered, her face hidden by a tangle of black hair. Her pendulous breasts hung free of the robe, which had belled open, and her fingers clawed obsessively at the floor. Beheim delighted in seeing her in this submissive posture.

"Why did you do it?" he asked her.

She started to lift her head, but he warned her not to look at him, to keep her eyes fixed on the floor. Then he repeated his question. When she replied that she did not understand, he asked why she and Felipe had killed the Golden.

"I've killed no one," she said, and then, with fresh malice in her voice, she added, "At least, not recently."

"So it was Felipe."

"No, he was with me here." She gave her hair a toss. "You're an idiot to think we're involved. What could we possibly hope to gain?"

Giving the weird black maw at the center of the room a wide berth, Giselle came up beside Beheim and took his arm.

"Perhaps gain had nothing to do with it," he said.

Lady Dolores kept silent, and he made menacing play with the torch.

"Damn you!" She stared up at him like a mad-woman through the disarray of her hair, the whiteness of her drawn face seeming an element of her ferocity, as shocking as ice on the spine. She lowered her head again. "You have no idea of how you're being used."

"And how is that?"

"I can only guess," she said. "But the Golden . . . don't you see? She was of no consequence. Who would be foolish enough to risk such an act for a taste of her blood? The murder must have been a means to an end, not an end in itself."

"I don't understand how that eliminates you from suspicion."

"Think, damn it! What was the next step follow-ing the murder? Who made the next move?"

"If you know, tell me."

"Agenor, you imbecile!"

"I don't understand."

"He had you appointed to head the investigation, didn't he? Do you actually believe that this was due to your investigative prowess? Are you that much of a fool? Agenor is using you to implement one of his schemes."

Beheim mulled over the implications of what she had said. "I'm at a loss to understand how this exonerates you."

"Who is Agenor's current adversary?" Lady Dolores tapped her breast. "I am! He has taken this opportunity to aim you at me. And at my lover."

Beheim saw that there might be some validity to this accusation, but he said, "My lady, if I were to disregard evidence on the grounds that one of my suspects had enemies who seek to harm him, then I would have no suspects at all. I'm afraid your attempt to undermine my confidence in Lord Agenor is as fundamentally unsound and simplistic as is the stratagem that you have accused him of using."

"You *are* a great fool," she said. "I wonder if even Agenor knows how great."

He decided to try another tack. "When I mentioned that the Lady Alexandra had provided me with information implicating Felipe, you put on a fine show of outrage. But given your relationship with her, I doubt it came as a surprise. What did you have in mind by trying to influence me in this direction? Don't you realize that I understand how she has succeeded in turning my investigation to her purposes? Perhaps to your purposes as well. It seems reasonable to me that this scheme to implicate Felipe might have been hatched by the both of you."

Was that a noise of amusement that escaped Lady Dolores's lips? He could not be sure, not having seen her face when she uttered it. But the words that followed were scarcely the product of an amused sensibility, and he was unable to determine whether or not she was acting.

"I will not hear it!" she said, an eager muscle working in her jaw. "I will hear no more of your poison against Alexandra! She is an innocent in this. Speak one more lie concerning her ..."

For a few seconds her words were reduced by the fierceness of her emotions to a fuming sputter more like animal speech. She drew a breath, her shoulders hunching, back bowing. For an instant Beheim had the idea that she was expanding, growing, becoming a giantess. He examined Dolores's anger in the context of Alexandra's characterization of their relationship. It was not out of the question that she had been telling the truth. If Dolores had seduced her against her will, it might have been because she had been obsessed with Alexandra to begin with—and this would explain Dolores's description of her as an innocent. He wanted to believe this, he wanted to believe in everything that happened between them. But he did not think he could sustain belief against his growing suspicion that she had sent him to Felipe's apartment for reasons other than she had revealed.

"I have lived for nearly three centuries," Dolores said huskily, giving the impression that she was holding back a shout. "I have loved five thousand men, five thousand women. I have seen Siberia burning and I have walked in the hidden cities of the Khan. And now, to be cowed by a pitiful thing like you." She let out a labored sigh. "Three centuries. Perhaps it is enough."

She glanced up at him.

"Don't do this," he cautioned, guessing her intent. Giselle whispered, "Michel!" and tightened her grip on his arm.

Lady Dolores gave a distressed laugh, one that seemed reflective, a self-commentary.

"Turn your eyes away from me," Beheim told her.

"My eyes?" she said. "Is it only my eyes you fear?

Not my hands, or my hair? Not these?" She cupped her breasts as if assessing their weights, her thumbs making idle circles about the chocolate-colored nipples. She gave another distraught laugh, and her voice acquired a burred, urgent tonality. "Oh, cousin, cousin, I am made of fearful stuff! My heart is poison, my mind is fire and a rhyme. My flesh is death itself. Beetles lay pearly eggs in the crannies of my brain. There is no more fearful thing than I, no more desperate and conscienceless an enemy. Do you believe I lack the courage or the will to drag you down to hell on fire in my arms? If so, you are wrong, mortally wrong, for I fear death only as I might fear to satisfy a lover of whom I've dreamed a thousand nights. He is with me always, and I have always yearned for him. He is endlessly alluring, endlessly patient. Those who do not know him, they fear him. But not I. Though he is Mystery itself, he is no mystery to me, no undiscovered country. I have traveled each night along his stygian rivers, along the moon-colored roads that lead forth from the desert of the skull. I have run with the beast whose beauty is the sun that creates the beautiful shadows of our lives. I have taken his demons in my mouth and drunk the juice of their decaying fecundity. The homunculi who burrow in his nightsoil have crawled inside me. I have given myself to the parasites that feed on the residues of his terrible dreams." She gazed with daft intensity at the black opening that Felipe had conjured, as if newly aware of it. "Death. Say it, cousin. Say it and listen how it vibrates in the air! The word has a windy, solemn sound, does it not? Like the expiration of a great passion, or the first breath of a storm."

She buried her face in her hands as if overborne by her lust for death. But then, moving more quickly

than Beheim had thought possible, catching him un-
awares, she reached up and seized his wrist,
immobilizing the arm that bore the torch. With her
free hand, she knocked Giselle aside and, rising to her
feet, flung Beheim against the door. The torch
dropped to the stones, scattering sparks, and rolled
away behind her.

"Yet if needs be," she said gleefully, "I am willing
to endure life awhile longer." She secured her hold on
his jacket, lifting him so that his feet dangled. "Long
enough, at any rate, to oversee your final passage."
She called out over her shoulder. "Felipe! I am free!"

Beheim butted her in the face, and she staggered
backward, losing her grip on him. Blood spurted from
her nose, filming thick as gravy over her lips and chin.
Her tongue flicked out. She lapped at the bright flow
from her nostrils and smiled.

Felipe began to hurl himself against the study
door; the wood bowed outward with each impact.

Then Lady Dolores shrieked. She looked in horror at the smoke that had begun to billow up about
her, for in recoiling from Beheim's blow, she had
stepped close enough to the fallen torch that a spark
had caught on the train of her robe. Now the silky fabric was alive with flame. She let out a howl of agony
and rage and threw herself at him, but he ducked
away. He caught Giselle by the arm, and veering to
the right of Felipe's magical void, which still held its
form in the center of the room, he dragged her back
from the alcove and the burning woman who tottered
after them, screaming, arms outstretched, rapidly becoming a gigantic torch that brightened the air till it
seemed like day. The study door splintered and
cracked. Lady Dolores's skin blistered and grew dark,
her screams shredded into a raw grating noise barely

audible above the snapping of the fire that was consuming her. The crisping mask of her face was horrid to see, and Beheim now felt nothing of vengeance, no hint of triumph. She made a rush at them, shedding gouts of flame, but when they eluded her, she changed direction and, taking a wobbly step to her left, poising for a fraction of a second as if to orient herself, thus leaving no doubt in Beheim's mind that this was a conscious act, she toppled into the black maw hovering in midair just as Felipe burst through the door in a shower of splinters, an explosion of snapped boards, looking—with his bared fangs and reddened eyes— like the emblem of nightmare. Aghast at the sight of Dolores, he caught her wrist, and as she fell she in turn—perhaps thinking he was Beheim, or perhaps in mere reflex—clasped him in an embrace. For a moment they teetered on the brink of a mortal balance, half in, half out of that chill black emptiness; the flames crawled up Felipe's arm, licking at his face. Then Beheim, recognizing that he could not chance their survival, ran forward and shoved them in.

Their disappearance into the void created a harrowing stillness. It seemed impossible that so much vitality could have been snuffed out so quickly, and Beheim experienced a central uneasiness at the suddenness and finality of the deaths ... if death it was. Perhaps Lady Dolores had believed that the blackness would muffle the flames. But it did not. Even after she and Felipe had receded to a great distance, Beheim could see them burning: a tiny reddish star in the midst of pale, swarming lights. The silence in the room made a kind of prison for him, turning his thoughts inward and forcing him to contemplate his ineptitude, his naïveté.

How easily he had let her distract him!

He was assaulted by the prospect of immortality lost. They would kill him for this crime, they would force him to undergo an Illumination. Lashed to the turret stones, he would bake and blister in the rays of dawn, the sun would boil away his spirit, send it fuming ahead into the future, and as he died he would howl out what he had seen, praying that his vision would be of sufficient worth to the Family that the Patriarch would signal a servant to make play with a wooden stake and end his agony. He recalled hearing how Giuseppe Cinzal's Illumination had lasted for hours, how his visions of the future had been of such clarity and import that the Patriarch had been loath to cut short the process. Cinzal, it was said, had turned into a thing of sticks and carbon, still spitting up roses of blood and clairvoyant fragments of the truth in a voice like ashes.

What was the sun that it could distill such mystical diamonds from the heat and pressure of a death?

And what was the soul that it could fly so far afield, that it could pass forward into time and still maintain a connection with the flesh?

Beheim stood bewildered, trying to make sense of everything that had happened, to fit together the pieces of the event and make it display some evidence of hope; but the only evidence available was that of his folly. And of Alexandra's betrayal. Oh, she had used him right enough. And in doing so she had brought him to the end of his days. The strange doorway through which Lady Dolores and Felipe had fallen appeared now to be a black mirror reflecting his future.

Panic crackled in his brain. Fear was thin, yellow, sour in his throat.

Chapter EIGHT

Giselle urged him toward the door, tugging at his arm, too stunned, apparently, to speak. Though unmanned by fear, Beheim was still able to feel pity for her. She must know there could be no escape, not with these deaths upon their hands. Yet he could not bear to abolish whatever hope remained to her, and since flight seemed preferable to waiting, he acted out the gesture of survival, and they went down from the drawbridge, down through the precipitous maze of arches and stairways, down and down into the bottom places of the castle, passing along byways so deep and obscure that whenever he chanced to look up, the great hanging lanterns overhead appeared as faint stars burning in a murky heaven. At any second he expected to hear shouts behind them, but no pursuit came. Was it possible the crime had gone undetected? He could think of no other explanation. Yet even so, sooner or later Felipe and Dolores would be discovered missing, and Alexandra would implicate him. She could not have presumed that he would kill the lovers, but he was certain now that she had been trying to discredit him or Agenor in some way; she would likely have a net poised to drop upon him. And yet she had led him in a profitable direction, for the suggestion of complicity between Agenor and Felipe was intriguing, though how it might relate to the murder of the Golden was still unclear.

He was tempted to convict her of betrayal, but there was as yet too little real evidence to draw a final conclusion. He needed time to let the mud settle from the waters and the hard facts sift down. Yes, that was exactly what he needed. Time, and an implausible amount of luck.

After more than two hours of running, ducking into shadows, they reached a yawning tunnel above whose entrance was inscribed an intricate graffiti of nymphs being raped by satyrs, flung onto their hands and knees, and mounted from behind, their mouths twisted, hands outflung, as if somewhere in the darkness beyond lay salvation. Beheim, overborne by a weariness less physical than spiritual, shared their longing for surcease. Beneath the drawing were scrawled lewd comments in German and French and Hungarian, many of which contained words unfamiliar to him. He had the irrational urge to let this be his final place, to stand there and translate each and every phrase, deducing nouns from verbs and vice versa, and composing of them an obscene ode, an epitaph charged with moral sickness.

There was a thick silence, the damp smell of sunless waters and rotting stone. He could see scarcely a dozen feet ahead, but straining his ears, he made out the beating of hearts nearby: two mortals in hiding some fifteen or twenty yards away. Males, he decided, judging by their odor. Either servants, advance elements of a pursuing force, or—and this he thought more probable—refugees who had once served the

Family and had abandoned their hopes of life immortal. The notion that he had become like them, a cowering outcast, sparked feelings of shame and outrage, and glancing at Giselle, who hovered patiently beside him, vulnerable looking with her hair come all unpinned, he experienced a flash of resentment. How could he have let himself be swayed by such a creature? If he had not fled, he might have been able to convince the Patriarch that he was the victim of deception; he should have stayed and demanded a confrontation with Alexandra.

And with Roland Agenor.

Especially with Agenor.

That old villain's touch was everywhere in the scheme of his undoing. Oh, he was likely innocent. Innocent of murder, at any rate. But Lady Dolores had made a telling point: Agenor might well be using him to turn the Golden's death to his advantage. What Beheim had taken for paternal solicitude and noble motive might have merely been the formal dress of a cunning stratagem, and he damned himself for not having recognized that altruism such as Agenor pretended to espouse was a virtue alien to the Family, that few favors done were not freighted with duplicity, no kindness untainted by greed or some other form of perversity. Agenor's pose of an ancient grown to ruddy wisdom through centuries of academic solitude doubtless masked appetites as feral and conscienceless as those of the de Czeges.

Agenor and Alexandra, Alexandra and Agenor.

Did that axis hinge upon some crucial fact, something that might bear upon the investigation?

Impossible to say.

He had lost everything and learned nothing.

Beheim's despair planed away into anger, and his

anger grew so profound, so liberating, he began to feel that he was soaring high above the bleak plain of his thought, no longer grounded in the rational concerns that had provoked it. And in that furious flight, distanced from all gentler considerations, it seemed that he had at last completed the arc of his being, embraced the lineaments of an inky, sharp-winged soul, and inhabited it fully. He thought he sensed a thousand vital potentials that a moment before he might have found loathsome, yet now appeared intriguing and inviting, promising new styles of dominance, fresh angles from which to approach the problem of forever. It was exhilarating, this knowledge. Intoxicating. His heart pumped with the robust rhythm of one just fed, and in his mind's eye—or perhaps it was no inner vision, but a product of the walls of the moment breaking down and permitting him a view of some netherworld through a ragged breech in the stones of Castle Banat—he saw vague figures gathering round him: slim, darkly clad men and women with pale skin and lustrous eyes. They drifted toward him with the processional slowness of creatures in a dream, wreathed in streamers of mist. Frightened, he sought to will them away, and when they did not disperse, he grew even more afraid; but then he realized that these were the hosts of the Agenor branch, both the living and the dead assembled in a place of witness, there yet not there, an immaterial splinter of each drawn to attend the ceremony of this, his enlightenment. He seemed to hear their names in his blood, a hushed droning like the shadow of a song, music that filled and enriched him like darkness thickening in a crypt; he could feel the specific force of their presences, a thicket of energies as intricate as fern shadow; and from all this, steeped in those spiritual pressures, he derived a fresh appreciation of his history.

These decaying villains with ruptured chests and stitched-shut eyes; these manly young beasts with their elegant manners and glinting teeth; these women with fanged smiles whose combination of beauty and unhealthy vigor was a lash to the senses—they all shared, he realized, much more than the specific strain of a blood infection, for that infection was the crucible from which a great harmony was being forged. As they crowded close, closer, their features growing increasingly distinct, he identified several of his acquaintances among them: Danielle Hinault, her chestnut hair piled high; Monroe Seaforth, the American financier; Claude St. Cyrille, Paul Widowes, and Andrew McKechnie, three men—like him—relatively new to the Family. And there was old Agenor himself. His shock of hair, like a white flame, struck Beheim—contrary to his previous assessment of his mentor's character—as reflecting a whiteness of spirit. Not an actual virtue. Virtue was too limiting a term. It was more a purity of intent, an absolute clarity of purpose that Agenor had transmitted to each of them, a signifying quality that would attach to all their deeds. The treasure of his blood, their chemical birthright. Beheim began to know himself as a figure in a centuries-long tradition, its heir and—more pertinently—its implement, his essential purpose being to assist in the completion of a scheme whose ultimate goal was clear not even to Agenor, but was an imprint of the blood, a cellular labyrinth whose ornate patterns they were foreordained to duplicate with their schemes and violent actions. He could almost envision its eventual result, and he could almost make out those of the branch—some yet unborn, others living yet unjudged—who would one day fashion its final structures. Perhaps, he thought, he would be among them, for the grand design was nearing completion. That much was apparent, a wisdom of his blood. And it was, he understood, his *blood* that was truly wise, not his mind or his soul. Just as that red juice was moved along the passages of his veins by the beating of a heart, so he himself was moved along the passages of the design by the workings of some mystic engine, its true nature obscured by time and the exigencies of mutant biology. Yet he could hear it churning in the song of his blood (oh, the Lady Dolores had been right about that; it was a song he had not heard till now, and now that he had heard it, he knew it plainly for what it was). And he imagined he could see the embodiment of the melody shining like a beacon in the black sky of his solitude, a simple device such as a cross or an ankh, yet emblematic of a deeper passion and a more fundamental truth.

As if their function had been merely to shepherd him toward this peak of understanding, the shades of the Agenor branch began to recede, undulating like the shadows of flames; their droning song rose like a steamy perfume, imposing upon him an awareness of great destiny and enormous truth and infinite belonging. He felt drugged and delirious. It was as if after having been lost for years in an enchanted wood, he had suddenly grown to the stature of a giant and was now capable of overlooking the treetops and orienting himself amid the Family's arcane metaphysical geography. He had the urge to shout, to roar his exultation; but a sense of calm potency washed over him, an emotion that had the richness of a cathedral silence. All of this might be, he thought, merely another dark symptom, an acceleration of the fever that possessed the Family, and thus might signal a slackening of good judgment rather than an evolution of awareness. Yet though he feared this to be the case, he could not reject the feeling, for it recast his confidence, allowing him to disregard the hopelessness of the situation and to concentrate upon what he might achieve.

Giselle made a frail noise, but Beheim was too involved with his own purposes to pay her heed. He stepped forward into the tunnel, imagining the shadows fitting about him like a cape, and held out his arms to the darkness beyond. The hearts of the two men in hiding beat faster. To see one of their former masters so close at hand must, Beheim thought, have returned to them all the fearful allure of their former service.

"Come here to me," he said. "You will not be harmed, I swear it."

One set of footsteps retreated, but before Beheim could set out in pursuit, a rusty, quavering voice called out, "Have mercy upon me, lord! I am weaponless against you!"

Like an image surfacing from a black pool, a thin, angular figure with tangles of iron-colored hair and a prophet's matted beard, wearing a hooded robe bleached to an indefinite gray, came haltingly forward from the dark recesses of the tunnel. Beneath the brush of whiskers was a hollowed, haggard face, but Beheim saw that the man was not old, as his stooped posture and seamed countenance indicated, only ill-used. The small, closely set eyes were an icy blue, lending an impression of canniness to his features; the neck was unwithered, and the squarish hands callused, powerful looking. Beheim could smell the fearful toxins in his blood, yet he also sensed that the man's fear did not run deep, that his cowering attitude was at least in part an attempt to hide feelings of contempt.

"Tell me your name," Beheim said.

The man stopped an arm's length away, averted his eyes, his left shoulder drooping as if preparing to receive a blow. "Vlad, Lord," he said, and then, continuing in a chatty and altogether incongruous tone: "My name is Vlad. Yet I am no impaler as was my namesake." An unsound laugh that went too high and cracked. "No, no, not at all. An unhappy coincidence, nothing more."

"Lucky for me, eh?" said Beheim, and gave Giselle an amused glance, eliciting from her a wan smile. "Where is your companion, Vlad?"

"Lord, he was afraid. In awe of your magnificence. He could not stand before you."

"And you ... you are not afraid?"

"Oh, but I am, lord. I am terrified. My blood"—he pressed a hand to his chest, striking a dramatic attitude—"runs cold. But I am practiced at fear. I have learned to be a witness to my urges, not their slave." His eyes darted toward Giselle, lingered a moment; then he returned his gaze to the worn stones at his feet.

"Truly, that is a practiced answer," Beheim said blithely. "I suppose I believe you."

For the briefest of instants Vlad met his gaze, and Beheim had a sense both of the unstable process of the man's thoughts and of the consolidated principle of his loathing, the product of years spent slinking through the dark, shunning the brilliant presences who ruled the upper reaches of his stone universe, lusting for a power that would never be his.

"I have heard," Beheim said, "that you who dwell here below know all the secret ways of Banat."

"Perhaps not all," said Vlad. "Some we know."

"I have heard, too, that you travel freely to every part of the castle."

Vlad inclined his head in a slight nod.

"Even to the Patriarch's chamber?"

"Even there, lord."

"Excellent! I would have you lead me to the Patriarch at once."

Vlad hesitated. "You will forgive me, lord, but I must be so bold as to inquire, why do you wish to travel secret paths rather than seeking an audience directly?"

"That is not your concern."

The man gave forth with an unsteady humming noise, like the drone of a drunken bee, and nodded rapidly, as if in agreement with some inner urgency. "It is evident, lord, that you have fallen into disfavor, or else you would not be asking for guidance. This being so, I would be a fool if I did not seek a reward for my service."

"Your reward," Beheim said, barely able to hold his temper in check, "will be to survive this encounter."

"For many that would be more than sufficient," said Vlad, sounding ever more assured despite his subservient pose. "But as for myself, lord, I am plagued with many fears. Death is only one of them, and life"—he gave a dismayed laugh—"life is sweet, but its sweetness has grown of late unsatisfying." He looked straight at Beheim; his bony, bewhiskered face, gemmed with those glittering eyes, appeared fierce and ratlike; the pink tip of his tongue poked out. "Give me the woman. Your beautiful, beautiful lady. Give her to me, and I will lead you to the Patriarch."

Giselle moved behind Beheim, her hand going to his shoulder, and Beheim laughed coldly.

"Hear me, lord!" Vlad retreated a pace, yet maintained a certain poise, like—Beheim thought—a mongoose withdrawing briefly from the fray to judge a cobra's weariness. "What will it harm you to make this promise? I realize that your word when given to such as I cannot be your bond. Promise her to me. Then, if it suits you, you may retract your promise. And after I have led you to the Patriarch, you may punish me for my impudence."

The illogic that buttressed these words muted Beheim's anger. "What could you possibly hope to win from such a contract?"

"Why . . . the woman, lord. You see, I believe by the time we reach the Patriarch's chamber, you will have realized that I can be of far more value to you than she. Though my uses, I admit, will surely be less pleasurable." He favored Giselle with a discolored, gap-toothed smile. "What is your name, dear heart?"

"Pig!" she said, clinging to Beheim. "He will butcher you for this!"

"Will he, now? My lord can always find another bitch from which to guzzle. But help in a time of need? That is the rarest of commodities in Castle Banat." Vlad, seeming almost merry, made a scuttling run deeper into the tunnel; he wound a strand of hair about his forefinger and gave it a yank, causing his head to bob like that of a puppet as he peered at Beheim. "Have we a bargain?"

"To this degree," said Beheim after a pause. "You will lead me to the Patriarch, and then, if I deem it wise, I will punish you."

"Michel, you can't—" began Giselle, but Beheim drew her into an embrace and said, "I would never sacrifice you. Surely you must know that?"

Vlad chuckled.

"He's mad! How can we trust him?" Giselle tried to engage Beheim's eyes, but he was gazing at Vlad over the top of her head, giving thought to a new consideration. What if the man proved correct in his assumption? Who could say what might happen on reaching the Patriarch's chamber? In circumstances like these, the assistance of an expert on the geography of the castle might mean the difference between life and death. Again he recalled Alexandra's contention that soon he would discover how little Giselle meant to him. He wanted to put the lie to her words, but now was riddled with doubts.

"Oh, I *am* mad," said Vlad. "Never doubt it. I am mad as morning light. One must be mad to dwell in Banat. We are all mad here, even the greatest among us. Is that not so, lord?"

Beheim gave the merest hint of a shrug.

"But," Vlad went on, "mad or no, I recognize the intrinsic functions of my place and time. I once served the Patriarch himself. Did I tell you that? Well, I did . . . and served him well. I understand the needs of the Family, I know their hearts and minds. In matters concerning them, my judgments are ever sound."

"Listen to me," Beheim said to Giselle, keeping an arm about her waist. "If he leads us astray, he will die. That he knows. Then I will simply find another guide. If he leads us truly, that will change nothing for you. I must put my case before the Patriarch. And soon. This is our best hope, perhaps our only one. I believe we should chance it, but since your fate is also in the balance, I will leave it for you to decide."

Her lips parted as if she were about to speak; then her face clouded; after a second or two she lowered her eyes, rested her brow against his chin.

"I cannot decide this," she said. "I must trust to you. How can I do otherwise?"

"Are you certain?"

A nod.

Beheim smoothed down her hair, felt her heart beating against his chest. Once again he stared at Vlad, who remained smiling at Giselle, shifting his feet, looking—with his snarled hair and beard, his snappish eyes—like someone halfway through a transformation into the animal.

"Betray us," said Beheim flatly, "and I will visit upon you the torments of hell. Do you understand?"

Vlad might not have heard. "What is the good lady's name?" he asked. "I wish to know her name."

Giselle ducked her head onto Beheim's shoulder. Beheim remained silent, exploring the possibility that the man's show of instability might be part of an attempt to make him incautious. It did not seem likely that Vlad—devolved and living like an animal in constant fear of the raptors high above—would be capable of this subtlety, yet the entire castle was a world of false appearances and clever deceits, and in such a world even the rats might wear disguises.

"No matter," said Vlad, moving deeper into the tunnel. "I'll name her myself. Something classic, something Latin. Lavinia. Or Calpurnia. Portia. That's it! Portia! Such a round, buxom name. A name so palpably fleshy it stiffens the tongue." He let out a whinnying giggle and beckoned. "Come, my lord! Perhaps you are in no hurry, but I am eager for my reward."

For twenty minutes or thereabouts they followed Vlad through a system of narrow unlit passages, through patches of evil stench and cloying dampness. The man must have known every turn by heart, for the absence of light appeared to bother him not at all. He capered ahead as they groped their way along, unable to see their hands before their faces, now and again calling back to Giselle, offering salacious endearments and then apologizing profusely to Beheim, explaining that he was not to be held responsible, as his heart had been stolen by the beautiful lady. The confidence that Beheim had felt prior to meeting him began to dissipate and he grew less secure with his decision. Though they were ascending, it was gradual in the extreme—he doubted they could have climbed more than seventy or eighty feet from their starting point. He had lost all real sense of where they stood in relation to the upper reaches of the castle. And it was becoming apparent that Vlad was not the expert guide he claimed to be, or else he had some hidden purpose.

He should have heeded Giselle, Beheim told himself; it was evident that his own instincts had been badly eroded. Any number of times he thought to menace Vlad, to demand resolution; but on each occasion he realized he could not trust the man's reactions. If deranged, he might in panic lead them further astray; and if he was attempting to confound them, then how could Beheim depend upon anything he said or did? No, the best course was to continue on, to be watchful. Another half hour. Then he would reconsider. High above in the aeries of Castle Banat, men and women to whom the bloodiest of violences was as casual an act as the swatting of a fly might even now be planning his fate. He could not hope that they would stay their hand much longer.

At length they came to a wall that blocked their path, but Vlad told them there was a stone pipe sunk into the base. They would have to crawl along it, he said, for some considerable distance.

"Is there no other way?" asked Beheim, uneasy with this prospect.

"Not unless we retrace our steps and start anew," said Vlad. "I chose the shortest route, lord. It is not the easiest to negotiate, but there is none more direct. None more hidden from prying eyes."

Beheim had no choice but to accept this. And so, with Vlad leading and Giselle bringing up the rear, they set forth.

The pipe was scarcely wide enough to admit them; from the fecal stink and sticky surfaces, Beheim assumed it to be part of a drainage system. The air was warm, and the sound of their breathing caused the heat to seem more oppressive yet and the darkness to seem tarry, like black glue clotting Beheim's nostrils and lungs. He kept close behind Vlad, so close that now and again his hand would brush one of the man's feet, but the farther they went, the less attentive to their guide he became. His thoughts whirled in desolate orbits. To be reduced to this! Crawling like a bug along a crack in a world he had once dreamed of ruling. Hate expanded in his skull with such tangible force, he imagined his body inflating, filling the channel, conforming to its shape, being molded into a bullet that would be spat forth into the brains of his enemies. Hatred became a kind of brilliant perception, and he saw how he would exact revenge for this humiliation. He had been too much in awe of his cousins, too impressed by their physical superiority to dare challenging them; but he realized now that their penchant for games and deceits led straight into his strengths. He was not afraid to match wits with them; in that sort of contest, it might be they who were outmanned. And, oh, what a game he would devise for them! What a cunning sequence of misdirections! Of course it would all depend upon his first impressing the Patriarch and gaining his confidence. He needed a perfect lie, something that incorporated the truth— whatever fragment of the truth he knew—and embroidered it with implication, delivering nothing of substance, yet making it seem that his intuition had forged a track to the heart of the crime. Once the lie had done its work, he would draw his enemies into the web it created. Agenor, Alexandra, and whoever else came to pose a difficulty. They were all his enemies in this. And despite his moment of enlightenment that had come upon hearing the song of his blood, even those of his branch were suspect. That, he realized, was the nature of the Family: it was a league of mortal enemies, a trait that sometimes proved both its most profound weakness and greatest strength.

His thoughts were interrupted by a choking noise behind him, a rustle, the sound of something being dragged away. Then a grinding, a thud, as of a heavy weight being slid down along a track.

Alarmed, Beheim tried to turn and struck his temple on the side of the pipe; pain blinded him for an instant.

"Giselle!" he said, clutching the injured place.

"So that is the lady's name," said Vlad. "I like it."

"Where are you, Giselle?"

"Beyond your clutches, vampire."

Vlad was speaking from a goodly ways off, and Beheim realized he must have scrambled on ahead.

"What have you done with her?"

"She is no longer your concern," said Vlad, his words betraying none of their previous eccentricity. "I suggest you now give thought to your soul. If you have one."

Beheim recognized that Vlad would never have addressed him with such disrespect unless he had some powerful form of defense at hand, and so he did not rush forward precipitously. He edged toward the sound of the man's voice and, despite his growing anxiety, essayed a laugh.

"And what of *your* soul, Vlad? What will become of it when I have done with you?"

"You have no power over me. You're a dead man. A dead thing. In a moment all your murderous days will be done."

" 'Thing,' is it?" Beheim edged a little closer, straining to see Vlad in the blackness. "Yet you once yearned to be such a 'thing,' did you not? Perhaps you still are servant to that yearning. Perhaps you still long for judgment."

Closer, closer. Inch by inch.

"It is true," Vlad said. "Once I longed for power and life immortal, but I became frightened and fled my office. From fear, however, I have learned much, and whatever I may have lost, I have more than gained its equal in the restoration of my humanity."

"Indeed? Then why remain in Castle Banat, why not go back to the world of humankind?"

"Life here has poisoned me. I can never go back to the place that bore me. But I can kill you, vampire. That should firmly establish my human proofs, don't you think?"

"Others will come. They will exterminate you all."

"You already hunt us. Why should we fear you more than we do already? And I doubt under any circumstance there will be a call for our extermination. There are dangers for your kind in these depths. We would not be easy to ferret out. It is likely that the Patriarch does not wish us to die. We cannot threaten him, and he may decide that our little community provides an intriguing danger against which he may test his subjects. In fact, I would not doubt that he has already assessed the situation and chosen to maintain the status quo. He has an affinity for such ironies as our existence here comprises. At any rate, if your cousins come to avenge you, I will hope to kill them, too. That will, in some small way, repair the wrongs done in my days of evil service."

Judging by Vlad's voice, Beheim estimated that he was no more than half a dozen feet away. He gathered himself, preparing to lunge; but before he could move, Vlad said, "Think on this as you die, vampire. Tonight I will have of your beautiful lady all those pleasures you have tasted. And more besides."

Another grinding noise, another thud. Beheim scuttled forward and met with a barrier. A stone slab had dropped down to block his path. It was immovable, though he pried at it with all his strength. He scooted backward, knowing that he would find another barrier behind him, yet hoping, hoping, his heart constricted by claustrophobic terror, his mind reddening with panic.

There was, as he had guessed, a second barrier.

He was trapped in a space not much larger than a coffin, encysted in an immeasurable tonnage of stone.

For a moment he was unable to breathe. He sucked at the dead air, tasting blackness and decay. He could hear the drumming of his heart, feel it swelling in his chest. Then a scream burst from his throat, and he began to kick at the walls, to beat upon them with his fists. His fear was so animal and despairing, he might have gone on in this fashion for some time, but no more than a minute had elapsed before a section of pipe swung open beneath him, like the dropping of a trapdoor, and he went sliding feetfirst into a second pipe, hurtling downward at a steep angle, snatching at the slick, damp stone, trying to find a crack, a projection, anything with which to slow his progress, bumping his head with blinding force. Then he was falling free, screaming, flailing at the air . . . but not for long. A second or two, no more. He landed on his back, the impact sending pain lancing through his limbs, shocking him into unconsciousness.

When at length he opened his eyes, dazed and aching, something was tickling his cheek and nothing he saw made any sense. Overhead was an expanse of smeared, sickly blue, like a poorly painted ceiling, daubed here and there with tendrils of white and splotches of dark green, and figured also by a glowing yellow and purplish mass, all diffuse and cloudy, as if he were gazing at it through a volume of water. There was a sighing noise. Wind, he thought, it sounds like the wind. The thing tickling his cheek feathered across his lip; annoyed, he plucked at it, held it to his eyes: a slim curve of brownish green. Slick and cool to the touch. Unidentifiable. He blinked, trying to clear his vision. A bit of definition appeared in the green splotches above. Pine needles? Couldn't be, he told himself. He sat up, painfully, dizzily. He lowered his head, closed his eyes to clear the cobwebs. His thoughts moved slowly. Rudimentary, childlike thoughts. This hurts, that hurts. What's this on my hand? Dirt? He wondered what he should do next. Find Giselle? Head for the Patriarch's chambers? He had no idea of where he was—how could he hope to find anything or anyone? He opened his eyes again and was relieved to discover that his vision had returned to normal. There were rips in his trousers, his knees were abraded. Grass blades all around him. Winter grass, sere and dry. That made no sense, either, that there would be grass growing inside Castle Banat. He was just beginning to worry about this when he glanced up and stared directly into the sun.

It was not the sun he recalled from his youth, not that warm, lovely golden-white burn. It was larger, much larger. Monstrous. A warped yellow round with a purplish corona and a surface mottled with incandescent whorls and boils of hideous fire. And so he did not at first recognize what he was seeing, but instead thought how similar it was, this grotesque orb, to the moon that he had imagined the murderer had seen atop the turret. Even after realizing it must be the sun, that the green swatches were, indeed, pine boughs, that the blue ceiling was the sky, and that he was surrounded not by stone walls but by hills and cool air and light ... even then he did not credit his senses. Sunlight would burn him, blacken his bones. And then he thought it must be killing him at that very moment, that he must not be feeling the attendant pain. Perhaps his senses had been seared away, perhaps he was beyond all feeling.

He began to tremble. Hot urine spurted down his thigh. It seemed he was falling toward the sun, or else it was growing larger yet. The flares of its writhing corona stretching out to ensnare him, bubbles of fiery plasma bulging toward him and bursting as from the surface of a vile, molten soup. He let out a whimper and tried to burrow into the earth, digging up clods and swatches of grass. Breath whined in his throat. He rammed his head at the ground, wanting to batter his way into the black earth. When this failed, he turned onto his back and stared about in abject horror at the landscape.

He was lying on a tufted mound some ten feet from the castle wall, about fifty feet below a gaping hole—obviously the terminus of the pipe down which he had slid; in many places the mortar had eroded from between the granite blocks so that the entirety of the wall was mapped with cracks and fissures, making it appear that the structure was on the verge of crumbling. To his right, the hillside—ranked with dwarfish pines—fell away sharply into a valley. Pine boughs overhung the spot where he lay, and whenever the wind pressed them down, it was as if intricate green paws were groping, trying to scoop him up. Something tiny and black was circling the depths of the sky, tilting back and forth on currents of wind, lending perspective to his view. The castle wall went up and up, a mile or more of gray ruin, and the sun, an evil eruption burst through from the other side of the sky, was pushing closer, and the woods hissed with wind, lisping the noxious secrets of the day, and that stupid winged thing was mindlessly circling and circling, and talons of pale cloud were uncurling, fraying into nonsense script, and the pines, shaking their burly tops like green beasts just emerged from a river, were attempting to uproot themselves and lurch forward in an attack. There was too much light, too much movement, too much of everything. The profusion of sights and sounds disoriented Beheim, kindled a fire in his mind that he could not extinguish. All the familiar constructions of his thought and expectation were burning, breaking apart, tumbling in showers of sparks down into a chaos of light, and unable to restore an internal order by means of reason, ignoring the pain in his legs, he leaped to his feet and ran, covering his head with his hands. He ran without regard for direction, simply bolting, praying that he might stumble into some benign darkness, a hole, a crypt, a cave. He darted in among the pines, avoiding patches of sunlight as if they were pools of yellow poison. But as he negotiated a steep defile bordered by an outcropping of boulders, he slipped on the carpet of needles and went sprawling, winding up crumpled on his side, panting, and once more gazing directly into the sun.

Fatigue made him wise. He was not dying, not burning. Somehow a miracle had occurred, and he had lived. There was no point in running any farther. Yet he could not overcome his terror of the boiling, fuming thing overhead, nor could he stanch his uneasiness with the world revealed in its light. For a long while he lay pinned by a beam of sunlight, expecting at any moment to be incinerated. Finally he drew up his knees, wrapped his arms around them, and with his back against one of the boulders, he sat hunched and miserable, harrowed by the warm sun that fingered his scalp and shoulders. He searched inside himself for a reservoir of strength, something that would shore him up and permit him to think, to analyze, to get a grip on this patently ungraspable situation. What could have happened to cause this? What had he done—or what had been done to him—to so abrogate the laws of his being? And he wondered as well how—despite the hours he had spent remembering the life of a day, despite the poignancy of his nostalgia—how he could ever have longed to experience the sun again. It must be, he decided, a benign illness of the eye that allowed humans to regard the thing without blanching. Even its minor side effects were perturbing: the air rippling and inconstant, rife with translucent eddies and drift-

ing opaque shapes; specks of dirt floating up like pep-
per grains in a clear fluid; patterns of pine needles on
the ground shifting about like thousands of muddled
hexagrams rearranging themselves. Watching all this
motion, both real and apparent, he felt vertiginous,
sick to his stomach. Everything was too bright, wrong
in its obscene welter of detail. The patchy grooves of
pine bark exposed by ugly light rather than made
cryptic and simple by moonshadow; the blotchy mineral complexion of the boulders; the diseased intricacy
of pine cones; the gray-green infections of moss. It
was alien, unnatural, ruled by that hellish fire in the
sky, the source of all wrongness, and he was reminded
again of the scene atop the turret, his hallucinatory impressions he had received of the murderer.

"Shit!" he said, suddenly jolted by comprehension, having made a connection between what had
befallen him and the Golden's death.

The murder might have been done in the daylight. No, it *must* have been done then! That would explain the retardation of the rigor.

Had he reached this conclusion under ordinary
circumstances, he would have laughed at it, and he
would further have rejected the validity of what he
had imagined atop the turret regarding the murderer's
state of mind; no matter how accurate such intuitions
had been in the past, he would have believed it impossible that a vampire could have withstood the sun's
rays. But he was living proof that a vampire could survive direct sunlight. And it *had* been a vampire who
killed the Golden, not a servant emulating his master's
lust for blood. Beheim's perceptions of the day as a
perversion of darkness confirmed this fact, validated
the impression of the murderer's perceptions that he
had gained at the scene of the crime.

But how, he asked himself, how could this have happened?

He took a deep breath to quell his uneasiness and began to consider the events of the past hours. An answer—the only one possible, it seemed—soon came clear. The liquid he had drunk in Felipe's hidden study. It must have been a drug that enabled one to walk abroad in daylight. The list of dosages and Felipe's journal entry supported this assumption. And there was something else. The fact that the windows of the study had been without shutters. Even were it a place that Felipe frequented only at night, no one of the Family could have borne for very long the presence of a shutterless window unless made confident by some other form of protection. Otherwise an accident might occur, one that would leave them helpless and exposed to the sun. He had been an imbecile not to see this before.

Panic flared in him again.

How long an immunity did the drug guarantee? He had to return to the castle . . . and quickly!

Then he remembered the flask he had taken from Felipe's study.

It was still there, still tucked into his shirt pocket.

So frightened he was unable to breathe, he fumbled with the silver cap, unscrewed it, and put the bottle to his lips; but then, recognizing that he exhibited no ill effects, he refrained from drinking.

He was going to survive, he told himself; he had only to stay calm and take his time.

Nothing had changed. The first order of business was still to return to the castle. Of course, even were he able to get back inside, he would find himself in the same situation as before. But armed with the knowledge of Felipe's researches, with the evidence of his experience, he might be able to influence the Patriarch to allow him to continue his investigation. There was hope for him now.

And what of Giselle, what hope for her?

He trotted toward the east turret, which loomed above the pine tops, and as he went he concluded that the safest method of reentering the castle would be to return the way he had exited it. Vlad and his accomplice would likely have removed the barriers from the pipe, assuming him dead. If he could scale the wall, using the cracks for finger- and toeholds, and retrace his steps, perhaps he would be able to find Giselle. He could not afford to waste time in a prolonged search, but he would very much like to encounter Vlad again.

Coming out from the shade of the pines and under the bloated eye of the sun was no less disturbing than before, but he mastered his fear and walked briskly toward the castle without looking up. He had little difficulty in scaling the wall, and as he neared the mouth of the pipe, that circle of sweet darkness, he began to feel secure and, if not wholly confident, then at least somewhat capable. He hauled himself up onto the lip of the pipe and dared another glance at the world of light and heat he was abandoning. As his gaze swept across the ground below, he caught sight of something nestled in a depression between two hillocks not fifty feet from the spot where he had landed. Something wrapped in a black widow's shawl, something with pale twisted sticks protruding from a bloodied skirt—legs, he realized, badly broken legs.

An old woman, perhaps.

A servant, the one whom the Patriarch had charged with the care of the Golden?

Who else could it be?

He did not feel sufficiently secure to risk climbing back down and examining the corpse; he wanted darkness and quiet and still air, and though he realized how slovenly and unprofessional this was, he could not endure the thought of staying outside another minute. At any rate, he no longer believed he could win this game through a process of deduction. How could he trust any clue the body might provide? There would probably be none, but even if there were, it might have been planted. No, the thing to do would be to use the corpse to his advantage.

And that could be managed.

Despite everything against him, if he could survive this next bit, he believed he would be in a position to make moves of his own, to send others scurrying for cover. He was no longer governed by the rules of evidence or the necessity for supporting witnesses. He was in effect a Columbus of the daylight, a voyager in uncharted seas. Who would doubt the integrity of his witness? If the murderer could remove or plant his clues, could not he do the same? If anyone sought to debunk his evidence, by displaying such knowledge they would implicate themselves in the crime.

It was really quite a simple game. Now that he had stepped off the board and taken note of its parameters, he saw how primitive were its conceptions, how clumsy and unschooled its players, how overly dependent they were on the tactic of fear.

He forced himself to take a final look at the sun, holding on to the idea that this was the world he would someday inhabit, that he would have to learn to bear whatever horrors it presented.

It seemed to hurtle toward him again, but he did not cower from it this time, though his genitals shriveled and his stomach knotted. The thing resembled, he decided, the underside of a yellow jellyfish with purplish tentacles and serious internal disorders. Thinking about it in that way, diminishing it, made him feel easier. He wondered if there was truly any beauty here, the remembered beauty of soft warmth and summer winds and thistles drifting through the air, the harmonious buzz of dragonflies, the universe in which small children played with hoops and lovers blithely wandered. Or was what he saw now the reality? Had all previous seeing been blighted by a lovely curse, the world's coarse truth hidden from mortal eyes? Could he ever learn to resurrect those old perceptions?

He stared out over the hilltop, past the valley and the hills, trying to overcome his fright, to discern some fraction of beauty in the sickeningly pale sky and its unruly configuration of clouds and sun, seeing only what struck him as the products of dementia and nightmare. But just before he turned away, there was a moment—a fleeting moment almost lost among flutters of panic and shivers of revulsion—when he seemed not to reinhabit that old childhood world of clean golden sun and soothing warmth, but to perceive in this place of garish light and turbulence a raw perfection such as might have existed during prehistory, a time when a crimson sun beamed down its killing rays, and giant ferns lifted in silhouette against clouds of mauve and copper and gold, and grasses seethed with furies of infinitesimal life, and there were poison butterflies as big as birds and beetles the size of sewer rats, and the screams of winged reptiles ripped through the sky, and nightmares with needle teeth coupled in a bloody rage, and somewhere in the depths of a vast forest, a new monster lifted its head and—as Beheim did then—gave a cry of shock and bewilderment, an expression so terrifying in itself that it abolished fear and reminded him that he was first among all the terrors of this world.

Chapter NINE

It took Beheim the better part of an hour to retrace his path to the tunnel mouth where he and Giselle had encountered Vlad. He made his way tentatively at first, but with increasing confidence—he was determined not to be taken by surprise again. Once the element of surprise had been removed, he did not believe that the vermin who inhabited the depths of Banat would be any match for him. From time to time he heard delirious shouts and laughter reverberating in the distance, and as he drew near the tunnel mouth, glancing to his left along a cross corridor, he spotted a reflected glow of torchlight. He headed toward the light and soon turned into another corridor whose far end was stained by a flickering ruddy glare. A faint babble of voices carried to him, as did the scent of blood. There might be, he estimated, as many as thirty people gathered together. Enough to present a considerable danger, should they be of unified purpose. But he continued on, driven equally by a red desire to confront Vlad as by any hope of finding Giselle.

When he reached the source of the light—a half-open door, massive slabs of oak bound with iron bands—he peeked into a room so narrow it might have been an incredibly elongated closet. Sixty feet long or more, with a high arched ceiling, lit by torches set in iron brackets. The space had been hewn from the rock on which the castle was founded, the walls of glistening, unmorticed black stone decorated with brightly colored caricatures of bone-white, cadaverous men and women with cruel carmine mouths and ridiculously elongated limbs and exaggerated fangs. Evil cartoons posed in attitudes of menace, each fifteen feet high or thereabouts. Images so vividly rendered, they seemed capable of coming to life, of peeling up from the rock and committing two-dimensional violences.

There were not so many people in the room as Beheim had presumed. Only a dozen or so, all dressed in hooded robes like that worn by Vlad. Most of them were crowded about Giselle, who was shackled to the wall, naked and apparently unconscious, her skin washed orange by the torchlight. Fresh bruises dirtied her thighs and arms. Vlad was standing beside her, his hood thrown back, talking with a plump gray-haired woman. Every few seconds he would touch Giselle on the shoulder, the hip, in a casual fashion that made Beheim think he was using her as an example in his conversation; whenever he smiled, his teeth glittered with unnatural brilliance, and this enhanced the rat-like aspect of his bearded face. Several other people were idling about, examining the murals, now and again casting glances toward Giselle, as if they expected something to happen. Beheim feared the torches, but he knew that if he were going to act, he would have to do so quickly, before they set about whatever it was they intended.

Footsteps sounded farther along the corridor.

Someone walking at a rapid pace toward the room.

Laughter came from even farther away, deeper in the labyrinth of corridors.

Beheim flattened against the wall, and when a burly robed figure drew abreast of him, he seized the man from behind and broke his neck with a quick twist, choking off his outcry. He hauled the body farther into the darkness, into a niche that might once have been used for a sentry post. There he stripped off the man's robe and, ignoring its foul odor, pulled it on over his head. As he was adjusting the hood to hide his face, two more men came striding along the corridor, chatting happily, and entered the room. Beheim stood straining his ears. After waiting a few minutes more to allow for any further late arrivals, he himself entered, stepping in among the small crackling fires and the rich stink of blood.

Gone was every trace of his benign regard for mortals. He felt nothing but anger and contempt. As he passed in among them he glimpsed mottled faces and dull eyes and gaping mouths. Several members of the assemblage, he noticed, were sporting makeshift fangs: curved tubes of crudely forged metal that fitted over their canines. This aping of the Family intensified his loathing. They were aroused, he realized. Titillated. Anticipating some gory delight. A primitive version of the Decanting, perhaps. And in their arousal, whatever craftiness served to keep them alive had been subsumed beneath a veneer of lustful perversity. He had been concerned that they would know him at once, that he would have to strike before he was prepared. But they had not the slightest intimation of his presence. Sheep would have been more alert, chickens more sensitive to danger.

He stationed himself behind two men at the rear of the gathering, some twenty feet from Giselle. She was chained so that her head obscured the crotch of one of the huge, pale cartoons on the wall, making it appear that her face and hair were a clever form of pubic decoration. She moaned and tried unsuccessfully to lift her head. Drugged, he supposed. Seeing close at hand the full extent of her bruises, imagining how she had been used . . . this hardened his anger. How these things stank! Their blood was a vile carrion fluid, their bones were black sticks mortaring a spoilage of poisons and stringy meat. They were brutes, animals, incapable of anything other than the grossest of perceptions, the most rudimentary judgments.

There were whispers and rustlings as Vlad turned to Giselle. Then silence. He spoke softly to her, gave her a light slap. Her eyelids fluttered, but remained closed. Vlad grinned at his audience and shrugged—in his manner, he reminded Beheim of the buffoonish, third-rate illusionists who had sometimes appeared during intermissions at the Opéra Comique. His canines, too, were fitted with a pair of metal fangs, and in a show of mock ferocity, he clicked them together and let out a hissing exclamation. The audience tittered; several of the women pretended to be shrinking away from him in fright. He turned again to Giselle, stroked her hips as might a lover; then, with another sidelong, grinning look at the onlookers, he sank his counterfeit fangs into her neck. She stiffened, her fingers splayed, yet she did not wake. A line of lovely ruby-colored blood escaped his lips, eeled down her neck and onto her breast.

Afraid for her, but feeling mostly a sense of proprietary violation, Beheim placed his hands on the necks of the two men in front of him, squeezing gently as if in affection. As they turned to look at him, their faces betraying puzzlement, he squeezed harder. There was a grating sound, like gravel being crushed beneath the wheels of a cart: the vertebrae at the bases of their necks grinding into a rubble of bone. He stared at them fiercely, wanting to stain their last seconds with his hatred. They quivered like rabbits in his grasp. Borne along by the momentum of turning to his left, freed of skeletal constraints, the head of one of them made nearly a complete revolution, so that—as his eyes rolled up—his final sight was of a corner of the ceiling to his extreme right.

Beheim flung the bodies aside and confronted the others, who had fallen back to either side of Vlad and Giselle. The room was so narrow, barely a few feet wide than his outspread arms, they had no hope whatsoever of escaping him. As they huddled together, clutching at one another and making puling noises, they seemed as foul and anonymous as roaches. In some basement of his thought he recalled who they were and knew that—although pitiable—they were not very different from himself; but that knowledge was meaningless, rather like the knowledge one might have of the principles of combustion when one strikes a match, intending to burn down a house full of sleepers. What he chiefly knew was that they were his enemies, that no quarter should be given them. He had grown beyond them in every way, most particularly in the refinement and scope of his emotions, and it seemed his fury could no longer be gauged in terms of human reaction, but was an evolution of anger, a monstrous flame of an emotion that filled his brain as light might fill the glass sleeve of a oil lamp. It was so grand, such a symphonic sweep of feeling, he could scarcely contain it. He imagined how he must look to them, taking the Lady Dolores for his model, picturing his own mouth stretched wide, linkages of saliva strung between his fangs, and he preened before them, letting his breath hiss out, wanting them to experience fear in all its subtle increments, to anticipate the richness of pain, waiting for them to become desperate and attack.

It was a paunchy, heavyset man with a sallow complexion who finally tried Beheim, snatching up one of the torches from the wall and swinging it at him with a great *whoosh* and flurries of sparks. Beheim knocked the torch aside, caught him by the throat and drew him close. Curiously enough, the man relaxed. His eyes ranged across Beheim's face with an innocent, awed curiosity like that an infant might display when straining to see a dim figure leaning over his crib. Beheim had never experienced such a raw feeling of presence. The man's essence seemed to billow about him like a rising fog, damp and turbulent and rife with clammy secrets. He was ordinary looking, with grizzled cheeks and unhealthy dark pouches of skin beneath his eyes and a scatter of inflamed eruptions mapping his chin and neck; yet at the same time he was wonderfully vital, aglow, as if every ounce of life were being sweated out of him by the pressure of the moment. Beheim was, for a brief moment, fascinated. Then fascination gave way once again to disgust, and he slung the man headfirst into the wall, crushing the top of his skull. He could feel the suddenly created absence of the death, like a tunnel punched through the air into a dimension of slow reverberation, and silence like a chill fluid welling out into the breach. And the scattered energies of those things that could not be sustained beyond death, the petty colors of the ego, the scant, last-remembered things, all the excess baggage of the man's life, these he felt on his skin as barely perceptible flutterings, like ashes on a hot wind.

For a matter of seconds the others remained motionless, uniform in their horrified expressions, watching the limbs of their dead companion spasm on the stones, dark blood pooling wide as a table beneath his burst head. Then they crowded away from Beheim; they turned to the walls, trying to climb out of reach, to use the shoulders of their fellows for ladders, prying at cracks, milling together, surging this way and that like rats in the bottom of a barrel. One of the women screamed, then a second woman, and Beheim screamed, too, taunting them in part, yet the cries ripping out of his chest almost as if in sympathy, making a natural counterpoint to their singing. Another man, a gangly sort with a crop of gray stubble on his cheeks, snatched up the torch that the heavyset man had dropped; but before he could take aggressive action, Beheim struck the torch to the floor and drove his fist into the man's face: three short, powerful punches that obliterated all feature and dappled the robes of those nearby with gore. He kept hold of the man's robe, letting him dangle, limp and lifeless, as inconsequential as the corpse of a game hen. His right hand was gloved in blood, and he displayed it to the others as if it were a sword, wanting them to comprehend the sharpness of the edge, to anticipate its bite. He was shivering with eagerness and hate. It grew quiet in that glistening, black room. The white creatures of the murals appeared to be trembling in the unsteady light; the crackling of the torches and sobbing breaths were the only sounds. One of the men began to weep. Vlad remained standing beside Giselle. His eyes darted to the left, the right; his lips were wet and scarlet, stupidly parted, like a clown's.

Beheim pictured himself moving among them, plucking out hearts, tearing limbs, shattering bones. But recalling the greater circumstance of his peril, he found the capacity for restraint. He herded the survivors against the side wall and crossed to Giselle. When he spoke to her, her eyes opened, but she did not appear to see him. He wrenched the bolt anchoring her shackles from the wall and caught her up in one arm; with his free hand, he caught Vlad by the front of his robe and lifted him. Vlad's mouth worked, and he made an unintelligible noise that had the flavor of an entreaty. He made a second try at speech and succeeded in asking, as he had done on their initial meeting, for mercy.

"Mercy is not always a kindness." Beheim smiled thinly. "But if you insist, I will be merciful."

He laid Giselle down against the wall, well apart from the rest, all the while maintaining his hold on Vlad. She had lapsed into unconsciousness; her breathing was labored and her pulse ragged. When he turned from her, some of the survivors sank to their knees and began to plead with him. It was easy to ignore them, yet he found that he no longer enjoyed the sight of the dead, that feelings of self-loathing were beginning to color his thoughts. Nevertheless, he refused to accept the full measure of guilt for what had happened. They had violated Giselle and tried to murder him. He had acted in the interests of their survival.

"This"—Beheim gave Vlad a shake, extracting a squeal—"this has tried to kill me with the sun. And he has failed. Do any of you wish to try me further?"

They were silent.

"Good," he said. "For it would serve you nothing. I am the first of my kind to have no fear of light or fire."

"Not the first, my lord," came the voice of a young woman standing to his immediate right. Quite an attractive piece, he noticed. Pretty in a country way, with generous features and fair skin and straw-colored hair. A mole like a drop of ebony figuring the corner of her mouth. Though she was far more buxom, her face coarser by a degree, she bore a striking resemblance to the Golden. Beheim was put off by her attempt to curry favor, but he could not help admiring her resourcefulness and courage. He told her to come forward, and once she had obeyed, stopping less than an arm's length away, he asked her to tell him what she had seen.

"Nothing, lord. At least not with my own eyes. But a man *was* seen yesterday outside the castle while the sun was high. He was no servant ... or so I'm told. He was of the Family."

"How do you know this?"

"That he was of the Family? It is not something any of us would mistake, lord."

The girl's eyes were a brilliant, almost chemical blue. Her blood scent, also reminiscent of the Golden's, was remarkably complex. Beheim found himself growing hungry. And more than a little aroused. She had not, he recalled, been one of those outfitted with metal fangs. An evidence in her favor. Until Giselle regained her strength, he would need someone to serve him, and this girl, with her strong spirit and her forthrightness, might just do.

"What is your name, child?" he asked.

"Paulina."

"Who told you of this, Paulina?"

She pointed to the corpse of the gangly man. "It was he, lord. And another who is not here."

"They told you nothing more?"

"Only that the man was very tall. And that he wore a wide-brimmed hat and spectacles with tinted lenses. He was interested in the body."

"A body?"

"Yes, lord. An old woman fell from the heights of the castle just the other morning."

Morning, thought Beheim. A term that, when used by one of the Family, might refer to any time after midnight. But when used by a mortal, might it not refer strictly to a period of daylight before noon?

"After sunrise," he said. "She fell after sunrise?"

"Yes, lord."

"Did anyone else see this man?"

There was a muttering negative consensus.

"My lord," said Vlad. "If you will permit me, I will send my agents throughout the castle and inquire of—"

Beheim shifted his grasp to Vlad's neck, choked him into silence.

Spectacles with tinted lenses. A wide-brimmed hat. Signs, Beheim thought, that whoever it was had been practiced at walking in the daylight, prepared for its terrors. Felipe, perhaps. Searching for the body of the Golden's servant, concerned lest it provide a clue that would reveal his identity. And yet this explanation did not sit well with him. If Felipe had murdered the Golden, he would have boasted of it while tormenting Beheim. To maintain silence and secrecy, to deny himself an opportunity for gloating, that would have been completely out of character. No, it had not been Felipe.

For another thing, Felipe would never be described as tall.

But Alexandra, that creature of secrets, she was tall, she was capable of all this misdirection and subtlety.

Her specific motives were still a mystery to him, but given the rumors concerning her ambition, her connections with Felipe and Dolores, given the general furor concerning the Family's possible migration to the East, there was potential motive aplenty. In light of what he now knew, Alexandra's intervention in his investigation and in his life was more suspect than ever, whether or not it had come as a result of an alliance with Agenor.

Could she have killed the Golden?

It would be foolish to doubt it, Beheim decided. After all, who of the Family was not capable of violence? From what little experience he had of Alexandra, he would not have thought her prone to such an excessive nature as was evidenced by the mutilated body of the Golden. But what rule did logic have over the matter, anyway? He was dealing with creatures whose hearts were mad, whose natures were governed by the need for lavish brutality and wild failures of the spirit. Even the most reasonable among them were infected with madness, and though he could be certain of nothing, he was tempted to conclude that Alexandra was the one he sought. Had she not more or less told him that her intervention was purely self-serving? In retrospect, he saw that her analysis of how he would be manipulated by the Family members stopped just short of being a confession. And as for the rest of their involvement, who could say what it had meant? Perhaps some honest emotion had been involved, but essentially it had been part of a game, perhaps a game that he had also wanted to play. The fact that he had allowed himself to become involved with her at such a critical time might be a symptom of his own madness, an expression of an unconscious urge to flirt with death. The thing to do, he realized, would be to test his hypothesis at once. If the deaths of Felipe and Dolores had not been discovered—what the odds on that were, he could not guess—he might be able to perform a valid test. If he were proved right, there might yet be salvation for him. If wrong, he would not have long to regret his error.

"Listen to me," he said to the little group of survivors. "For this man's recklessness"—he gave Vlad another shake—"some of you have paid a dear price. If you think you can resist me, then take the torches and come at me now. But if you wish to live beyond this day, I urge you to enter my service. After I have done what I must, I will set you free."

He studied them a moment, watching their reactions; once he had satisfied himself that they were thoroughly cowed, he turned his attention to Vlad.

"Lord, I have secrets!" Vlad said, squirming in his grasp. "Valuable secrets. I can give you blood to drink that will—"

"The torments of hell," said Beheim. "Do you remember?"

He took one of Vlad's metal fangs between thumb and forefinger, and snapped it off, bringing with it a tooth and its bloody root.

Vlad howled, he twisted and jerked. Crimson juice flowed down his chin, matting his beard. Beheim held him aloft by the hood of his robe, and after a short while Vlad hung limp and groaning. Then Beheim slammed him against the wall, stunning him, and pulled back his head to expose his throat. Most of the others were watching with what seemed renewed interest. One bloodletting, Beheim thought, was doubtless as desirable as another from their debased point of view.

"Think of your soul," he said to Vlad, and sank his fangs into the man's neck. The sinewy tissues were reluctant to part; Beheim had to worry at the flesh in order to penetrate the vein. His mouth flooded with a bitter taste, and when the blood spurted forth, it was too sweet, the basic flavor fouled by a gamy undertone. He pulled away and spat a red mouthful into Vlad's face.

"Drink that," he said, "if you wish to imitate your betters."

Still taken with the rapture of the bite, Vlad stared foggily at the wall. To enliven him, Beheim snapped off the second metal fang, and as Vlad writhed in pain he spoke to the others, saying, "I must reach Felipe de Valea's apartments unobserved. And after that, the Patriarch's chamber. Is there a safe passage by which you may lead me? Answer carefully. I will not tolerate betrayal."

Several assured him that there was such a passage. Paulina met his eyes and nodded. She seemed less frightened of him now, her fear replaced by an anxious curiosity.

"Very well. Lead me there, and I will reward you. Otherwise"—he closed a hand on Vlad's face, his palm covering the mouth, the thumb and fingers gripping the sides of the jaw—"otherwise, you have no hope at all and only this for a reward."

He began to squeeze Vlad's head, gradually increasing the pressure, all the while staring into his eyes, trying to probe to the center of the man's little rat soul, hoping to add a generous serving of humiliation to his agony. Vlad attempted to fling himself away. He kicked, clawed, his heels battered the stones, his squeals muted by Beheim's palm. His eyes widened, and soon thin crimson rims began to show around the whites. His entire body was alive with vibration.

"Does it hurt?" Beheim asked in a tone of mock concern. "I imagine that it must."

Vlad's arms flailed. A shrill keening leaked out from the muffle of Beheim's hand. With a crack like a pistol shot, his jawbone fractured. His eyelids slid down, and he appeared to lose consciousness. Beheim continued to squeeze. First one eyelid began to bulge, then the other. They were being slowly forced open by the protruding globes of the eyes themselves. He gave Vlad a light slap to revive him and then covered his mouth again. Vlad's neck inflated with a choked-back scream. A cheekbone shattered, his limbs shuddered. Bulging crescents of white became visible beneath the lids. His face felt like a sack of broken tiles, and when at last Beheim dropped him to the floor, he sat there like a great baby with his legs spread, his arms outstretched, his head rolling, and his breath making a windy, shrieking noise in his throat.

"There," Beheim said, wiping spittle and blood from his hand. "I have been merciful. Live if you can."

Vlad toppled onto his side, feebly groping for purchase on the stones. His eyes were open now. Red-rimmed, leaking bloody tears, they bulged like hard-boiled eggs from their sockets; his eyelids were stretched across the upper portions of the globes. Judging by the way he probed for the edges of the stones, Beheim believed that he must be blind. He turned his gaze to the other survivors, who were cringing back against the wall. Only Paulina had succeeded in maintaining her poise.

"Take the clothing of your dead," he told them. "Tear them into strips and make ropes. Lash yourselves together. I will hold the end of the rope, and you will walk alongside me into the castle. When I have won through to the Patriarch, I will reward you. Is that clear?"

They murmured their assent and set about doing as he had instructed while he tended to Giselle. She did not respond to his ministrations, and he became worried that the abuse she had suffered and the drugs they had given her might have a cumulatively mortal effect. He would wait a little while longer, he decided. If she did not improve, then he would do what he must.

"Paulina!" He beckoned to the blond girl, led her toward the door and out into the corridor, leaving the door ajar so he could keep watch on the others. He stood Paulina against the wall and, keeping his distance, studied her again. There was some quality about her, a clean sensuality, and he thought that this was the thing that had initially inspired his lust. That, and her blood, with its heady, pungent bouquet. Not so compelling as the Golden's blood. A less refined vintage, but a prized one nonetheless.

"Have you never served one of the Family?" he asked.

"No, my lord."

"Then how did you come here?"

"I was born in the castle, lord."

"Here . . . in this low place?"

"Yes, lord. As were my mother and father. And their parents before them. More than twenty generations of my family have lived in Castle Banat."

This fact engaged Beheim's curiosity, but he had

neither the time nor the inclination to question her about it further.

"I would have you serve me, Paulina. Do you understand what this entails?"

"I do, my lord."

"And would you enter my service?"

She gave no reply. Tension showed in the set of her shoulders and her neck; some of the color had drained from her cheeks.

"Are you afraid?"

"I was, lord. Very afraid. But now . . ." She lowered her eyes. "Now I'm not so afraid as I was."

He reached out and lifted her chin, fixed her with a stare. The line of her mouth lost its firmness, and her eyes widened; he saw reflected in them an orange wash of torchlight centered by a darkness that he recognized to be himself.

"Answer me, Paulina," he said. "Answer me now. I cannot permit you a long deliberation."

"I would serve you," she said in a faltering voice; she glanced at the doorway, at Giselle, who lay as if sleeping. "But my lord already has a servant."

"Surely two are permitted," he said, amused. Yet in his heart he understood how pragmatic an act this cursory seduction was. Should Giselle fail to recover, should he submit her to judgment and she fail at that as well, he would need to replace her. Another betrayal. Not so bald a one as his infatuation with Alexandra, but a more profound one, perhaps, in that he was trivializing Giselle's plight, preparing to do without her. More damning, too, in what it told about the depth of his feelings for her.

With the tip of a forefinger he traced the blue vein in the hollow of Paulina's neck. Her eyelids drooped, and she swayed ever so slightly, as if weakened by his touch.

"Answer me, Paulina," he said.

Her answer, a whispered affirmation, seemed to come from a place deep within her, a place in which she was dazzled and dazed, liberated from all fear and inhibition.

He stepped to the doorway. The others looked up from their grisly work, faces expectant. He did not speak, only urged them to caution with a stare. At length he pulled the door shut, closing them in, and went back to Paulina, who had not moved. He caressed her cheek, her hair, then slipped her robe from her shoulders. Her breasts were tipped with childish, rosy pink areola. They seemed improbably large, monstrously beautiful. White animals with soft, nodding lives of their own. He lifted one, testing its heft, and felt a surge of eagerness in his groin. Yet his thoughts did not focus entirely on Paulina; they drifted back to memories of Alexandra, her smaller, firmer breasts, her almost feral ardor. That annoyed him. He did not want to dwell on her except as a suspect, and to banish her from his thoughts, he bent to Paulina, inhaling the musk of her white skin and the sweetness of the river flowing through the thin blue channel in her neck. He nuzzled a spot, moistening it with the chemicals of rapture. His hands clamped her waist. When he drove his fangs into her, the flesh giving way as readily as might a piece of cork to a steel needle, she tensed and let out an aggrieved gasp; but then her head lolled to the side, allowing him better access. Her blood rushed forth as if it were eager to be drunk, and he was astounded by the complexity of its flavor. It was easily the most wonderful blood he had ever tasted. Rich with essence. Strange shapes came before his inner eye, shapes that assumed color and proportion, and to his vast surprise, he began to have an uncommon sense of Paulina's history. He seemed to see her in a poorly lit room of soot-covered stone with several other blond children—her brothers and sisters, perhaps—and someone was watching, always someone in the darkness, watching and waiting for something. There were other images, a flood of them, all passing too quickly to register, moments of love and fear and pensive solitude, all weighted with that same oppressive feeling of being watched, and at the heart of these impressions was an intimation of her nature, her soul, stained by the violent, degrading culture of Banat's outcasts, yet somehow maintaining a core of innocence and strength. Then this curious apprehension of her was swept away by his absorption with the taste of the blood, a dark syrupy sweetness with tart undertones and a body of wild, furious life that stimulated a hunger of unparalleled urgency.

It took every ounce of his self-discipline to pull back from her, and when he did, still dizzy from the richness, she presented a gorgeous sight, with her eyes closed, her straw-colored hair tousled about her face, causing it to appear all the more delicate in contrast to this unruly frame; there was a seepage of blood from the incisions his fangs had made, filming over the upper slope of her right breast, and this excited him again. But he resisted the temptation to lick her clean and instead concentrated on the disturbing elements of what had happened. The hallucinatory effect of the blood; the image of the blond children. He recalled what Vlad had said: "I can give you blood that will—"

That will what?

Drive you mad? Intoxicate you as would the blood of the Golden?

It occurred to Beheim that he had never inquired of Agenor where the breeding stock that produced the Golden lived. He had assumed that those involved in the breeding program inhabited the surrounding villages, but now it seemed apparent that the most logical of dwelling places was the castle itself. And Paulina. The product of twenty generations of life within the castle walls. Might she not be a vintage off from perfection by a degree, not quite subtle enough a flavor to serve as centerpiece for the Decanting? The Golden's cousin, perhaps, or her sister? He believed this must be the case, for he had never drunk such blood before, never experienced such an overpowering response. Even if so, however, he doubted it would have any bearing on his investigation. It only furthered his comprehension of Castle Banat, of its intricate environment, and reminded him of how ill-equipped he was to deal with those intricacies.

He pushed open the door and looked about the room, his eyes resting on the mutilated dead and the defiled living; on the bloody, bulging-eyed Vlad whimpering and twitching in some dream of finality; on the hideous murals depicting Beheim's peers, and the chaotic painting of red streaks and puddles he had made on the stones; and lastly on the moribund Giselle, whom he had loved, whom perhaps he still loved, though now he was not confident of his capacities in that regard. Despite the air of perversion and brutality, he saw a tragic grandeur in the particulars of the scene, and he had the notion that no matter what the future held, no matter how long that future would last, he would always think of this room as the place where he had taken a final step away from his old life. He was different, he believed, from the man he had been prior to entering it. Larger and wiser. More dangerous.

Different, too, in ways that beggared categorization, ways that he could not separate out from the welter of his new experiences and comprehensions. But some great dark thing in him, that entity newly wakened during his sojourn in the depths of Castle Banat, seemed to be raising its head and taking a first long look around, gathering information that would fuel its preliminary conclusions. He did not know whether to be happy or dismayed by any of this. That, at least—his essential confusion—remained unaffected. However, he doubted that he would remain confused for long.

Chapter TEN

Felipe's apartments were as Beheim had left them, and though he suspected this good fortune, though he wondered where Alexandra might be and to what end she might be occupying herself, he concluded that the deaths of Felipe and Dolores must thus far have gone undiscovered. The black portal that had swallowed them remained floating at the center of the living room, but it appeared to be decaying, its dark substance eroding, losing cohesion. If Felipe and Dolores still burned within, Beheim could not make out their particular fire from among the myriad lights that swarmed in its strange depths. He stood a moment before the portal, not in memorial for the dead, but rather in obeisance to its Mystery; he put his palm close to it, felt again that cold pressure, felt also the alternation of revulsion and allure it bred in him. It was not so frightening, this little patch of death, when one could choose to enter it or not. Indeed, the choice seemed much more problematic, a decision between an endless journey into madness and another journey whose most frightening landfall would be the porches of oblivion.

As soon as he was certain that the apartment was

empty, he released the outcasts, first allowing them to scavenge for valuables, then charging them to return to their habitations and say nothing of his business; but Paulina he kept with him, directing her to stand watch over Giselle, who lay unconscious at the foot of the stair leading to Felipe's secret study. Once she was settled, he sat at Felipe's desk and began poring over his journals, trying to gain some understanding of the dosages required to protect one against the light of day. Apparently Felipe had not ascertained the precise dosages necessary to protect for specific periods of time—though he had noted that he believed continued consumption would result in a permanent immunity—and Beheim was forced to make educated guesses. After he had copied the formula and gathered all other available knowledge, he opened the cabinet where Felipe stored the drug and set about diluting his supply with water, working feverishly, fearful of being discovered—according to what Felipe had written regarding Agenor's insistence on a test, it seemed unlikely that Alexandra or anyone else would possess a supply of the drug; thus they would be forced to invade his sanctum in order to obtain it. If that occurred, Beheim planned a surprise for them. The image of Alexandra burning into charcoal beneath that grotesque sun did not delight him; but this was, he told himself, a game of her design—at the very least, of her choosing—and she had persuaded him to join in it. As troubling as was the idea of her death, the idea of his own troubled him still more.

When he had finished, he tucked three flasks of the undiluted drug into an inner pocket, a sufficient supply, he estimated, for months of protection against the light—it might be that he would have a chance to run if things did not go well, and he did not want to be limited to night travel. He also took a dagger from the drawer of the desk. Then he hurried to the stairs, caught up Giselle in his arms, and—preceded by Paulina—made his way along dark and untraveled passages toward the heart of the castle. As he went he tried to unravel the skeins of rivalry and coercion that had led him to this pass. It was an inconceivable task. But he believed that whatever personal whims and political machinations were in play, they were all somehow subordinate to the debate currently engaging the Family. For the first time he wondered if, when standing with Agenor and Dolores in the great hall on the night of the murder, he had only been parroting his mentor. Now, cut off from Agenor's influence, he was not quite so firm in his opinions. Who knew what bewildering eventualities the East might hold? Perhaps there were unknown dangers there more inimical to the Family than those known ones they faced in Europe. Perhaps they could undertake a change in Europe, become more devious and circumspect in their actions, and that alone would ensure survival. But then it might be that immersion in the East was the only tactic that would allow them the time necessary to adapt to such a change. In the end, he realized, the whole question would most likely be decided by the requisites of a design or game that none of them completely understood, with the possible exception of the amazing creature whom he was seeking to interview. It might be no more than the inevitable result of some operation of fate, like the one whose presence he had sensed just prior to meeting Vlad, on hearing the song of his blood, the weaving of an unimaginably large tapestry reaching its conclusion, a thready signature writing itself in the bottom corner. Alexandra had been right: he was a pawn. But so, for all her guile, was she.

The most that they might hope to learn was whether they were of a color, moving together across the board toward the possibility of higher rank, or if they had been set one against the other, a minor engagement that would have some peripheral significance as to the ultimate outcome.

The entrance to the Patriarch's chambers was an adit that led to a hidden door. Beheim laid Giselle down at the mouth of the adit and knelt at her side, trying to detect some change in her that would signal her imminent recovery. Though the flickering of Paulina's torch lent her false color, her pulse remained erratic and the corners of her mouth were down-turned, as if she were in terrible pain.

"What in hell's name can he have given her?" Beheim said, smacking the flat of his hand against the wall.

"Laudanum, perhaps." Paulina shook her head glumly. "Vlad had many drugs, many poisons."

Beheim could not make up his mind whether to risk judging Giselle, to take the chance that she would survive judgment, or to do nothing and hope she would recover on her own. At last his indecisiveness persuaded him that the time was not right for judgment. He would see how things stood once he returned from his audience with the Patriarch.

If he returned.

There was no point in dwelling on that.

"Wait with her," he told Paulina. "Be patient. I don't know how long this will take."

She made no reply, but he needed none to confirm her fidelity. He remembered how it had been immediately after he had succumbed to Agenor. He had not been able to take his eyes off the man; he had cataloged his every twitch and habit: how Agenor's laugh descended into a hoarse, broken chuckle; how he sometimes would throw back his head in an almost feminine gesture before speaking; how he would fold his right arm across his chest when in a deep study, bracing his left elbow on the right hand, his left hand held open as if to catch the substance of his thought that was due at any moment to be spat forth from his forehead. Paulina was, as Beheim himself once had been, utterly captivated, enraptured, staring at him with unmodulated adoration.

From his waist he removed the dagger he had taken from the study and handed it to Paulina. "Should anyone of the Family find you here, you must kill Giselle and then yourself. I realize this is a harsh command. But, believe me, you will both suffer less that way."

She gazed at him through strands of blond hair, as mutely adoring as a hound. He was disaffected by her single-mindedness, and this disaffection was not related to who she was, he realized, but to the character of the relationship, the same relationship he had with Giselle. It struck him as unchallenging now, devoid of intrigue. The pleasure he had once taken from such dominance seemed childish, and looking at the two of them, he understood that though they were useful to him, neither of them, not even Giselle, was as dear as he might have thought. It was Alexandra, a woman for whom at times he could manufacture a substantial hatred, and whom he was probably going to try to kill, who challenged and intrigued him. Alexandra who fired his imagination. Alexandra whose mysterious and doubtless pathological obsessions stimulated his own obsessions. As far as Giselle and Paulina were concerned, he had reached a point of development from which there was no returning; all his declarations of love and responsibility for Giselle had, he saw, been a means of holding on to the familiar, the known, a hedge against the uncertainties of his new life. He refused to admit to this completely, telling himself that by thinking this way, he was attempting to cushion his sensibilities against the likelihood of Giselle's death; yet as he prepared to enter the Patriarch's chambers, he felt that this would be a final parting and was dismayed by his relative lack of emotion, the watered-down quality of his guilt and affection. It seemed he was more engaged by the prospect of facing a perilous future than he was of clinging to the security of his past.

"Be watchful," he said to Paulina. "You mustn't fall asleep."

He thought there should be something else to tell her, something that would give her faith in his eventual return; but it was not in him. Nor could he bring himself to look at Giselle, humiliated by her steadfastness and her sacrifice. He only wanted to leave them, to put them from mind for a while at least. He took a quick step away, but as he started along the adit Paulina caught up his hand and kissed it, and would not release him until he had kissed her in return and comforted her with lies.

On passing through the hidden door, Beheim stepped out onto a stone pier extending from the bottom of an enormous chamber—some three hundred feet in height, he reckoned; perhaps half that at its widest—and was met with a sight that, as its particulars came clear, spiked his backbone with cold and prickled the hairs on the back of his neck. There was no light source, at least none he could detect. Yet there was light. The chamber was filled with an eerie, grainy, blue radiance; it seemed something akin to the humming silence and the cold and an ozonelike stink, as if light had been transformed into a liquid with these same properties. The radiance was sufficient to cast vague shadows, yet was so dim that it took several minutes before he could make out much of the detail of the place: bats making looping flights in the cobalt reaches; pornographic bas-reliefs on the walls, many having a melted look, like stalactites, giving the impression that they were natural productions of the rock that had not yet finished taking shape; the various piers and the passageways opening here and there above him, some with massive iron-bound doors, others mere cracks; more of the ubiquitous statuary— none of the figures he could see had faces, just blank ovals resting atop torsos both bestial and human. The most curious of these conceits, however, covered the floor of the chamber, which lay some twenty feet below and had been sculpted into a representation of thousands upon thousands of bleached, twisted, undernourished bodies with agonized features. The sculpture had been rendered with such a remarkable kinetic feeling, Beheim imagined that the bodies were inching along, slithering one over the other, all moving in the same direction, all trying to reach the same unguessable goal. And then, to his horror, he saw that, indeed, they were in motion, they were not stone but flesh, alive in some measure, enlivened, perhaps, by a tendril of the Patriarch's will.

As he stood there, shivering in the crepuscular light and moist air, growing more and more uneasy, Beheim realized that the chamber could not be considered ordinary even in relation to the extraordinary potentials of Castle Banat. The place was Mystery itself. He could feel it. It was part of death, part of the infinite country whose only border was the act of dying, and like all Mysteries, it was a realm where one could lose oneself utterly, where the concept of life after death was transformed from a philosophical concept into a bleak physicality, a region whose unfathomable logics could in an instant fold up a tuck of black essence into the shape of a monster, a dream, an endless array of dread events and objects. He felt now the same dissolute gravities as he had when he passed through judgment, the same enfeebling despair and loss of orientation, as if he were falling and falling, hoping for a fire to catch in his blood that would lend him the strength to swim against the currents of death and strive toward one of the faint lights that picked out the distance. Somehow the Patriarch had succeeded in wedding the continuums of life and death, and here he dwelled in both, at home in fire and in ice, fullness and nothingness, steeping himself in these pure contraries, hardening over the long centuries into a god.

More frightened than he could remember, Beheim backed away from the edge of the pier, eyes fixed on the mass of seething bodies; but then he spotted something on a pier almost directly opposite, perhaps a hundred feet away, that gave him pause: a blazing figure, a man made all of white fire, so sharply defined against the blue-dark backdrop, it appeared inset into the air. Though it possessed human form, it was featureless, its effect rather like, he was later to think, a wizard's mark stamped at the bottom of a mystic scroll. After a few beats the figure lifted its arm and pointed toward a ragged opening resembling a cave mouth some forty feet above and to its left. Beheim had the idea it was pointing out a path to the Patriarch, commanding him to take it. But the thought of

stepping down among those half-alive things mindlessly churning their way to nowhere . . . He could not
bear it. He continued backing toward the door, but as
he spun about, preparing to run, he found himself
face-to-face with another blazing white figure. (Or was
it the same? When he glanced over his shoulder, he
saw no sign of the original.) It stood an arm's length
away, blocking his exit. Though the face was without
feature, as he stared into that white oval, into such a
fiery absolute of whiteness it seemed to flow with dazzling hints of every color, he had a sense of insane intellect, a soul in furious disarray. One touch of that
glowing hand, he thought, and blistering energy would
spread through his flesh, magicking him into a raving,
featureless thing, a soul imprisoned within an armor of
fire, demented by pain, capable only of this sentinel
obedience.

Beheim's first thought was that the figure had
once been a man like himself, one who had displeased
the Patriarch and been punished in this fashion; but
then he was seized by the knowledge that this was not
someone *like* himself, but was by some uncanny process the image or reality of his future, the infernal thing
he would become if now he tried to flee. He could not
tell whether this impression was purely premonitory
or if it had been planted in his mind by the Patriarch
. . . though he suspected this latter to be the case. Yet
whatever the character of the premonition, he did not
question its truth. Hesitantly he moved toward the lip
of the pier and was relieved to find that the bodies below had cleared a pathway for him, forming a long,
curving avenue that stretched across the chamber
floor; however, this turn of events only marginally diminished his fear, and it was with unsteady legs and a
growing sense of hopelessness that he scrambled down

a crumbling slope to the floor and set out for the cave mouth to which the fiery figure had pointed.

He tried to avoid looking at the bodies, heaped slightly more than head high on either side, as he negotiated the crossing; but now and then something would attract his attention, a throaty noise, a susurrus of breath, a despondent sigh, and he would glance in reflex toward the sound and encounter a staring eye, a slack mouth, a tangle of bluish-white limbs, a pallid scalp from which sprouted scant dark hairs, a pair of emaciated buttocks, all in a tumbled, haphazard arrangement such as might have been conceived by a lunatic artist. He did not permit his eye to linger, but even a glance was sufficient to inform him that despite their horrid state of repair, these pathetic creatures still possessed minds and wills. There was pleading in their tortured faces. Pleading, and what Beheim interpreted as fearful recognition. Their flesh was wasted, desiccated, imbuing their features with an androgynous aspect; yet here and there were visible withered genitals and flaccid female breasts. Overall, they seemed to emit a thin radiation of emotion; he could almost hear it, less a keening than a whine, an expression redolent not—as he might have thought—of agony and loss, but of milder emotions, petulance and frustration, as if they were not truly unhappy with their lot, merely dissatisfied.

After walking among them for half a minute or thereabouts, Beheim became somewhat accustomed to the surroundings. Though daunting, the chamber embodied a sufficiently grand conception so as to mute its more horrific qualities. If, he thought, one managed to quell one's initial revulsion and view it as a continuation of the castle's bizarre decor, it was possible to gain a perspective, to see it as otherworldly, even oddly sublime. But on rounding a curve, coming in sight of the opening he was to enter, Beheim's hard-won perspective went glimmering. Dozens of the creatures had piled themselves high in order to create a crude stairway that he would have to ascend in order to reach his objective. He made to turn back, unwilling to be so intimate with them, but discovered that the avenue had closed behind him, dammed up by a wall of distended bellies and grubby elbows and horny shins. There was nothing for it but to press ahead.

Climbing that stair, clutching at crooked knees and cleft buttocks for handholds, stepping on foreheads and breasts and backs, encountering thready pulses and hearing shocked exclamations as he put his weight on stomach or chest, clinging to a pair of shoulders and leaning so near to the face of a staring, gawking woman that her graveyard breath warmed his cheek, feeling the bodies striving not to give way beneath him—not even crawling through the sewer pipe after Vlad had been as oppressive an experience—and by the time Beheim reached the top and went stumbling forward into the opening, into the tunnel beyond, he felt so soiled and defeated he was ready to take his place among these damned and nearly empty vessels, and go slithering with them this way and that, creating roads and dead ends for new recruits. He rested against the wall, gathering himself. Blue light struck inward from farther along the tunnel, glinting on the rock faces, signaling the presence of another chamber. He supposed it would be no less horrid than the first.

With a weary step, he headed off along the tunnel, stopping once to consider his options, deciding that he had none, then going on again. A short walk brought him, as expected, to the top of a broad marble stair that led down into a second chamber, equally vast, but much longer than it was high, shaped roughly like an egg laid on its side, its pale gray floor smooth yet slightly undulant, like well-worn limestone—it made him think of a great natural cavern, an underground vista such as might be described in the work of a baroque fantasist. Here, too, there was sourceless blue light; here, too, the walls were ornamented with disturbing bas-reliefs and the chamber floor was occupied by hundreds of human figures, but these were not crawling, they were standing and walking about and even dancing. Bathed in that sickly radiance, dressed in elegant rags, the remnants of ball gowns and evening clothes, their movements graceful albeit somewhat stiff, pale couples circled to the inaudible rhythms of a sedate waltz—one inaudible at least to Beheim's ear—avoiding the numerous small black pools, round as periods, that dotted the expanse, passing in and out of the shadow of colossal statues, warriors, beasts, and so forth, nine or ten of them, that sprouted up at irregular intervals like chess pieces in an endgame. It was a gathering similar to that held in the banquet hall on the evening of the murder, except here there was no music, no laughter, no conversation, only a thick silence that seemed to be welling from the blue shadows at the opposite end of the chamber.

Despite the morbid eccentricity of the scene, this chamber struck him as being more hospitable than the first; but whatever complacency that idea had bred was dashed when he noticed a woman ascending the stair toward him. She was, he saw as she drew near, quite beautiful, though her pallor and rigidity of expression—typical, he had heard, of the most venerable members of the Family—did nothing to enhance this impression. Her black hair was fashioned into a

heavy braid that hung down over her shoulder; the
smooth curves of her belly and breasts showed
through rents in her gown of white brocade, and her
features were strong, almost too strong to be in harmony with the delicate bone structure that supported
them. It was a Mediterranean face, with large dark
eyes and high cheekbones and full lips, its olive tone
gone waxy, yet overall managing to retain a sensual ap-
peal; in fact, the longer he looked at her, the more her
deathly coloring and lack of expression came to seem
positive facets of her beauty, perverse accents that be-
spoke a haunting sexuality. Though enormous potentials for violence and vindictiveness were implicit in
who she was, he could not help marveling at her and
feeling a need to be close to her, to gain through an intimate association some portion of her knowledge and
power. How long, he wondered, had she lived? A
thousand years and more, he'd wager. She might have
trod the Byzantine world, the Roman, walked with
Darius and Caesar. She might be Helen, Magdalene,
Cleopatra, a Cretan sorceress. Compared with her,
compared with the force of the cold fire that flowed
from her, numbing his fear and rendering him increasingly vulnerable to her charms, all the women of the
Family he had known, even Alexandra, were children
of their sex.

She opened her mouth, then closed it and sighed,
as if speech were difficult for her. When at last she did
speak, her voice was frail, rusty, some of the words in-
corporating pauses between syllables, hinging them
with hoarse breaths. "You are most welcome, Michel,"
she said, offering him her left hand, which was
adorned with a moonstone set in a wide silver band.
"Come, let me introduce you to your elder cousins."

Her grip was deceptively gentle. She could, he

knew, wrench off his arm and sling him halfway across
the chamber with only a minimal effort; yet as she led
him down the stairs and out onto the floor among the
gliding dancers, he did not focus on the dire possibilities attendant on her touch, but on the frisson of
arousal he experienced whenever her hip brushed
against him; the sensational perfume of her blood; the
rippling of milky flesh across the tops of her breasts
caused by the shock of her footfalls; the charge of light
in her eyes that flashed each time she glanced at him,
like silver fish surfacing briefly in black ponds, barely
a glint, yet too brilliant to be mere reflection; the be-
mused half smile that came to her lips when she
caught him staring; the entire subtlety of her presence, a potent emanation in which he thought he
could detect the essences of ancient magics and for-
lorn histories, desolate kingdoms, burning cities. He
was so enthralled by her, he scarcely registered the in-
troductions she made. The men's arrogant, dismissive
nods, the hot eyes of the women trying to pin down
some fluttering corner of his soul, the illustrious
names of the branches they represented, Vandelore,
Moritella, Agenor, Pescalco, de Czege, LeMiron,
Sepulveda—these were irrelevancies. It was *her* name
he wished to know, *her* gestures and looks he yearned
to interpret. And not until a waltzing couple passed
too close, jostling him, did the spell she had cast lift
and permit him to remember why he had come. Nor
was it until that precise instant that he fully appre-
hended where he stood, feeling with redoubled intensity an awareness of Mystery, the disorientation and
flagging spirits that derived from a propinquity with
the country of death, which lay everywhere, attached
to the skin of life like a dark subdermal layer and, in

places such as this, showed in patches through the flimsy cover of the living world.

He broke free of the woman and gazed wildly about. They had come more than halfway across the chamber and were standing about thirty feet from one of the statues: a monolithic iron-colored rock thrusting up from the pale stone of the floor, atop which was perched a massive throne of some pitted blue mineral, and seated thereon, a sculpted male figure with coarse, brooding features and taloned hands and dark corroded skin almost the same color as the throne, making it seem either that he was sinking into it or emerging from it. Several of the black pools ringed the base of the monolith, and four couples were negotiating a path among them, dipping and swaying, their heads tilted at gay angles; the only sound was the sibilant scrape of their dancing pumps on the stone. As he gazed out into the chamber at the statues, immense court pieces, their pawns whirling over the undulant gray floor, Beheim felt diminutive and lost, entirely out of his element.

"I must see the Patriarch!" he said, turning to the woman, trying to inject mastery into his voice, but hearing a quaver in it. "I must see him at once!"

She remained imperturbable. "He hears you now, Michel. You have only to let your wishes be known."

"Where is he?" Beheim spun about, searching for a sign of an unseen eavesdropper. "I must see him!"

"Michel!" The woman's peremptory tone shocked him into stillness. "*He* sees you. That is the important thing. Now say what you have to say, and he will answer you."

Recognizing that he could not succeed in imposing his will, Beheim summoned a degree of calm and began to tell of what had transpired, of his plan and all he hoped to achieve, directing his words toward the woman. She kept her eyes on him, yet there was no force to her stare as there had been previously. It was as if some essential part of her machinery had been switched off. Except for the rise and fall of her chest, she stood motionless, her white gown glowing in the half-light.

When he had finished, she maintained her silence for a time; finally, with no more animation than she had displayed while listening, she said, "We were of course aware that Felipe and Dolores had passed into Mystery. But we did not know the agency of their fate." A pause. "They were much loved."

This last bore a hint of accusation, and Beheim was quick to offer a defense. "I had no choice. I was obeying the Patriarch's charge."

"Perhaps. Though it seems to us you may have been overzealous in your obedience. Be that as it may, once this matter is behind us, the Valeas will seek to square accounts with the Agenors. I trust you will not lose sight of that."

Beheim caught movement out of the corner of his eye, but when he turned, he saw only the statue of the enthroned man. Ice seemed to melt along his spine. Had not those taloned hands shifted ever so slightly along the arms of the throne? He was certain they had. And those pale slivers showing beneath the heavy lids, were they imperfections in the stone or the whites of two globed eyes? This statue, he thought, might very well be the Patriarch. If so, it was terrible to contemplate the extent of his deformities, his state of near petrifaction; the price for millennia of life was high, indeed. He gazed at those hooded eyes, trying to connect with the great cold mind, still vital in its prison of stony flesh, and said, "I cannot proceed with-

out your assistance, lord. Were I to spread the rumor
that an important clue in the murder of the Golden
lies outside the castle, it would surely be seen as a potential trap by the murderer. If, however, you were to
let slip the news, it would not be doubted. Further I
require a number of servants to help me dig the pits
before daybreak. It is essential that we begin at once.
By my reckoning we have but six hours of the night
remaining, and it will take some time to organize
things."

Again the woman let a few moments pass before
speaking. "What you have asked is now being done."

Beheim had detected no movement on the part of
the enthroned man, and he wondered if mental signals
could be passing between him and the woman.

"You understand that this must be done with subtlety," Beheim said. "The spreading of the rumor, I
mean. And you must not inform anyone before daybreak. Tell them that I am planning to inspect the
body of the old woman shortly after dusk, and that I
wish no one else to touch the body until I have had a
chance to look at it myself. Some tale may be needed
to explain the absence of Felipe and Dolores. I will
leave that for you to determine."

"Everything will be done as you require," the
woman said. Another lengthy pause. "However, here is
a condition that attaches to my assistance. My agent
must accompany you. Do you have with you a supply
of the undiluted drug?"

"I do."

"Enough for two?"

"More than enough."

She held out a hand and, reluctantly, he passed
over one of his three flasks. "I will send her to you after daybreak."

"A sip should provide sufficient protection for the day," Beheim said. "Another thing, lord. Two of my servants are waiting outside your chambers."

"Yes," said the woman. "We know. One is sorely in need of judgment." She tipped her head, as if trying to see him in a better light. "Shall we judge her for you?"

The prospect of unburdening himself of his responsibilities was appealing, but he resisted temptation. "No, my lord. But I beg you to watch over them while I am gone."

She inclined her head. "It will be done."

"I am curious about something, my lord," Beheim said. "I have been told that all this, the investigation, the murder, is part of a game, that games are the order of the day, and that I am only an unimportant player. That much I can accept. But I find it difficult to be so ignorant of the goal of the game. The stakes."

The woman said nothing.

"The matter of our common argument," said Beheim. "The question as to whether or not the Family should go into the East . . . is this, perhaps, one of the things at stake? The resolution of that argument?"

"Perhaps," said the woman.

Frustrated, Beheim said, "By 'perhaps,' do you mean it is one of many things at risk, or is it that—"

"The answer to all your questions is 'perhaps,'" the woman said. "Each moment brings a new answer, yet as far as you are concerned, they are all 'perhaps,' for you do not have the discretion necessary to perceive the nuances of the questions."

Beheim started to speak, but she waved him to silence.

"This matter of a possible migration," she went on, "it is of some small interest to us. And that being so, it is to an extent involved in all of our deliberations and our actions. But only to an extent. Should disaster come upon us, some here"—she indicated the onlookers, the dancing couples—"have other means of escape at their disposal apart from fleeing to the ends of the earth. Others have no wish to escape. Others yet no longer have any real understanding of the concept of escape. So you see, while it is a question that concerns the majority of our cousins, here, among this most illustrious minority, it merits spotty consideration at best."

"But surely you have at heart the welfare of all the Family, not just that of its most powerful members?"

"If you could see what is in my heart," the woman said, "your eyes would go dark with that vision. If you could perceive but one hundredth of the logics that assail me at every second, your brain would burst. Play your part. Learn from the playing of it. That is all you can do. At any rate, you will eventually draw your own conclusions, no matter what I tell you."

Beheim was disappointed. To have endured so much, to have passed through that harrowing antechamber and to have received such a flimsy answer, to have discovered that the Patriarch had been reduced to statuary, to a grotesque garden ornament capable of communicating only by means of a proxy, it was worse than disappointing. He had expected a more dynamic presence, someone whose power and clarity would act as a solvent upon his doubts and crystallize his wisdom.

The woman let out an amused hiss. Her smile widened until the tips of her fangs were exposed, lending a newly sinister aspect to her beauty. Some of the couples had stopped their dancing and were regarding Beheim with what seemed sly anticipation.

"You wish to confront the Patriarch?" the woman asked in a dry voice. "Truly you do have courage."

Beheim glanced in confusion at the statue of the enthroned man, with his corroded blue skin and dour mouth and slitted eyes. "I thought this was—"

"Perhaps someday. For now he waits his time." She moved close to Beheim, took his left hand. "Come with me, Michel. If it's the Patriarch you wish to see, I will take you to him."

She drew him to the extreme edge of one of the black pools, and on glancing down, seeing lights drifting beneath the surface, fans of pallid radiance like a fading aurora borealis, he shrieked and threw himself backward, realizing that this pool, and likely all the rest, were not incidences of underground water but portals into the pure medium of Mystery, into the country of death. The woman held him fast, squeezing his hand with such force, he thought the bones would shatter. She turned a shriveling stare upon him, and he soon found himself absorbed by the shifts of color within the irises, the minute contractions and expansions of the pupils. His fear dwindled to a flickering anxiety. When she told him to step forward, he felt a twinge of alarm, nothing more, and did as she instructed.

Breaking the surface of the pool was like breaking through the crust atop a churn of thickening butter. The crust slid greasily between Beheim's legs, up his chest, across his face, like a blind thing groping at him, trying to acquaint itself with his shape. Then he and the woman were plunging down into a chill nothingness, a void populated by clusters of starry lights, scattered here and there like the flowers on a black bush. The presence of the lights wounded him; they seemed unattainably distant and bright and hopeful, antidotes to the fathomless darkness in which he was foundering. The cold was so intense, he could not feel the woman's hand, and he was startled to find that she had maintained her grip. She floated half facing him, the classic lines of her face warped by a demonic smile, her skirt pushed back between her legs by their momentum, the stiff fabric molding to her belly and thighs; her hair lifted from her shoulders, merging with the blackness. She looked so fierce, so full of heat and viciousness, he expected her to burst into flames. He managed a quick glance behind him. There a solitary blue light winked and glittered—the pool, its surface seen from beneath. He made out the black walls of death curving on all sides away from this particular light, as if it were the neck of a bottle into which he had been dropped; but in every other direction he saw a perspectiveless depth, and when he glanced back again, he discovered that the blue light had shrunk and now occupied a position on the rim of a cluster of lights, and he could no longer detect any sign of enclosure.

Chapter ELEVEN

In the beginning he had little sense of the speed at which they were falling, because he did not struggle as he had on his day of judgment, content to plummet feetfirst, becoming if not totally relaxed, then accepting of the situation. Why, he reasoned, should he struggle? He was doing the Patriarch's bidding. No harm would come to him. But when he noticed the woman's hair flowing straight back behind her and recognized that their speed had increased markedly, then reason fled. He thought he felt the blackness seeping into him, insinuating itself into the corners of his eyes, his pores, flushing out what was left of his soul. Filling his brain with zeros, choking his heart, icing his bones. He pried at the woman's fingers; he tried to rip away the blackness, to swim back the way he had come, but able only to use one hand, he made no headway and all his flailing succeeded in achieving was to send them spinning out of control. Light pinwheeled in his blurred vision; the breath was sucked from his chest. It took every ounce of his strength and determination to right them. The woman offered no assistance whatsoever. Nothing, it appeared, could disturb the pathological rectitude of her smile.

"Damn you!" he said, surprised that he was able to hear even his own voice in all that whirling emptiness. "Let me go!" He tried unsuccessfully to pull free. Her smile broadened, and she shook her head mockingly, as if he were a child from whom she was withholding a treat.

He drew back his hand and, marshaling all his strength, slapped her face. Her head did not move an inch; she might have been made of stone. He hooked his fingers, clawed at her eyes, but she knocked his hand aside, numbing his wrist with the blow. He wanted to plead with her, to beg, but his pride would not allow it.

The current drawing them into the void was stronger than any he had heretofore experienced. Even had he had both hands free, he doubted he would have been able to make much progress against it. And there might, he decided, be no need to do so, for the current—gaining speed with every passing second—appeared to be bearing them toward the distant lights, toward salvation, not away from them as had been the case during his judgment. Perhaps, he told himself, his thoughts once again tinged with panic, with a touch of hysterical glee, perhaps the Patriarch was not at home, off doing errands or some such, and a swift-moving current was performing butler service, whisking whoever stopped in for a visit back to their point of origin or else to some other safe harbor. Yet as they approached the nearest light, a yellow pinprick that had swelled into a radiant golden sun, he realized that its center, into which he might have wished to steer, preferring whatever place it opened onto to this endless fall, was blocked by something. A woman, he saw on drawing closer. Sinewy;

olive-skinned. With apple breasts and muscular legs and a frightful gash in her throat that must have nearly decapitated her. Dried blood stained her breasts and belly, matted her secret hair. She hovered in the midst of the golden fire, immense, a giantess; but Beheim knew her size was only apparent, a product of the visual distortions that afflicted all who passed through Mystery, and when he drew closer yet, he would find the light diminished and the woman shrunk to normal proportions. Initially he had assumed her to be an Imago, a scarecrow left by the Patriarch to warn off the uninvited, but as they flashed toward her she reached out her arms as if in welcome. His heart stuttered on seeing her more clearly. Red teeth filed to points, pupils cored with fire. Her fingernails were ebony-colored, long and curved and sharp. He tried to alter their course, to lunge aside, but the current proved irresistible and he was borne into the golden halation, then to within inches of the woman's grasping fingers. So close he could see the streaks of gray rot surfaced from beneath her skin, the collapsed humors of her eyes, and he thought he saw something else, something moving sluggishly in the blackness of her mouth, an insect god perhaps, secure behind the scarlet portcullis of her teeth. Then, as she slashed at him with those razoring fingernails, the current spun him off to safety. From behind him there came a shrill cry of disappointment.

Once again he attempted to break free from the woman in white; once again he failed.

"Bitch!" he cried, and hurled himself about; the woman's nails punched into his wrist.

He tried to reel her in by the forearm; he clawed at her, but she blocked his hand away. He swung his

fist, and this time, instead of blocking him, she let the
blow glance off the side of her head and returned a
blow of her own. Her fist caught him flush on the temple, leaving him stunned, dangling limply in her grasp,
watching the darkness flow past and the lights turn
first into stars, and then into demon cages. He realized
now it was useless to contend with her, and rather
than wasting his energy in plotting an escape, he
sought comfort in his memories, searching for something that would ease his fear. He was not surprised
when his thoughts settled on Alexandra.

Though he had come to suspect almost everything about their involvement, it was the one time that
he could recall since his judgment when life had sur-
passed his expectations, when something untrammeled
had been attained, even if that something was mere
intensity, a bright flash of being that seemed to exist
outside of time, apart from the chains of events that
bound them to a path of conflict and distrust and betrayal. One could not, he thought, derive much hope
from such a moment. It was a freak, a sport born of
lightnings that had struck and transfigured the body of
their soiled emotions. Yet the simple fact of its existence was in itself an embodiment of hope, like a sign
in the sky presaging some miraculous advent, and as
he reclaimed those memories, tasting their flavors and
wrapping himself in their colors and sensations, he felt
if not hopeful, then at least cleaner for having them
within him. He tasted Alexandra's mouth and heard
her whisper, experienced the sly touches of her long
fingers, rocked with her again in that immense funereal bed. He grew certain that among these glints and
quivers there must be a single moment whose purity
outstripped the duplicitous origins of the act, an instance of sheer connectivity that offered some whole-

some proof and held a promise more lasting than that of sexual delight. An exchange of looks, a peaceful interval in which they had known some heart's truth. If he had the time, he told himself, to study those memories in sequence, surely he would be able to isolate that one absolute. But he could not sustain the images, and on opening his eyes, he discovered the woman in white watching him, trying to blight with her poisonous dark stare whatever solace his memory had yielded.

Each time they approached one of the lights, they would accelerate, sweeping past it in a dizzying rush, and every one was as the first: a bright passage blocked by some horrid creature or another, all snapping, biting, slashing, narrowly missing Beheim. He had the idea he was being shown that there was no way out, that this was a pocket of death the Patriarch had isolated and made his own. What this signified, he could not guess, but he did not believe it augured well. They hurtled past a scorpion prowling the innards of a blue star, a wolf raving in crimson fire, a white sun at whose heart nestled a gigantic worm, past a variety of deformed men and women, past a fly wearing a crown, past twists of darkness like living flaws at the center of burning jewels, past a shifting puzzle of glowing silver bones, past winged rats and apes with human genitals and bloated corpse faces with adders' tongues, until at last, beyond the clustered lights, he made out a wire-thin strip of dead white that bisected the blackness, lending the illusion of a horizon to that horizonless depth. Though it seemed bland by contrast to the terrors he had already encountered, he believed that this was either signal or symptom of the ultimate terror of the place: the Patriarch. He felt an eerie, cluttered sensation in his head, as if his brain were clogged with an overabundance of thoughts, and this developed into a mental discordance, shards of rage, peals of disgust, interludes of gloating joy, blasts of implacable anger, and lustful thoughts like knives, a mosaic of impressions that together composed a unity, a whole. He understood that in penetrating the surface of the black pool, the country of death, he had also penetrated the calm, chill surface of the Patriarch's mind and fallen into the chaos beneath, into this little death he had made of all his years of feasts and dreams and despondencies, an inky fever in which he endlessly soaked himself, having no better way to pass the time, no greater use for life, for he was growing ever closer to death, and yet because of his nature he would never die, only grow more deathlike, just as in that schoolboy theorem, the first mathematical clue one receives of the utter incomprehensibility of the universe, it is stated that if one attempts to travel from Point A to Point B by going half the distance, then half the remaining distance, then half what is left after that, and so on and so forth, one will never reach Point B but will continue to fall short of one's destination by increasingly infinitesimal fractions, and thus one is fated to travel forever between what was once the beginning and the end, or between the towns of Reims and Mornay, or between whatever poles one has chosen, poles that have by now evolved into two ludicrous abstractions. It was, Beheim thought, this capacity to withstand the bleakest and most irrational of environments, to thrive in the absolute negative, that neutered the Family's will to survive, that persuaded them to twist each hopeful strand of being into something even darker than the darkness of their origins, and caused them to try to destroy that which was virtually indestructible. And now he, too, was being contaminated by these tendencies, for though the Patriarch's ravings were resounding in his head and he was traveling hand in hand with a woman who was nourished by corruption and treachery, he was beginning to adapt to Mystery—and not merely in order to survive as he had done after receiving Agenor's judgment. He was coming to appreciate its qualities, to derive sustenance from it. It was not that he had grown less afraid; it was rather that he had acknowledged fear instead of reacting against it; and having acclimated to this degree, he was capable of looking without prejudice at his surroundings, of understanding that they were not absolutely inimical.

Suddenly the black silence and the false stars and the cold rang a familiar change in him, as if he had scented an old friendly smell or had of the place a sense of commonality such as long ago—not so very long, he thought, barely two years—he might have taken from a row of plane trees standing sharp against a milky dawn near his father's house outside Irun, a white mist blanketing a potato field, the powdery green burst of a myrtle bush, things that have seated themselves so firmly in our hearts, we no longer notice them, but that, when we are brought hard upon them after a lengthy absence, cause a tremor in our souls. Things of home. That, he realized, was the secret call of this darkness, the thing that softened his dread; the knowledge that his birth could no longer be considered to have occurred in Irun. Mystery was now his birthplace, the soil from which he had sprung on his day of judgment and to which he would always hereafter return. This emptiness, this abandoned well with its demons and lights and torments had supplanted the spicy odor of his grandfather's venison stew, the purring of a favorite cat, the tinkling of his mother's piano with its ill-tuned high C souring a Schumann waltz. Understanding this harrowed him, yet it also gave him strength, attached him to a mooring that made his fall seem less precipitous and in the end provided him with a ground on which to stand, from which to wield whatever lever he could carpenter against fate.

They were nearing another golden light, one at whose center there capered a scrawny, red-eyed old man with unkempt, shoulder-length gray hair, all rags and fangs and bony, clutching fingers. Beheim, who had lost confidence in the notion that the nature of his mission would assure his safety, devised a plan. He engaged the eyes of the woman in white, floating superimposed upon the black backdrop like an angel of death and desire, her flesh showing sleek and gleaming through the rips in her gown like the skin of a succulent. He beckoned to her with his free hand, inviting her into an embrace. "I'm frightened," he said. "Let me come close for a moment." He knew that she would not be afraid of him, certain of her physical superiority, and though she would suspect his actions, she would delight in teasing him with the prospect of hope. He concentrated with all his might on presenting an image of fear and entreaty.

She let him pull her close, but did not relax her grip. Her hips settled plushly against him. Seen at that intimate distance, her face dissolved into a pale blue dominated by those compelling eyes—to avoid being mesmerized by them, he drew her into a kiss. Her lips tasted of stale blood, and when she probed his mouth with her tongue, it felt thick and clammy and snail-slow, like those mindless things one finds half-alive in a spadeful of turned-up dirt. Yet that soiled kiss claimed far more of his attention than he had wanted, and he had to remind himself to keep watch over her shoulder as they closed on the golden light with its aged sentinel, knowing he would have to time his actions perfectly. Beyond the light, the strip of whiteness strung across the void was lumping up in spots and acquiring the lineaments of a smashed-thin face, a stretched toothy mouth flanked by slit eyes with inflamed rims and notched pupils, like a monster peering out from a corner of flatland that it was busy prying up. Beheim forced his mind back to the woman in white and the old man, but could not stop picturing the white thing taking shape in the distance.

Rays of light fingered them. What had appeared to be a star now became a golden tunnel with a devil at the bottom, and as they fell toward him Beheim saw that the old man's red eyes were not eyes at all, but empty, bloody sockets, and his cadaverous cheeks were covered with a dead man's growth of stubble, and his tongue was bloated, dark red, looking as if a slug had crawled halfway out of his mouth, and his hands opened and closed, opened and closed with the spasmodic reflex of someone freshly killed, and what he had taken for capering was in reality a palsied jitter like the dance of a hanged man.

Beheim locked his hands behind the woman's back and deepened their kiss. She pressed against him, apparently unsuspecting, still consumed by her own treachery. A few seconds before they were to sweep past the grasp of those groping, gray fingers, he doubted the wisdom of his plan, perceiving its potential pitfalls and reversals; but there was no time left to deliberate, and as they reached their closest point of approach, using all his strength, he spun them about, going with the pull of the woman's hold rather than against it, changing their course by a fraction, sufficient to bring her in range of the old man's right hand.

His fingers hooked her shoulder, yanking her away from Beheim. Shock hardened her face into a white mask. She clutched at Beheim, but he fended her off, letting his momentum carry him onward along their altered course, and slung himself toward the heart of the light, catching sight—as he twisted and flailed—of the two of them tangled together, biting and clawing, their fangs bared, shining, disfiguring blood spreading everywhere. And beyond them, blurred into an indefinite shape by sprays of light, something huge and pale was coming fast.

Fear was so bright in him, he felt it leaping up inside his body, like a cat leaping from a burning window, adding its force to his straining progress. Fresh doubts assailed him. What if there were no portal at the heart of the light? What if some even more terrible guardian had been set to block his path? Someone screamed behind him. Man or woman, he could not say. Only the pain was indisputable. He surged on blindly into the light, powering upward with the crude strokes of an unschooled swimmer against the current that would have swept him back into the void, reaching for something that might not exist, an edge, a mortared rim, a projection of rock. . . .

He had it!

His fingers curled around a knob of stone, squeezed it for his life.

His other hand touched a flat surface, then a crack. He inserted three fingers into it, dug for a solid hold.

And then he was hauling himself up and out of a pool into flickering torchlight, onto cool rough stone. As he lay gasping he saw that he was lying in a corridor, ranged in both directions by iron-mounted torches. He did not recognize the place. It might be anywhere in the castle; it could lead to a world of terror. But no terror, he thought, more profound than that he had just escaped.

If, indeed, he had escaped.

The thought that the chase might not be over put a charge in him. He scrambled up and was dumbfounded to see drips of blackness slither from the creases of his clothing and plop onto the stone, where they rolled about like animated punctuation, then combined, first into a puddle, then into a rivulet that went flowing back to merge with the surface of the pool.

He started along the corridor, choosing a direction at random, but had not gone three steps when there came a ripping sound behind him, as of heavy fabric being torn down its seam. He turned to see the woman's head and shoulders emerge from the pool. Her hair was slicked back, negative droplets spilling like beetles across her skin. Her eyes, black and vacant as holes in a bedsheet, fastened on him; her mouth opened. Whether to speak or gulp in air, he did not know. Then a hand, an incredibly long-fingered white hand attached to a pulpy arm, reached from beneath the surface, caught the top of her head—as a normal hand might surround an orange—and yanked her under.

Beheim sprinted away, arms pumping, intent on finding a side passage, wanting to turn a corner on the entire experience, but there proved to be no side passages. The corridor appeared to extend into infinity, an infinite ranking of torches angled from iron mounts and glistening, dark gray stone brocaded by crusts of moss. He kept running until a stitch came in his side. When he at long last paused, leaning against the wall, his labored breath breaching the silence, he looked back down the corridor and saw a white figure—tiny at that distance—standing in or near the place from which he had fled. He could feel the chaotic pressure of that same mental discord that had affected him when he sighted the white horizon line announcing the Patriarch's imminence. His legs were shaking, his lungs on fire. He knew he could not run much farther. Resentment boiled up in him, and he cried out, "What do you want of me? I'm doing as you asked!"

The Patriarch gave no sign of having heard.

Beheim staggered off a few steps. "What do you want of me?" he cried again, and this time he received a response, though not of the sort he had hoped to elicit.

The corridor seemed to tip downward—it was as if he were staring into a well of perspective, a dwindling array of fiery red tears and gray slabs of stone in whose penultimate depth hung the figure of the Patriarch, more a white emblem than a living thing. A feeling of vertigo assaulted Beheim. He clutched at the damp stones and shut his eyes.

After a while, cautiously, he opened them.

He would have liked to scream, to release the fearful pressure that was building in his chest; but the sight before him seemed to possess its own crushing gravity, a force that cut short his breath and made any outcry impossible. The Patriarch's face filled his field of vision—he looked to be a giant peeking into the end of a tunnel a few feet from where Beheim stood flattened against the wall. It was a face with a surprisingly delicate bone structure, reminiscent of a bat, of a weasel, of every kind of vermin: nose reduced to a bump with slits; a lipless mouth from which protruded fangs the size of tusks; pulpy white skin laced with blue veins, their patterns having the intricacy of tattoos; the eyes were disproportionately large, with notched pupils centering irises whose murky substance appeared to be swirling, always in flux, picked out here and there by phosphorescent lights that bloomed and faded with the inconstancy of foxfire.

The mouth opened, revealing a complement of needled, bloodstained teeth; a gush of carrion breath followed.

Beheim soiled himself. He sank to the floor, his strength gone, turned his eyes to the wall, and waited for the end.

But the end did not come.

Instead he heard a cultured masculine voice say, "Come, my child. Sit and talk with me awhile."

Chapter TWELVE

The man who had spoken was slender and young, several years younger, it appeared, than Beheim, with a wide Byronic face framed by dark curls; he wore a billowy shirt of white silk and loose gray trousers, and on the fourth finger of his right hand was a massive gold signet ring. He was occupying a wrought-iron chair at the center of a moonlit courtyard, enclosed by crenellated walls of three stories in height—they must, Beheim realized, be at the very top of the castle—and ringed by potted ferns and flowering plants; it was paved with a mosaic of flagstones and divided into nooks by an arrangement of vine-tangled trellises. The moon was almost directly overhead, cutting a sharp slice of shadow across the westernmost quarter of the courtyard, where a short stairway led up into a room with shuttered windows. With a foppish gesture, the man indicated a second wrought-iron chair, flanked by a table of like design, and again urged Beheim to sit.

Though he was still afraid, knowing the man was only a more presentable incarnation of the ghoulish creature in the corridor, he wanted to believe that some accommodation had been reached, some test passed, and that things would now proceed at a rational pace and measure. Supporting this hope was the fact that his fouled clothes were missing, and in their stead he was now wearing a shirt and trousers identical to those worn by the Patriarch. He came to his feet and walked unsteadily to the chair. The Patriarch's smile was charming, guileless; he seemed to be beaming his approval of Beheim's every action.

"Would you care for some refreshment?" he asked as Beheim settled himself. "A glass of wine, perhaps. Or something stronger, if you wish? Ordinarily I would have the necessities to hand, but I was not prepared for your visit. Always best to come announced. That way"—with an avuncular wink, he reached out and patted Beheim on the knee—"there'll be no surprises."

Beheim had an apprehension of the madness dammed up behind this pleasant facade. He gave an involuntary shudder. The fanciful iron pattern of the chair bottom seemed to be branding him with cold arabesques.

"I'd welcome some whiskey," he said.

"Whiskey it shall be!" The Patriarch called for a decanter to be brought at once.

He stretched out his legs, folded his hands on his stomach. "You've done well, my boy. Better than I've any right to expect. You've displayed uncommon courage and a modicum of cleverness. With luck, we'll have put an end to this tiresome business by tomorrow evening."

"I hope as much, my lord," Beheim said, trying to present an image of firm competency. "But there is no guarantee of success. The trap is a simple one, and obvious. Too obvious, perhaps, to catch a subtle creature like our murderer."

"Why subtle?" the Patriarch asked, leaning forward in his chair; his voice grew strident. "What subtlety is there in butchery of the sort he has committed? True, your cousins do have their subtleties, but they are moved chiefly by fear, by every manner of irrational concern. The simplicity of the trap is not necessarily a liability. The simple logic that informs it will make it a great temptation. Perhaps the murderer will think I have forgotten something, overlooked something. And as for its obviousness, well, subtle creatures will often see in the obvious the most convoluted of possibilities. I'm quite certain you will find a rabbit in your snare tomorrow." He tapped his brow. "I have a feeling for these things." He glanced toward the stairs. "Ah! Here's your whiskey."

The woman in white was descending the stairs, bearing a tray upon which rested a decanter and a glass of cut crystal. As she moved out from the shadows Beheim saw that though her body had remained voluptuous and smooth-skinned, her face had decayed, the tendons coming unstrung, the flesh in tatters, the lips eroded, so that rotted gums and gray teeth and a portion of the skull were all laid bare. Her eyes were awful vacancies and leaked a viscous fluid. It was all Beheim could do to keep from leaping away when she offered him the glass.

"You may leave the decanter, Christina," the Patriarch said, and she set the tray down upon the table next to Beheim. Her breath was a liquid sibilance, and as she leaned close he heard a faint creaking and imagined this to be the sound made by some fleshy construct stripping away from the bone.

He gulped down two fingers of whiskey, drawing strength from its fire, and poured himself another.

"Such a pretty thing," the Patriarch said as

Christina returned to the shuttered room. "Under ordinary circumstances, anyway." He lifted his voice. "Not pretty at all now, are you, my dear?"

Christina did not seem to hear.

"She's incredibly vain," the Patriarch went on. "We'll just have to hope this teaches her a lesson."

"For what reason is she being punished?" Beheim asked.

The Patriarch gave him an arch look. "For invading my privacy, of course. And, as a consequence, risking your life."

"Risking my life," said Beheim musingly, wondering how to put his next question without eliciting an enraged response.

"That's right. I might have killed you."

"But"—Beheim hesitated—"you knew who I was, did you not?"

"Ah!" The Patriarch waggled a forefinger in the air, as if to mark a moment of revelation. "Of course! You're puzzled as to why I would hunt you, knowing that you were performing a service on my behalf. Well, that's an easy enough question to answer." Once again he leaned forward, but on this occasion he did not seem at all avuncular. "There are rules," he said in a sepulchral tone. "Rules that must not be broken." He nodded, as if he had just imparted a great wisdom. "Rules that demand obedience. There can be no excuse to justify their violation."

"I see," said Beheim.

"No, child." The Patriarch leaned back and crossed his legs. "You do not see. Not yet. And perhaps you never will. It is not given to everyone to see these things."

Ragged clouds were passing in front of the moon, causing a rush of thin shadows across the flagstones, and Beheim had an impression of the instability of the place, of the unstable mind that had conceived it. It could all be whisked away in an instant, he thought. The chairs, the moonlight, the nodding ferns. It was a veil, a seeming. Even if real, it was nothing that was capable of resisting the power of the man before him, a man to whom the centuries were years. Fascinating, to think of all he had seen and done. But Beheim did not covet the Patriarch's experience or his power, nor did he desire to understand it. He wanted to be away from Castle Banat, away from everything associated with it, and he decided to hold his tongue, hoping that his silence would speed the end of the interview.

"You know," said the Patriarch, shifting in his chair, "I'm not quite clear why this is so important to us. This business of the Golden. Naturally there's the matter of an impropriety. A gross impropriety at that. We really can't permit such goings-on. But there's more to it than that. Something of greater consequence involved. I just can't seem to put my finger on it." He studied his left hand, as if considering the inadequacy of his five fingers; then he glanced up brightly. "So perhaps in this instance I have obeyed the dictates of reason, for I firmly believe that your participation in all this is the key to resolving some deeper question. Not merely your participation. Something allied with it, something . . ." He made a frustrated noise. "I can almost grasp it. Almost! Ah, well. It's obvious that I need you. I'll have to be satisfied with knowing that, I suppose. How odd to need anyone, especially one so callow."

Beheim said nothing, and a strained smile came to the Patriarch's lips.

"I wonder if Agenor truly understands your part in this," he said. "I think not. He does not have the

command of the situation that he believes. It's all so
interwoven. Roland. Felipe and Dolores. The Valeas.
Alexandra." He let out a wry chuckle. "Alexandra! Now
there, there's a piece of work for you!" He looked to
Beheim for a reaction, but Beheim maintained a stub-
born silence.

A single frown line marred the smooth expanse of
the Patriarch's brow. It was the perfect emblem of his
mood, the line an artist might have chosen to express
stern displeasure.

"Well now," he said with impatience. "How shall
I reward you for this invaluable service? A treasure,
perhaps. Secrets. Something substantial is called for.
What shall it be?"

The dark air above his head had begun to stir, becoming rife with furtive glints, a physical symptom,
Beheim thought, of his internal struggle between reason and mad desire. He did not think he could risk annoying the Patriarch further, and yet he did not want
to ask for a reward, fearful that he might ask for too
much or too little, and that this might increase his ag-
itation. At last he said, "I am happy to serve you, my
lord. In truth, I can hope for no reward greater than
to earn your continued solicitude. However, I wonder
if we might discuss something that has been a matter
of concern to me, and may, I believe, have a bearing
on my investigation."

This appeared to please the Patriarch. His frown
vanished, he settled back in the chair and told Beheim
to proceed.

"Earlier in your chamber," Beheim said, "we had
a brief exchange regarding this matter, and though I
understand it is not something that has commanded
your interest to any great degree, I believe neverthe-

less that it merits your attention at this moment in time."

The Patriarch's sigh was one of patience sorely tried. "You intend to bore me again, do you not, with talk of the East?"

"I hope I will succeed in—"

"I have said all I will on the subject."

Beheim let a few seconds pass before responding. "You have placed me in an awkward position, my lord. I do not wish to offend, but I would not be serving you well if I did not press this matter. I feel, and I have felt from the beginning, that the murder and the possibility of a migration were somehow related. You yourself have stated that there is more to the investigation than my solution of the crime, that you sense some deeper question may be involved. I submit that this question of migration may be the very thing you have sensed."

"And what if it is?" said the Patriarch.

Confused by this, Beheim said, "I assume that if such is the case, you would want to study the materials available, to—"

"There is nothing to study. Either some of my children will go into the East, or else they will not. I leave that for them to decide. Rendering decisions of this sort will enable them to develop toward a higher plane, and perhaps someday they will be capable of deciding more significant issues. Issues such as those I must decide. Issues"—he raised his voice, preventing Beheim from breaking in—"that have nothing to do with anything you would understand!"

"But, lord," said Beheim, "if this is so, why do you use words such as 'important' and 'significant' when referring to it?"

"In the first place," said the Patriarch coldly, "it is

not at all certain that I was in our comments referring to the question of a migration. That has yet to be made clear. However, if I was referring to it, perhaps it had some significance to me at the moment. Now, I can assure you, it is of no consequence whatsoever."

The irrationality of this statement left Beheim thoroughly bewildered. Yet then he wondered if this mutability of concern on the Patriarch's part was not evidence of insanity, but an important clue to the nature of a character that had evolved into the alien. And could any marked difference between the two conditions be detected by someone who had experienced neither one?

"What of your welfare, my lord?" he asked. "And what of the Family? If the world changes as Agenor believes it must, does the question not become significant to us all?"

"Should the need arise, there are places beyond this world to which I and my court will travel. The rest, as I have said, must make their own decisions. Now, enough!" The Patriarch's head fell back, his eyelids drooped; it looked as if he were contemplating some abstruse philosophical turn. "I have not enjoyed this conversation, but I intend to reward you nevertheless. I think it just in this instance, however, if your reward were to take the form of instruction."

The moon brightened, as if a film had been washed away from it. It hung low above the courtyard, so low that a slim figure standing atop the battlements was cast in silhouette against it. A boy, Beheim thought, dressed in a sleeping robe. He could not quite make him out.

"Tonight you have learned much of Mystery," said the Patriarch. "More, I daresay, than you can at this moment encompass. More even than you are aware. It might be decades before you acquire sufficient experience so as to order your knowledge. Because I love you—and I do love you, my child—I will attempt to clarify what you have learned and thus spare you decades of fruitless effort. I'm afraid that the first part of this instruction, however, will be somewhat bitter."

He made a graceful gesture, one directed toward the boy on the battlements, and the boy stepped off the edge into space. Beheim sprang from his chair, expecting a fall, a terrible impact, but the boy did not fall. He hovered in midair, his robe taking the wind, belling, then collapsing, pressing tightly against his body, revealing that it was no boy at all, but a young woman with full breasts and flaring hips. She began to drift down toward them, arms at her sides, becoming a shadow as she passed below the edge of the roof and out of the moonlight. As she reached the level of the second story, she came into full view again. Her chestnut hair was done up in an untidy bun; her eyes were quite large, and her mouth was pouty, the lower lip exceptionally full.

It was Giselle.

The recognition bred a chill hollow in Beheim's chest. He turned to the Patriarch, seething with anger; but the Patriarch kept his eyes on Giselle, smiling what seemed to Beheim a doting, approving smile.

She drifted lower, still lower, until her feet were inches from the stones. There she floated, no more than fifteen feet away, the fingers of her right hand touching a sword fern, the hem of her robe twitching in a ground current. Her eyes were unseeing, fixed on some point far beyond the world.

Beheim took a step toward her.

"Hold!" said the Patriarch. "Let her be."

Beheim stopped in midstride as if his strings had

been cut. The Patriarch nodded happily, like someone who had been proved right against the odds, but had been confident all along.

"She might have been the first of your line," he said. "Perhaps the lady of a new branch. The Beheims. That potential was clear in both of you. Now"—he shrugged—"now she will merely be another of my whores. A privileged position, mind you. But not one of such historical import." He heaved a doleful sigh that was too exaggerated to be genuine. "I trust this will teach you henceforth to act when action is required, to seize your opportunities. It should have been evident that she was long past ready for judgment, and that she had an excellent chance of survival. But then I imagine Alexandra had captured the bulk of your attention."

Still stunned by Giselle's reappearance, Beheim turned again to her. His thoughts of Alexandra were bitter, vengeful.

"She would have died had I not judged her," said the Patriarch. "Else I would not have usurped your right."

A sudden surge of anger moved Beheim toward her once again.

"I said hold!" cried the Patriarch, bringing him up short. He had risen from his chair and was standing with his fists clenched at his sides. "She is no longer yours. She is mine! Touch her and you forfeit everything." Then, in a less peremptory tone, he added, "I've left you the blond bitch, the one with the sweet blood. The castle slut for whom you neglected this beautiful creature. Still, that's more than you deserve."

At this mention of Paulina, Beheim experienced not even a flicker of emotion; he could scarcely call her to mind, so consumed was he by guilt and remorse. "What is happening to her?"

"She is with Mystery, of course. Striving toward life. Fear not. She will soon return to us."

"How can that be? She is here."

"Ah, now that relates to the second part of your instruction." The Patriarch reclaimed his chair. "You see, my boy, the Mysteries do not yield easily to analysis. It's true enough to say that they are death, the place to which death admits us, the place where we may—if we are properly prepared—choose the manner of our rebirth. For those who seek to enter the Family, the choice is simple. Either they will find their way to us, a fortunate few, or else they will fall forever through the dark, enduring torments that far outstrip those depicted in the popular representations of hell." He snorted in derision. "Hell! What an endearing notion! That evil could have so simple a geography and population. Red imps with pitchfork tails and goats' horns. Or for that matter, that evil could be so neatly and generally defined as though it were a bottled black juice you'd find at the local apothecary. These Christians and their God!" He made another derisive noise. "I've lived in times when gods were six a penny. As a matter of fact, I've spoken with several, and believe me, they're no bargain. Take this Jesus, for example. The famous Messiah. One of my children came just this close"—he held up thumb and forefinger together—"to giving him a little kiss. And would have done if chance hadn't intervened. Apparently the man—or should I say, the god?—was begging for it."

Beheim, still agonizing over Giselle, nonetheless found time to wonder at the Patriarch's moods, how quickly he flowed from menace to whimsy to senile rambling.

"But to continue," the Patriarch said, "Mystery has a more than passing similarity to the Bardos as described in *The Tibetan Book of the Dead*. One might assume from this that various Tibetans have experienced Mystery. If so, however, they have mistranslated the experience, for Mystery is far more malleable and complex, and less precise an entity than the Bardos. It would be more accurate to say that Mystery is a cosmic essence embodying a kind of metaphysical geography populated by failures of the spirit. Lost souls, if you will. Yet not even that is entirely accurate. To understand Mystery, to understand it completely, one must dwell in it as I do. But for the purposes of our conversation, it is only important for you to know that immersion in it does not preclude one's presence elsewhere." He waved carelessly at Giselle. "Voilà!"

At his gesture, the wall at Giselle's back and a section of the flagstones adjoining it melted away, replaced by the black, starred field of Mystery, a sight that was coming to seem commonplace to Beheim. The darkness bulged toward them, as if restrained by a meniscus. It appeared that Giselle was partially embedded in the field, her heels poised on the brink of an abyss.

"Watch now," said the Patriarch. "Watch as she flies."

A second, translucent Giselle materialized, superimposed on the first figure and identical in all respects but two: she wore no robe, and she appeared to be straining, struggling against the darkness, twisting about, rolling her head, as if the blackness were an oppressive cloth in which she was wrapped. Gradually this second image took on solidity and richness of color, while the first became as vague and ghostly as the second had been. The perfection and vulnerability of her naked body made Beheim's heart ache. Then her lips parted the merest fraction of an inch, and a trickle of blackness seeped forth, spilling onto her chin, showing as sharply as might a crack against the pale skin.

"So did you yourself once fly," said the Patriarch in a wistful tone. "So did we all. Steeping in the liquor of death, becoming permeated with it."

Shame flooded Beheim. Shame that was only incidentally concerned with Giselle's fate, and related chiefly to the fact that what he regretted most was his failure to judge her, the knowledge that he had forever lost his chance to control her. That would have always been the character of their relationship, he realized. Dominant and submissive. Of all the Family, only with Alexandra had he achieved even the semblance of equality. Yet none of these recognitions dissolved his feelings of remorse. "Bring her back," he said.

The Patriarch laughed. "I cannot. And even if I could, I would only succeed in prolonging the inevitable."

"Bring her back, damn you!" Beheim shouted.

"Are you mad?" The Patriarch got to his feet. "Control yourself. This is not seemly. Not in the least."

But Beheim was beyond control; he darted forward, thinking—against reason—that he might snatch Giselle from the void; before he could reach her, however, a blow to the back of his head dropped him to all fours and sent lightning shooting back into his eyes.

"It's clear," the Patriarch said, "that you will profit far more from this conversation once all distractions are eliminated."

Beheim lifted his head in time to see Giselle arrowing off into the void, swiftly dwindling to a point of white, and as if the blackness had been a sheet held up behind her and in moving away she was drawing the material close about her, the way a hand pushed into a black cloth might gather the cloth about it like a glove, so the void, too, seemed to dwindle, shrinking to a ragged patch no bigger than a window, then an irregular circle the size of a drain, then a speck, and then it was gone, leaving in its stead the flagstones and gray morticed walls of the courtyard.

The Patriarch grabbed Beheim by the collar, hauled him up as easily as he might have a kitten. "The sole reason you want her is because you've been denied a toy, a pet, and you're sulking." He lifted Beheim higher, so that his feet dangled, and forced his head up so that their eyes met. "You don't love her. If you did, you'd be exultant, overjoyed that she is soon to be one of us. Immortal and vital beyond her wildest dreams. Perhaps had things gone differently, you might have formed some sort of affectionate bond once she passed her judgment. But what you think you feel for who she was, that is pretense pure and simple. Do you believe you are a mortal? A creature of weak sentiment and puerile morality? Put that from mind. *This* is what you are."

That wide, pale handsome face began to stretch, its lines to dissolve, and the eyes, dark and expressive of an intelligent calm, came to be cored with hot red fires, and the curly black hair looked like a thicket of brambles that had grown up around but not yet covered a hideous marble head. Even after the dissolution had ceased and the face had returned to its Byronic poise, Beheim could still see the decaying thing beneath. He recalled how he had once thought he would lie to the Patriarch, coerce him into lending his support. What a fool he had been! So bedizened with the newness of his own strength and illumination that he could not for the moment imagine any greater force.

"Unrelieved black is the color of your nature," said the Patriarch, letting Beheim fall to the flagstones. "The color of the death in which you were reborn. The color of grave soil and nightmare. You know this is true, you feel its truth, yet you resist it and so fail to understand what it entails. You think of it as evil, but you have no comprehension of the word. You perceive the concept as erroneously as do the Christians. As a terrible, conscienceless process of violence against the order of all things. And so it is. But you fail to see the depths underlying that definition, the logic, the good plain country sense of evil. Therefore listen to me, and I will make you wise."

He walked a few paces away; he struck a theatrical pose with his back to Beheim, hands clasped behind him, face tilted to the night sky.

"Order, my child, is an illusion. At least it is in the common meaning of the word. Both the philosophies of evil and good acknowledge this, though they do so in disparate fashion. Those devoted to the good perceive themselves and everyone like them to be intrinsically imperfect; they seek to impose order on their lives, to delimit the natural urges, to counterfeit order through restraint and mindless devotions. And what has been the result of their efforts? War. Famine. Torture. Rape. The slaughter and incarceration of millions."

For an instant the flagstones melted away, blending into a flat gray expanse like the sea of an overcast morning; the ferns grew skeletal and colorless, and the walls of the courtyard lost definition. Then it all returned to normal. It was as if, Beheim thought, the Patriarch, badly affected by his consideration of the good, had experienced some fleeting doubt concerning the substantiality of his worldview.

"Now we who favor evil," said the Patriarch, "profess ourselves to be natural creatures and strive only to express our natures. We feed when we must, we give vent to rage and lust, to the full range of our emotions, and we do so without self-recrimination, without the unnatural reining in of our basic urges. We deny ourselves nothing, and we accept the truth of who and what we are. And what comes of this? Some die at our hands, a few are granted immortality. Some unpleasant physical and mental conditions arise, but are these any worse than the cancers and senility and derangement that afflict mortals? On occasion we overindulge, but never on such a grand and fulminant scale as the overindulgences of the Christians. We do not make war on them. We feed upon them, yes. But that is a natural thing, this cutting back of the herd now and again. It is they who seek war with us, they who attempt genocide. That is their way. They have no understanding of moderation."

He glanced over his shoulder at Beheim. "Both philosophies have at their core the same yearning for peace, the same vision of a perfect serenity. On the one hand, this is seen as a stainless white radiance; on the other, as an infinite darkness. But there are few salient differences between these two apparent poles. In fact, their sole distinction lies in the method of attaining peace. Our method, what is called evil, the exercise of license and power on an individual basis, a stable kind of anarchy with only the loosest form of restraint, that is the most humane way, the way that causes the least pain. It has been argued that this is so only because there are not so many of us as there are devotees of the good. My answer to that has always been, there will under no circumstances ever be as many of us as there are now of the good, for we will keep our own numbers down, we will harvest the weak and legislate against the abusers of power. So which is truly the good? I ask you. And which the evil? The gaudy, blackhearted, self-indulgent way of least pain? Or the pious, psalm-singing, selfless way of war and desolation?" He came back toward Beheim. "The secret of our virtue is this, child: not to care. None of us care. Not you, not Alexandra, not Agenor, not any member of the Family. Oh, it can happen that a kind of caring may spring into existence when two or several of us become fascinated with the other, and admittedly this is sweet, this is a delight. But it is not caring as defined by the Christians. It is a playful delusion, a costume in which we dress our lust, our selfish needs. And this essential lack of concern for others, our almost total self-absorption, that is what makes us less dangerous and ultimately more compassionate than our foes. They have been poisoned, driven mad by the pursuit of those hypocritical eidolons: generosity and love for their fellowman. By contrast to their penchant for mass violence in the name of salvation, our own madness is a balmy distraction."

Once again the entire courtyard appeared to flicker into unreality, becoming for a moment a vague sketch of itself, almost lost in grayness. The Patriarch seized hold of Beheim's shirtfront and pulled him erect so that they stood face-to-face.

"Evil," he said, evoking the essence of the word by his menacing pronunciation of it. "It is no satanic pageant play, it has no infernal city as its capital. Evil is simply what you are, Michel, the stuff of your life. It is the taste of blood, it is the slack feel of a drained supper limp in your arms, and as you lift your head, the sight of the pitted moon like a dead god sailing the dark between the forked limbs of a gallows tree. You can deny what you are for a little while, but in the end your own nature will overwhelm you. As it has begun to do this night. And if you continue to deny, to resist"—he pushed his face nose to nose with Beheim's, lowered his voice to a savage whisper—"then you will displease me! That, my child, is by far the worst of the fates that can enfold you. That is something I should avoid were I you." He held Beheim aloft at arm's length. "Now go! Finish the task I have set you. And when you have finished, think on all I have said this night."

He shoved Beheim away, and Beheim, having no desire to anger him further, walked briskly toward the stairs that led away into the depths of the castle. From behind him came the sound of laughter, laughter so liquid and resonant he did not believe it could have issued from a human throat, and thus when the stairs—as he mounted them—and the stone walls began to fade into flat, unrelieved gray, he did not hesitate, but continued on, less fearing the insubstantiality of the place than what he might see if he were to turn back. The ground remained solid beneath his feet, and the air, though colder than it had been in the Patriarch's chamber, was sweet to breathe. As the final traces of form faded, enclosing him in featureless gray, he felt a twinge of claustrophobic panic, but he maintained his resolve and took heart in the fact that the laughter had faded along with all else; after walking for several minutes, however, and finding no end to the gray, he wondered if panic would not be more appropriate than self-control. Evil, he thought, could not find a more fitting expression than this limbo. Perhaps

it was another conceit of the Patriarch's, an object lesson of sorts. But that was something of a leap. More
likely the Patriarch had been distracted and had forgotten what he had done with Beheim, forgotten all
about him. Left him to wander, to become the ghost of
this supreme emptiness. It was quite possible, he decided, for the image he had gathered of the Patriarch
was one of erratic, brilliant decay. But then he realized
that in conjuring up the Patriarch's essence, he was
only considering that last, more genteel guise and was
failing to add in the ghoulish demon the man had
seemed at first, the all-powerful dweller in Mystery.
That creature would forget nothing. He might pretend
to have forgotten in order to increase one's anxiety;
but he would so delight in every potential for torment
that nothing would elude his mental grasp, though he
kept a thousand souls dangling at once over the fires
of his majestic disdain.

Beheim cleared his head of these morbid considerations and plodded on, gradually becoming as gray
and indefinite in his mind as his surround. If there
was a thought in his brain, it consisted of a dismal,
primitive chant, a wordless beat of failure and futility
that kept marching time with his footsteps. He was
heavy in his flesh, his heart, permeated with fatigue
both physical and spiritual, and when at last he saw
the gray begin to clear and glimpsed the dark shapes
of pine trees and a hill, other hills, and realized that he
had passed through the imponderable, magical stuff of
the walls of Castle Banat, actually walked through
them, a ghost in effect if not in reality, and reached the
place to which his duty bound him, he felt not a whit
of relief, only the weary recognition that yet another
phase of his ordeal was about to begin.

Chapter THIRTEEN

The Patriarch's servants, following Beheim's instruction, dug several pits in the woods close to the castle, each one four meters deep. These they lined with heavy canvas to slow drainage and filled three quarters full with water, not enough in itself to entrap a member of the Family, but enough to render him helpless for a few moments so that sheets of iron—shutters removed from castle windows—could be drawn over the top of the pits, thus sealing in the murderer. Given the water level and the mucky condition of the soil, Beheim thought it doubtful that she—or he—would be able to achieve sufficient leverage so as to climb up and push the iron sheet away. Once this was done, he had the sheets and pits camouflaged with branches and dirt, and then sent the servants back to the castle. Shortly before dawn he took up a position behind a small hillock some sixty feet from the depression where lay the body of the Golden's companion, whose decaying scent was borne to him on the night wind.

Soon a blade of carnelian light slipped between the horizon and the sky. Beheim, benumbed, too distanced by the evening's events to give more than passing attention to the consideration of his peril, watched it spread, illuminating the humped blue-dark geography of the hills, the crimped valleys with their star-struck tinsel rivers and the towns with a few early lights burning like a scatter of embers. He could smell the wet grass, the heady spice of pine needles, bitter smoke from some far-off burning, and from these odors, these sights, it seemed to him that the faces and forms of his past were being extruded, some still-vital essence of each being released into the air and growing more vital yet on being kissed by the rich nitrogens and stinging ozones of the moment, rearing up before him like the fabulous visions that come to a dying man who can no longer feel the terrible insult done his body by wound or disease, but rather is drifting in a blissful nowhere between Mystery and the end of time.

The things that came to him then were not the things that he would have assumed he would remember, the memorial moments, the birthdays, the promotions, the successes, but were lesser, brighter, and more convivial bits of living. Eating fish stew from a can on a Marseilles dock and trading insults with the fishermen. Spending a night in a cave in the sun-browned, god-thronged hills above Corinth. Drunk in the company of other students, diving into the Seine off the morning bridges to impress a girl. Another girl with whom he had lived for a summer, a dancer in one of the tiny family circuses that passed back and forth across Europe like gaudy platoons; the kid from Reims who sold him a gold watch without any works inside; the lady who invited him in when he had been hiking near Strasbourg, cooked him a meal, prayed over him for an hour, and then—as if this had effected a sufficient purification—took his virginity; the old soldier

serving now as a cook in a country inn near Avignon
who had prepared fresh trout with mushrooms and
told bloodcurdling stories of the Napoleonic wars.
Meeting a woman who had just been released from an
asylum in Quercy and claimed she was on her way to
keep a rendezvous with her dead husband in a bistro
near Les Halles; meeting a group of albino children
whose parents were educating them to be psychics;
meeting a priest who hated God, a Gypsy who refused
to read his cards, a drunken dog trainer whose trick-
performing pets had been stolen. Wrestling a giant at
a carnival in Irun and getting his arm broken. Going
to the cockfights in Salamanca, a night under olive
trees lit by torches, and winning a thousand pesetas on
a black cock whose guts at the end had hung from his
belly like fringe off a general's epaulets. The great cathedral in Köln where he first heard *The Messiah*; a
cantina near San Sebastián where cryptic designs were
painted on the doors to ward off evil, as if evil were an
incompetent lout who might be sent fleeing by the
sight of a few daubs of color and some misspelled
Latin words; a riverboat owned by a young widow
whose windows were all of stained glass and whose
walls were illuminated by crude murals of the saints;
a waterfront bar in Calais where one night, while having his first after-dinner calvados, he watched a ten-
year-old girl pierce her cheek with steel needles in
return for whatever change the patrons tossed her
way.

It was all running out of him, he realized, like violet water down a drain, all that brilliant particularity
of life and history emptying, as if it no longer found
him a suitable vessel. And it was being replaced by . . .
by what? He could put no simple name to it, but it
seemed a new pilot stood at the helm of his soul.

Someone informed by a dark, cool competency, yet in whom there burned a lust so feral it was almost indistinguishable from rage, so potent that it outshone even his fear of the day now dawning. It was this entity who now looked out from his eyes onto the brightening world, who contemplated the patch of weeds around him, yarrow and vetch, mint and sorrel, with stony displeasure, annoyed by the rich, moldering scents of the autumn woods, and who watched unmoved as the sun smeared scarlet and orange and purple along the horizon beneath galleons of cloud, bringing the forested crests of the surrounding hills into sharp relief. Yet he did not quite conform to the Patriarch's definition of an indulgent and self-absorbed mentality, for there remained in him more than a sliver of conscience, of moral regard, of all his old compulsions, and he did not believe these things to be mere residues. He had changed, yes, but he was still himself in some wise, still Beheim the man, and while understanding this did not please him as once it would have, he was nevertheless satisfied to know that the change had not utterly overwhelmed him. The Patriarch's wisdom apparently had its limits, and recognizing that was also an occasion for satisfaction.

Soon the world came to be filled with the great vibration of the sun. Beheim lay flat, refusing to look up, feeling waves of killing heat on his neck and shoulders, his eyes on the castle, which blotted out nearly half the sky, as still and silent as the corpse of some immense stone-colored animal. The pale blue sky distressed him, as did the winded greenery and rippling grass and the incessant play of light and shadow; yet he experienced no panic and furious disorientation as before. He did not think he could ever come to love the light, but if tolerate it he must, then tolerate it he would. A black beetle sporting pincers nearly twice as long as its body began climbing a stalk of sorrel in front of him, blindly proceeding into midair. He felt an odd kinship with the thing, but when it reached the top of the stalk and swayed there, turning its antennae this way and that, he became annoyed with it and also with the analogy he had drawn between its progress and his own, and flicked it away with a forefinger.

Not long after sunrise someone emerged from the castle. A very tall, very slim someone dressed in a long gray skirt and a dark blue shawl that covered her head and shoulders, and shadowed her face. Alexandra. Beheim had no doubt that it was she, but was perplexed by the hesitancy with which she approached the body, stopping and starting, casting quick glances overhead, displaying none of the calculation that he would have predicted. And when, instead of going directly to the body, she negotiated a wide circle around it, paying no attention to it whatsoever, and went plunging about in the tall grass, pausing now and again to peer into the pine woods and call his name, he did not know how to take this.

"Michel!" she cried. "Where are you?"

She darted a glance toward the castle.

"Damn you, Michel!" she shouted. "Show yourself! We may not have much time!"

She stumbled, fell, disappeared into a grass-filled depression; then she staggered to her feet. The shawl had slipped down onto her shoulders, revealing the spill of her auburn hair, and in the instant before she pulled it back over her head, Beheim saw a look of abject terror on her face. She stood without moving, and he had the idea that she was fighting for control— again, this was not behavior he would associate with the murderer, who would, he surmised, be acclimated to this environment. She was reacting in the same way that he had when he first experienced daylight. Yet when she peered into his hiding place, he knew she must have detected some sign of him, his heartbeat perhaps, and he got to his knees, ready to run. And when she came toward him, he jumped to his feet and backed away.

"Stay down, you idiot!" she said. "You'll be seen!"

She stumbled and fell once again and, rather than regaining her feet, crawled toward him through the high grass. Fear was written in her tightened mouth and round eyes. Nevertheless he continued his retreat.

"What in perdition's name is wrong with you?" she said. "Get down!"

She sank to her knees in the grass, gazing up at him balefully; but then her expression softened and she reached out a hand as if to give him a caress. He did not allow it, retreating even farther away, and she stared at him in obvious confusion.

"What's the matter?" she asked. "Why are you behaving this way?"

"How do you expect me to behave? Fawning, pawing you? Begging for a kiss?"

"I think some show of affection would be appropriate," she said stiffly. "After all, we . . ."

"We what? I'd like to hear your interpretation of the event."

"We made love," she said after a pause, her voice gone small. "At least that's what I did."

He could find nothing of a disingenuous character in her words, in any facet of her reaction, and he wanted to believe her; but belief was not in him.

"I'd like to hear your interpretation," she said.

"What I thought about it has no bearing on this,"

he said. "I did what you wanted me to do. That should be enough for you."

"Michel . . ." she began; then she broke it off and gazed despondently back toward the castle. "Sit down. Somebody will see you."

He made no move to obey.

"Are you deaf?" she said. "You'll be seen if you keep standing there like a damned statue!"

Puzzled, still uncertain of her, but admitting to a sliver of uncertainty concerning her guilt, Beheim dropped into a squat, maintaining the distance between them.

Alexandra reordered the shawl about her face and sighed. "How can you stand this?" she said dispiritedly. "It's horrible!" Her head gave a twitch, as if she had thought to glance up at the sun but had thwarted the impulse.

"It becomes less difficult with time," Beheim said. "What are you doing here?"

"I'm out for a Sunday stroll!" She gave him a pitying look. "Do you believe I would willingly experience this . . . this hallucination? The Patriarch sent me to witness your triumph." She colored this word *triumph* with heavy sarcasm.

He remained silent, studying her, not yet convinced; he had expected that Christina would be the Patriarch's agent. Alexandra, watching him, burst into laughter.

"You think *I* committed the murder, don't you?" she said. "Is that the reason you're acting so coldly toward me?" She shook her head in disbelief. "That's right! I'm the one! I'm the madwoman who tore the Golden apart just to have a taste of her blood. And naturally, being guilty, I'd be the one to steer you onto the right course."

"You may not have had that course in mind," Beheim said angrily. "In fact, even if you are innocent, I don't think you did. You knew nothing of Felipe's researches. What did you really want to happen?"

"I told you! Before we made love, I told you everything! You knew you were taking a chance. You knew there was the possibility of disaster."

"Perhaps you told me some of it, but not all. Did you want Felipe to kill me so as to compromise Agenor?"

At the sound of Felipe's name, she grew somber. "I did not mean for him to kill you. I could hardly have expected that. But neither did I hope for the opposite. I've already explained all that to you, but obviously you've dismissed what I told you as being part of some devious scheme in which I sought to ensnare you."

He chose to ignore her last comment. "I had no choice but to kill him. Felipe and Dolores intended to kill me."

"It's not important why you did it," she said in a brittle tone. "In fact, I suppose you've done me a great favor, you have raised me high. But that will count for little with others of my branch."

"I wonder how they will greet the news that it was you who sent me to Felipe's apartments."

"Badly, I expect," she said with sudden venom. "You make a strong case for my preventing that story from being spread. And since you are the only one who can tell it . . ."

"Yet you must bear witness to the Patriarch. What will you tell him? That you settled a personal grievance rather than letting his will be done? You have as little choice in this as have I."

Her anger faded as quickly as it had come. She

regarded him glumly for a few counts, then glanced down at the grass; she plucked up a blade, rubbed it between her fingers.

"What are you thinking?" he asked.

"I recall asking you that same question not so long ago. You had some difficulty in answering it."

"And I recall you telling me that it was the easiest question of all to answer, unless one had something to hide."

"I've nothing to hide." She continued fingering the grass blade, her head down, hair partially obscuring her face. "I had hopes, Michel. That was what I was thinking just now. I was thinking about those hopes, about how rare they were, how rare were the moments that inspired them. Does that seem foolish to you?"

"No, not if those hopes and moments truly existed."

"How can you doubt that they did?"

"I nearly died following your advice. Isn't that—"

"It wasn't advice I offered. It was far more than that."

"Whatever it was, I nearly died because of it. Reason enough to raise some doubts about the purpose of your counsel, wouldn't you say?"

Her eyes locked on Beheim, and he was again struck by the exotic character of her face, those green eyes, the extraordinarily wide mouth, the cheekbones as abrupt as scars.

"Agenor told me you could be pigheaded," she said. "Yet he also said that logic would never fail to sway you. Apparently he is not all-seeing."

"What is your relationship with Agenor?"

"Why should I tell you anything? To have you denounce me for a liar or worse? You were a policeman too long. You suspect even the good that comes to you."

"I won't deny that I've a suspicious nature," he said. "As to whether or not I've had reason for my suspicions, that's another story."

She plucked up a handful of grass, let the wind take it, all but a few stalks that remained lying on her palm in a configuration that reminded him of a cryptogram. That more than anything she had said or done, the way she watched the grass drift away through the air, wonderingly, with touching attentiveness, like a child seeing something simple and marvelous for the first time, that persuaded him that she had not been exposed to the daylight for a very long time, that she could not have committed the murder.

"You don't have to tell me," he said. "It's probably unimportant. I'm not sure any longer why I want to know these things. Habit, I guess."

"I don't believe it's important, either," she said. "Agenor is not himself these days. He rambles, he loses track. It would be foolish to give much weight to the things he does." She brushed something off her skirt. "I've no idea how he would describe our relationship. We have political views in common, but little else. After the murder he came to me distraught, more so than I have ever seen him. He asked if I knew anything that might help you with the investigation. He was afraid he had put you in a desperate position. I told him I might be able to help. Of course I had my own ends in mind. As I told you, I hoped you would find something to discredit Felipe. The bottle cap was a happy coincidence. Yet I will never believe he had anything to do with the murder. That was not his way. Had he lusted for special blood, he would have bred

his own Golden. Indeed, I know he was considering
doing just that. Look here."

From a voluminous pocket in her skirt, she removed a leather folder that Beheim recognized as
Felipe's journal. He was distressed, not because she
had stolen it, but because he had not thought to steal
it himself.

She began leafing through the loose papers inside, but he said, "Don't bother showing me. I believe
you."

It all made sense, he thought, though sense of an
extremely sketchy sort. He could not understand why
Agenor had bothered to seek an alliance. Instinct, perhaps. Or had he known of Felipe's researches? Could
he have suspected that the murder had been committed during daylight? If so, why then had he not
suggested as much to Beheim?

There was no point, he decided, in further analysis. He would have to wait and see if his plan bore
fruit. An unlikely prospect. It was evident that he had
misread most of the clues and all the tendencies of the
case.

He settled himself beside Alexandra, still wary of
her, but accepting her for the time as, if not a lover,
then a neutral observer, possibly an ally. He did not
know if he could trust her in a difficult situation.

"What do you want from all this?" she asked him.

He laughed bitterly. "I'm hardly in a position to
want anything. I'm just trying to survive."

She appeared to be waiting for him to continue,
to explain, but he did not feel in the mood to rehash
his experiences of the past twenty-four hours.

"Well," she said finally, "what would you want if
wanting were your motive?"

"Why does that interest you?"

"I'm interested to see what we might have in common. Perhaps we will become friends again."

"Friends? Is that what we were?"

"It will do for now."

"I don't think I've heard the word 'friend' used since I became part of the Family."

"It has, I will admit, something of a different meaning to most of us. But friendship and membership in the Family are not mutually exclusive."

With the shawl shading her face, she really looked quite beautiful, softer and more vulnerable than women of the Family were wont to look. But Beheim had learned to distrust beauty. He turned his eyes to the battlements of the castle high above, rearing dark against the pale sky. A few threads of gray cloud were gathering over the valley, netting a portion of the blue, and farther to the west, a flight of blackbirds whirled up from a copse, appearing as if an invisible hand were scattering the ashes of a giant.

"I'm not sure," he said. "I don't suppose I know enough to have reasonable wants at this juncture. But one thing I'm clear on. I want more than what I've been told is possible to want. I want something that would strike most of our cousins as being out of character. If I were to try to name it now, I would most likely seem foolish. Yet it is not a foolish thing to want. I'm clear on that as well."

She remained silent for a few seconds, then said, "Not a bad answer. I've felt that way myself."

"Indeed?" he snapped. "I imagine it's just another phase I'm passing through."

"Don't be an ass, Michel! I'm trying to befriend you, to help you."

"First and foremost, you're trying to help yourself."

"Granted. But our interests coincide in this instance. They have from the beginning. We can help each other. We'd be fools not to. No matter how isolated an instance was our time together two nights ago, it had to signify something. Some form of intuitive trust at the very least."

"Trust," he said thoughtfully, looking out across the field at the castle, like a god in its gray decrepitude and huge, imponderable mass.

"Yes, what of it?"

"I was considering whether or not I valued it least of all the bonds that could unite us."

She gave no response, and he glanced at her. She was staring with disgust at a beetle—perhaps the same one he had flicked away—that was crawling along the hem of her skirt. He supposed that her disgust was part and parcel of her distaste for all the daylight world; but there was something so fabulously normal about her reaction, so womanly, he laughed and laughed. Yet when she asked him why he was laughing at her, he felt so much, relief, hope, fugitive strands of deeper emotions, once again he was not certain that he knew the answer.

Chapter FOURTEEN

T he sun, a huge, golden, blistered sac of light, edged higher toward the top of the sky; gray clouds continued to gather over the valley. They talked intermittently, casual talk for the most part, Alexandra expressing revulsion for things of the day, having bouts of extreme anxiety, and Beheim comforting her by relating his earlier experiences. They shied away from speaking of what had happened in the white room, on the great carved bed, but it was there between them, almost palpable, a third presence in which they both had a part that sat by their sides and added an accent of warmth to their conversation. Before long they heard a church bell tolling noon, and as the last peal had died away, a man dressed in black came walking around the curve of the castle wall and stood in the shadow of the wall, gazing out toward the spot where the body of the Golden's companion lay. He wore trousers, jacket, a wide-brimmed hat, and had on tinted spectacles. Most likely, Beheim thought, by waiting he was trying to tempt anyone watching into showing himself, thinking that he could retreat into the castle before his identity was discovered. At length he came forward into the light. It seemed to Beheim that his gait was familiar, the way he swung his left arm farther than his right, and how his head fell slightly to the right as if to counterbalance the swing of the left arm. With each and every step, the man's presence struck new chords of familiarity. Beheim held his breath, strained his eyes, peering between blades of grass. The tension was such that he felt he was being pressed in a vise. And when at last he recognized the man, when he saw the white hair feathering from beneath the hat, when the craggy nobility of the features became apparent, he refused to believe the evidence of his senses.

"Agenor!" breathed Alexandra. "It's Agenor!"

"No," he said, trying to put his faith in denial. "No, it couldn't be."

She caught his wrist. "It is! Look! It's him!"

Agenor had stopped about five yards from the body; he turned his head in a slow arc, scanning the woods for movement. From his pocket he withdrew a scarf. After another look around, he tied the scarf over his nose and mouth, and stepped close to the body.

"What will you do?" whispered Alexandra.

"Nothing," Beheim said, still shaken. "I'll report what I've seen to the Patriarch. Or you can make the report. You're his agent."

"It's not enough. You have to force him to confess to the murder. If you don't, he may be able to invent an excuse for being here."

"What possible excuse could there be?" Yet even as he said these words Beheim found himself believing that Agenor would be able to justify his presence. No scenario in which he was the murderer held water. It was absurd, Beheim thought; he would not condemn him without a hearing. And yet if Agenor was the murderer—and he had to admit to the possibility—

then by giving him a hearing, he would be exposing himself to grave danger. He had been prepared for this when he had assumed Alexandra to be the guilty one, but Agenor was a far more formidable foe, and all of Beheim's preparations, his pits, his dilution of the drug, now seemed inadequate. What if Agenor had his own supply of the drug?

Alexandra was staring at him expectantly, those lustrous green eyes holding his gaze, but exerting no pressure of will.

"Very well," he said. "But keep clear of him. If he manages to overcome me, you alone can bear witness to this. If he attacks, you must assume he is guilty and return to the castle. Do you understand?"

She nodded, touched his hand—for luck, he thought, for assurance. He almost trusted her.

Standing up from the grasses that had hidden him, Beheim felt that he had grown enormous, that he was towering over the valley, the woods and rivers, towering over even the circumstance of murder, dwarfed only by the imponderable tonnage of Castle Banat. The sight of Agenor—his spectacles now removed—bending over the corpse and plucking at its clothing seemed no different than the sight of anyone he had ever arrested in the moment before the moment of truth. The old man looked vulnerable, small, oblivious to the fate about to close its jaws on him, and it was from this perspective, in this frame of mind, that Beheim spoke to him, saying as he walked toward him, "Nice day for a walk, eh?"

Agenor let out a yelp of alarm, dropping the tinted spectacles, and sprang to his feet. He gaped at Beheim for a second, but then his features relaxed, composed themselves into a calm mask.

Guilty, thought Beheim, stopping perhaps twenty feet away. Guilty as the devil.

"Michel!" said Agenor. "I'm surprised to see you here. I'd assumed you were still involved in your interrogations. A servant told me about this." He gestured at the body. "So I thought I'd investigate. See what was up. I believe"—his brow furrowed as if in deep contemplation—"that this may be the body of the Golden's companion."

"It won't do, my lord," Beheim said. "Really. It won't do at all."

Agenor's face was washed over by a succession of emotions: defiance, rage, sadness. "No," he said at last, his voice almost inaudible. "No, I don't imagine it will."

Wind laid undulant lines across the field, rippling and striping the tall grasses; the grass made a long, hissing sigh.

With a rueful laugh, Agenor looked up to the sun, then he waved at it. "Well," he said breezily, "tell me your opinion, Michel. Can we suffer this on a daily basis? Is it worth all the effort?"

Beheim had no answer for him.

Agenor's Adam's apple bobbed reflexively. "It seems I've gotten what I wanted. Whether I truly wanted it or not."

Beheim did not understand this statement, but he had no desire to pursue the matter. Each second he was assaulted by a complex of feelings, old feelings of devotion and allegiance, new ones of anger and resentment at Agenor's betrayal. "Will you come back with me to the castle, lord?"

"The castle." Agenor swept off his hat, ran a hand through his thick white hair. "Yes, well. I'm afraid I can't do that. I would like to. In fact, I intended to.

But I simply can't." He glanced up at Beheim. "I wondered if this was a trap. I suppose it was idiotic of me not to recognize it for one."

"My lord, if you do not return with me now, you will surely die."

"At your hands?" Haughtily. "I think not."

"I diluted Felipe's drug, my lord. I cannot guarantee that you have more than a few minutes of life remaining."

All sternness and rigor drained from Agenor's face, and it appeared his features would dissolve, melt like heated wax, and flow off the bone into a puddle. Then he regained his composure. "That is a lie."

"Your pardon, lord, but what would be the virtue of such a lie? I did not know the murderer's identity. I wished to protect myself. Dilution of the drug was my sole means of protection in the face of powerful enemies." Beheim took a step forward, suddenly wanting—despite everything—to save the old man. "Time grows short, my lord. I would not see you die in such ignominy."

"Ah, but it is precisely the death I sought! And not an ignominous one at all." Agenor, to Beheim's consternation, seemed merry, giddy with the prospect of immolation; once again he looked up to the sun. "If, indeed, you are telling the truth, and if, in that case, you knew what you were doing when you diluted the drug, which I doubt, I still do not believe that you will ever completely understand the irony of this moment."

"Then explain it to me, lord, if explanation pleases you. But be swift, I caution you."

"Yes, perhaps I should explain. If for no other reason than that you will be able to confirm my folly." Agenor edged a step closer to Beheim, a surreptitious movement that put him on the alert. "You see, my friend, I have been experiencing certain—how shall I put it?—certain discomforts of late. Mental difficulties. A tendency toward the erratic, a drifting in and out of delusion. I recognized these to be symptoms of the changes that attend the passage from one stage of this peculiar eternity into the next, and I must tell you I did not welcome them. They seemed like maladies, the products of a curse. Therefore, unwilling to subject myself to these changes, and gripped by the blackest of depressions, I determined to end my life."

Agenor shifted nearer, and Beheim prepared to run. He was feeling a bit separate from the world, light-headed, but this did not concern him. He was fascinated by Agenor's arrogance, his implicit denial of a circumstance that had placed him in mortal peril. It did not greatly surprise him, though; it was in accord with the Family's penchant for self-destruction.

"It was not a difficult decision," said Agenor. "But implementing the decision, that was another matter entirely. I did not wish my death to be the mere spending of a life, and I must also admit to a degree of cowardice. Then one morning—I had been experimenting with Felipe's drug—after returning from a walk outside the castle walls, I was passing the Golden's chamber, and it occurred to me that she could serve as the agency of my death. I thought this a stroke of genius. I had always aspired to participate in a Decanting, and now I could satisfy this yearning. I knew the Patriarch would not permit such a breach of tradition to go unpunished. He would sentence me to an Illumination. And therein, I realized, lay the value of my death. I would have questions put to me that would focus the dying light of my mind on the particular portion of the future that has so concerned me these past years: the question of whether the Family should abandon the West and go into the East for safety."

Beheim tried to take a step away, but he felt rooted to the spot. Agenor's tall black figure rippled like something seen through flame, and his voice had the resonance of a great bell; its vibrations dizzied Beheim, made him slow and uncaring.

"I planned to take a sip, no more. Only a sip. But once I had tasted the Golden, I was unable to stop. Oh, Michel, what a flavor the blood had! And it was not the flavor alone that commanded me. There were visions. It was as if I had become the Golden, as if by drinking I flowed along the river of her life and knew ... No, not knew. Felt! I felt all her womanly secrets, the hot pleasure waked by a first kiss, her monthly pains, her sharp virginal longings. I degraded myself in my abuse of her. And so with a single act of violence I rejected centuries of temperate life and scholarly ideals. When I saw what I had done, my desire for death grew stronger, and I set in motion a scheme that would both punish me and elevate you. You see, I believed that despite your inexperience you were the one who should take my place, that you would become the voice in our Family for policies of reason and restraint. I intended to lead you slowly toward the conclusion of my guilt, to make it look as though your brilliance had won the day. But now it appears that my decision to die was not a firm one."

He cocked his head as if hearing an inner voice and made a scratchy noise in his throat, as if what he had heard had afforded him mild surprise. His manner of speaking grew increasingly halting and distracted.

"It was never firm. Never. I ... I understand that now. My death wish, if you will, was merely another symptom of the mental erraticism that had so depressed me, a kind of morbid playfulness. Games. I was playing games. With myself, I suppose. With everyone, and everything. And my convoluted attempt at achieving death by means of your investigation, that, too, was a symptom. A game. I both did and did not want to die, you see. Equally attractive ends. So I constructed this scenario against which to play out my ambivalence. Even at this moment I am flirting with the ideas of death and noble sacrifice. But"—a cracked laugh—"I will not do more than flirt with them."

Agenor, Beheim realized, had moved quite close to him, less than an arm's length away. His white hair looked bright as flame. The deepened lines on his brow seemed to write an epic of concern, of deep study; his eyes were hooded, brooding; but there was a febrile slackness to his mouth that spoke of weakness, indulgence, an inner unraveling. That expression was a signal of terrible danger—Beheim knew it well. But all his observations and recognitions were futile. He could not stir a step. Agenor's lips parted in a slowly developing smile to reveal his fangs, and Beheim felt that he was shriveling away inside himself, as helpless as a bird before a serpent.

Then something came whistling down onto the side of Agenor's head, something that impacted with a solid *thunk*. He screamed and staggered away. Blood stained his white hair, rilled in a heavy flow down his cheek and jaw, and Alexandra, her hair in disarray, looking half-mad herself with fear, dropped the dead bough with which she had struck him and caught Beheim's hand and pulled him toward the woods. Still dazed, he struggled against her. She shouted, slapped his face, and stung to alertness, he let her drag him along, running clumsily over the uneven ground, lurching sideways whenever he struck a depression, flailing his arms to maintain balance. There was a roaring at his back, a sound such as a wounded animal might have made.

They burst through a fringe of chokecherry into shaggy green pines, dappled sunlight, ferns, boulders protruding from a cover of dead needles, the land sloping away sharply. Alexandra started straight downhill, towing Beheim along, but as they descended the steep slope, remembering the pits, he said, "No, this way!" and turned her back uphill, setting a course roughly parallel to the edge of the woods. The sunlight confused him. Every place looked more or less alike, masses of dark green and pine trunks glowing coppery in the strong light, and they were moving so quickly, so erratically, ducking left and right, he became uncertain as to where the pits lay. They were close at hand, he was sure, but he could not pinpoint their location. He could hear Agenor breaking through the bushes not far behind, and once again he thought how inadequate his preparation had been. The pits, even if he were able to find them, would likely be useless. And who knew how long Felipe's drug, even diluted, would protect Agenor?

After another minute or so it became clear that Agenor was gaining rapidly on them, and Beheim's tactics changed; rather than attempting to trap Agenor in one of the pits, he decided that the best course would be to elude him for as long as possible and let the sun do its work. And since his wind was weakening, he thought that they would be better off hiding than continuing to run. Not far ahead he spotted a tangle of secondary growth, a miniature jungle that had sprung up around two fallen trees, their huge root systems clotted with dirt, looking dark and mysterious, like strange ritual wheels just unearthed from a ruin,

the closely packed nodules of root tissue and clumps
of wet soil contriving an uncanny resemblance to those
myriad assemblages of the gods that adorn Indian
mandalas. The dead trunks lay one across the other,
and were shrouded in thickets of viburnum, spirea,
and elderberry, tangled further with ivy and thorny
devil's club, as well as with a crush of dead boughs.
Having satisfied himself that Agenor was not within
sight, Beheim jumped up onto one of the trunks, hauling Alexandra after him, and they tightroped out to the
junction where the two trunks crossed. There they
gingerly lowered themselves into the massy vegeta-
tion, pushing through tiers of wet needles and stiff
webs of branches and ropy vines into the dank cavity
beneath, a cavity, Beheim realized gratefully, that
deepened into a mossy hollow and would allow them
to crawl farther back beneath the tangle should the
need arise. They sat on the clammy ground. Dampness soaked through Beheim's trousers almost immediately, but he felt secure. The foliage was so thick
overhead that only a few needling beams of gold light
penetrated to their hiding place. He watched as one
appeared to glide over Alexandra's white cheek and
center on a glorious green eye. The pupil shrank to a
pinprick, the perfectly plucked eyebrow arched as if in
inquiry. He squeezed her hand, drew a deep breath
and let it out slowly, feeling all his muscles relax.

Seconds later Agenor came pounding past, his
breath sounding fierce and guttural, like that of a wild
boar. Beheim heard branches shredding in the surrounding thickets, the footsteps receding, then silence.
Somewhere a bird twittered. Wind stirred the leaves
and needles above them, admitting a shower of light.
Beheim's flurried thoughts began to settle, and as they
did he recalled the location of the pits in reference to

the landmark of the fallen trees. One was very near, about a hundred feet away and almost directly up-slope. A bit late, he thought, but he was pleased to know his own location, more secure for knowing it.

He gave Alexandra's hand another squeeze, but held up his own hand to signal that she should maintain silence. Their eyes met again. There was, he thought, a softening of her regard, a new color added to her view of him, another gold fleck glinting in that mineral iris. His fingers strayed along her wrist. He felt her strong pulse, the beat of her century-long life, as powerful and persistent as the rhythm of an African drum. Her hand was pliant in his. Receptive. He intended to be cautious this time in interpreting that receptivity, but he was tempted to believe it signaled real promise for them. Love? He was not sure their inconstant natures would support such an easily bruised passion, though lust might well find a fine expression in their promise. But what he sought most of all was something rarer than love. Trust. Commitment. Honor. Possibly she had acted in her own immediate self-interest in striking down Agenor—she may have feared being discovered by him and realized that her chances of survival would improve with an ally. But she had not acted for those reasons alone, he was sure of that much. The infant recognition that had made them lovers must also have been at work. The intuition that he was someone in union with whom she could achieve her heart's desire, someone whose influence would refine and make more precise her comprehension of that desired object. It was something he himself felt about her, and though he was not yet willing to embrace the feeling with open arms, he had the notion that sitting there in that clammy little womb beneath the dead trees, the darkness was putting a seal on their union, marrying them in some final and ultimately efficient way.

There was a creaking from somewhere close by, as of a clandestine footstep on an unstable surface.

Beheim held perfectly still, his ears straining.

Wind riffled the pine boughs; the distant chatter of a jay.

The rich smell of the soil around them seemed suddenly to grow more pungent.

But there was no further creaking.

He was about to risk a whispered assurance to Alexandra when someone began tearing at the layers of foliage above them, ripping away great swatches of vines and dead boughs and chokecherry branches.

Agenor.

Beheim saw him through rents in the greenery, standing atop the pine trunk, his features contorted with rage, half his face covered in drying blood.

He dipped his shoulder and his hand punched through into the cavity, groping for them. He smashed his fist into the trunk, and as if the fist were an ax, it clove the dead wood, scattering chips everywhere.

Alexandra shrieked; Beheim caught her about the waist, dragged her deeper into the hollow. He toppled over backward onto cold wet ground, and as he scrambled up, his head scraped against pine bark, against the trunk upon which Agenor was standing. "Help me!" he said, squatting and putting his shoulder to the trunk. "Help me lift it! Hurry!"

Agenor was grunting, cursing, continuing to rip and batter away at the barrier of foliage, at the wood itself, chewing out a wider passage with blows from his powerful right hand. Whenever his fingers caught the wood, they tore deep gouges in it. The vibration of his blows seemed to shiver the world. Beheim's heart felt hot and swollen.

"Now!" he said as Alexandra settled beside him, her shoulder pressing against the trunk.

Together they heaved upward, first merely shifting the trunk, but then—the full force of their strength engaged—pushing it up at an extreme angle, tearing loose vines and shrubs, warm gold light flooding the hollow, half-blinding them, and Beheim heard a shrill cry as Agenor lost his balance and fell.

With a fierce effort, they shoved the trunk off to the side of the hollow and clambered up onto level ground.

Agenor was ensnared in a mass of uprooted shrubs, visible as an arm and a shock of white hair; the trunk had rolled onto his legs. But as they gained their footing, shielding their eyes against the light, they saw him sit straight up, draped in vines and crowned with leaves like an old forest king suddenly woken from a long sleep. He wrenched a leg free and kicked at the trunk with it, rolling it aside with what seemed the slightest of exertions. Then he came to his feet, trailing strands of vine, moss in his hair, which was an unruly mess, sticking up in places, stray locks falling onto his forehead. Leaves and needles fluttered down about him. His eyes gleamed, pure black at that distance like beetles lodged in the orbits, and he stared cold death at them, the image of savagery and madness. With a backhanded swipe, he snapped the slim trunk of a sapling ash beside him; then he stepped toward them, appearing in no particular hurry, certain of his victory.

Beheim and Alexandra backed clumsily up the slope away from him, and Beheim, remembering the pits, steered Alexandra on an appropriate course. When Agenor increased his pace, he pushed her

ahead of him and they ran, darting in and out among
the pines, until they reached a circular clearing centered by an immense prow-shaped boulder that
marked the site of one of the pits. Beheim took a stand
beside it, positioning them in a patch of sunlight so
that the pit lay between them and Agenor, who was
moving purposefully toward them now, smiling, doubtless thinking that they had given up. Alexandra made
to run again, but Beheim restrained her.

"Stay here," he said under his breath. "We'll never outrun him. Our best chance is here. Believe me!"

Doubt caused her stoic expression to flicker, but
after a second's hesitation she nodded and turned toward Agenor.

The old man had regained his composure. Though
he was still dressed in vines and a few leaves, he
seemed only dissheveled, a gentleman who had, perhaps, taken a bad fall from a horse.

"That's better," he said as he approached. "Better
by half. It will be quick, I promise you."

Beheim tried to keep his eyes off the matte of
branches and leaves and needles that disguised the
pit. Could any water be seen through the latticework
of foliage, shining in the sun? To draw Agenor's attention away from it, he said, "No one need die of this,
lord. What you did was only an aberration. I understand that. I have no desire to punish you."

"Perhaps you do not, my young friend," said
Agenor, coming forward at a steady pace. "But others
will. The Patriarch will learn of my guilt. If not from
you, then by some other means. I can never return to
Castle Banat, and if I am to escape, I must make certain that I have a good head start. I wish I could spare
you, but"—he shrugged—"I cannot."

A dozen more steps, Beheim thought, urging Agenor on with a wish as intense as a prayer.

"It's I whom you have reason to fear," Alexandra said, startling Beheim. "For I am not of your branch. Kill me if you must, but you have no reason to kill Michel. You are his master, you can control him."

"Can I?" said Agenor. "I wonder. It strikes me that he has changed greatly in this short time. Had he not, I doubt he would have inspired such allegiance from you."

Beheim let his eyes drift to the side, making sure of the position of the iron shutter, buried beneath dirt and needles.

Five steps, maybe six.

He felt almost buoyant with a mixture of fear and exhilaration. The burning thing in the sky seemed to have intensified its radiance, flooding the clearing with light so substantially golden it seemed to be solidifying around them, threatening to preserve the pines and the boulder and the three of them forever like insects in amber.

Then Agenor paused, and Beheim's heart sank.

"Come to me, my friend," Agenor said, extending his arms to him. "Let me embrace you."

There was nothing sardonic or gloating in his tone; on the contrary, he looked rather wistful standing there, head tipped to the side, brow knitted, the corners of his mouth turned down.

"I cannot, lord," Beheim said. "I am not so easy with this moment."

"Nor am I," Agenor said sadly. "But there is no point in prolonging it, is there?"

He came several steps closer, stopping with his feet mere inches from the verge of the pit. Beheim could scarcely hold himself back from leaping forward and pushing him in.

"Strange," said Agenor musingly, "how this has all come round."

"Think on this, Agenor," said Alexandra. "Consider it well. We might compose a formidable power, you and I. Surely there is another way, a way in which you could make use of the assistance of the Valeas, whom I now represent, to further your ends."

"An alliance?" said Agenor. "True, if it were an alliance I could count on, such would be most helpful. But where are my guarantees?"

"A guarantee is easily achieved," Alexandra said. "Were I to kill your man here, were I to report that my actions came as a result of having discovered it was he who killed the Golden, would not my complicity assure an alliance?"

Beheim gazed at Alexandra in astonishment, but she paid no notice to him, fixed upon Agenor, her lovely face drawn with intensity.

"Interesting," said Agenor.

"Everyone witnessed his behavior toward the Golden on the night of the ball," Alexandra said. "His guilt would come as no surprise. Evidence could be planted in his rooms. You could claim that you suspected him from the start, and that you hoped by appointing him to investigate the crime, you were giving him an opportunity to reveal himself."

Agenor gave a sharp laugh and, addressing Beheim, said, "Is she not the most astonishing creature?"

Beheim was speechless, gone beyond fear into a state of confusion so profound it seemed a new kind of pain.

"Yet the very quality that makes her so astonishing," Agenor went on, "the marvelous spiritual agility that enables her to give herself wholly to first one and then another ..." He shook his head in awe. "I'm afraid I would find you too distracting, so I will have to forgo the pleasure of an alliance, dear lady, and proceed with my initial design. But first"—he glanced down at the ground, then smiled at them—"first I must decide how to negotiate this ridiculous trap you've set. Now let me see. Shall I leap across, or shall I go round? What do you think?"

Beheim's acceptance of defeat must have shown on his face, for Agenor—staring at him—proceeded to laugh heartily and then said, "There, there, Michel! Surely your hopes for this pathetic device were not high."

"No, not very." Beheim looked down at his hands, finding them in this moment before extinction odd in the extreme, little fleshy grips that moved with such craftiness—it seemed impossible they should cease to exist. Then anger knotted in him again. "Tell me, lord," he said. "All your ideals, all those hopeful schemes and noble designs with which you so enthralled me, were they only part of a game? Were they whimsy, a trait of the character you chose to adopt?"

Agenor did not answer at once, but gazed off into the deep woods, down the slope toward a trickle of bright water showing like a strip of silver ribbon left hanging in the boughs of an old Christmas tree. The blood had finished drying on his face, much of it had been rubbed away, and with his white hair and the ravaged beauty of his face, he resembled an old actor who had botched his makeup with an overapplication of rouge.

"I believe not," he said, genuine pain in his voice. "I believe what I have done is stray from the path of my spirit rather than returning to it. A great deal of worth has come of the philosophy I have helped to breed. That we stand here in this terrible light is itself a proof. But how can I be certain that even these things are not the by-products of willfulness and folly?" He stared at Beheim, his mouth working. "Do you believe I love you, Michel? In my heart it seems I love you well, and no matter how this day ends, that will not change. But do you believe it?"

"Why is it important what I believe?" Beheim asked, trying not to stare at Agenor, for it appeared that something was happening to his face, that the skin was coarsening, reddening.

"In the centuries to come, perhaps I will forget you, my young friend," said Agenor, assuming his familiar lectoral mien. "Then again, perhaps I will not. The question of your importance has yet to be decided. However, why the question is important remains another issue. I would like your opinion on my mental state. I realize it's much to ask, considering the circumstances. But nevertheless I would—"

"Yes, it is rather much, isn't it?" Beheim snapped. "But never mind, I'll be happy to oblige. You see, it's an incredibly easy question to answer. It calls for no consideration whatsoever. Just look at yourself. In the space of a few seconds you've gone from mawkish regret to the fatuous maunderings of an old poof, and you haven't noticed a damned thing that's happening to you. You're mad! And not just a little bit mad. You're as mad as that foul thing who calls himself our Patriarch!"

He was afire with elation—something was definitely happening to Agenor. The skin was darkening in patches, reddening overall, the wrinkles growing more pronounced. The effects of Felipe's drug were finally wearing off. Finally! Beheim was surprised that Agenor had not yet felt any pain.

"And as to whether you were ever sane, well, I'll admit that all you ever said about how we need to change ..." He made a derisive noise. "You're living proof of that! But it doesn't matter if sanity once gripped you, because you'll never be sane again. You're finished as a rational being. You might as well go hang in the trees with the rest of the bats!"

Agenor listened to this outburst with an air of haughty bemusement, like an adult tolerating an annoying child, and when Beheim fell silent, he gave a sigh in which it seemed years of dust and patience were collected, and opened his mouth to deliver what Beheim might have expected to be a pompous denial or a grandiloquent expression of superiority; but then his eyes grew distended, he touched his cheek with a trembling hand as if to reassure himself of its solidity, and what issued from his mouth was no condescending prattle but a raspy scream that built in volume and pitch until it became as full-throated as that of a terrified woman.

Very like, Beheim thought with satisfaction, how the Golden must have screamed on the eastern turret that morning when Agenor tore her apart.

Chapter FIFTEEN

The old man clasped his hands to his face. Wisps of smoke trickled between his fingers, and the fingers themselves began to blister. He made a gargling noise, and then, flinging out his hands, revealed the scorched surface of his face, the forehead charring, the blisters on the cheeks burst and leaking a clear fluid. His hair, too, was burning, the pale, sunstruck flames leaping merrily. He dropped into a crouch, hopping about like a bedizened dwarf, trying to pull his jacket up over his head, all the while emitting a quavery cry. The backs of his hands were crisping, the blackened skin cracking to reveal an angry redness beneath, and Beheim, without thinking why he acted, leaped across the pit and pushed him in.

As Agenor's body broke through the mat of branches and hit the water with a heavy splash, there was a great venting of steam, and when he surfaced, still burning, he groped wildly for the branches that had fallen in with him, attempting to arrange them like a thatch over his head. Beheim searched in the dirt for the iron edge of the camouflaged shutter, gripped it, and heaved it toward the pit, wrangling it sideways.

"What are you doing?" Alexandra shrilled, clutching at him. "Let him burn! He would have killed us! Burn him!"

But he broke free of her and maneuvered the shutter until it covered the imprisoning water and its agonized captive.

Alexandra grabbed at the shutter, trying to remove it from the pit, and Beheim shoved her away. She shrieked, enraged, and came to him, clawing at his face. Again he knocked her away. He spotted a pine branch lying beside the pit, one that had broken, so that its end was sharp and pointed, he picked it up, and as Alexandra ran at him a second time, he slapped her, driving her against the boulder. Before she could gather herself, he flung himself atop her, bending her backward over the boulder; he tore the front of her dress and her lace undergarment, fitted the sharp end of the pine branch to the inner side of her left breast and pushed until bright blood showed against the freckly white skin. She stiffened, ceased her struggles. Her eyes were wheels of reflected light, like frozen eddies in a green river. He did not look away, but met her dazzling stare with the hot press of his anger.

"I should kill you," he said. "I don't know why I'm even hesitating."

"You're as mad as Agenor! I've done nothing to deserve—"

"You were going to betray me!"

"And first I tried to trade my life for yours. Does it make sense that I would do that and then betray you? No sense at all. Unless, of course, I was trying to distract Agenor in both instances, to delay his attack."

He looked at her doubtfully. "You were most convincing."

"I'm convincing in everything I do. Especially in those things I do because of conviction."

"Even this . . . now?"

She made a clicking noise with her tongue and teeth. "Why don't you stop it? You're not going to kill me."

"I'm not, eh?"

"No."

"And why, pray, will I be merciful?"

"Because you want me."

He thought at first that she was mocking him, though there had been nothing of mockery in her tone. Her gaze was frank, open, and he had the impression that she was inviting him to intimacy. He tried a laugh, but it rang false even to his own ears. "If I release you," he said, "then you must leave Agenor to me. His fate will be decided by the Patriarch."

"That 'foul thing,' you mean?"

Beheim ignored this. "Will you swear not to harm him?"

"I've no wish to harm him now. I was overexcited. As to his fate, it is already decided. He will burn. Whether here or on the castle heights, it makes no difference to the Patriarch."

"Swear."

"As you wish." A shrug. "I swear he will be safe from me."

He eased up his pressure on the branch, tossed it aside; then he lifted his weight from her.

"You've forgotten something," she said, still reclining half atop the boulder.

"Have I?"

"This." She pointed to the bead of blood welling

from the side of her breast, a ruby droplet. "You've bled me. Now you must drink or break with tradition."

Beheim watched the droplet slide down her rib cage and onto her belly, leaving a slick track; another was forming in its place. The sight was powerfully arousing.

"I think," he said awkwardly, "I think this falls outside the bounds of tradition as it is defined."

"No matter," she said. "*I* want you to drink."

She lifted her arms, let them fall back behind her head, and smiled. Her tousled hair, almost red in the sunlight, made the perfect frame for her face. He could not keep his eyes from her pretty breasts. Warmth came to his face.

"This is ridiculous," he said. "Now's not the time."

"Pleasure's never ridiculous. It's serious business. And this now, this is particularly serious."

"I don't understand."

She said nothing for what seemed a very long time. Something broke through the underbrush nearby, made a hurried rustling in the leaves. The light dimmed, then brightened. There was a weighty feeling to the stillness, as if, Beheim thought, a god had turned his eyes their way. That weightiness nourished him. He felt almost at peace with all the trouble of the day. The pines were strange, enormous foot soldiers in shaggy, dark green coats, and the light was in that instant mild as honey, and the rustles in the woods were spirits and the boulder was an altar rock.

"Drink," Alexandra said, her voice so soft it was barely distinguishable from a sudden rush of wind through the boughs. "To please me. To please yourself. Drink."

Her breasts tasted of sweat and perfume, and her blood was a strong flavor, not complex, as he had presumed, but simple and direct. It warmed him, it renewed his strength, but did not intoxicate except in the way of all blood. After he had taken the new droplet from her breast, licked the flesh clean, he rested his head there where he had drunk. Her fingers played in his hair. The feeling, too, was simple and direct, easy on the heart. He wanted more of it.

"A kiss," she said in a lazy voice, tugging at him, trying to pull his face up to hers. "Give me a kiss. Just one."

Her lips parted for his tongue, her hands traced delicate, teasing patterns on his chest; her legs parted, letting his member push against the yielding heated place between them. He could feel how it would be with her again. Like stirring himself in hot resin, like falling through the sun into wind and silence, and sailing for a while in some white palace of the mind through which a sea of fevers flowed, and then after a timeless time, the time accumulating like a crowd around a street accident, a tension waiting to be dispersed, emerging from it as he emerged then from that one kiss, galvanized, one of those sensational moments when you step out from the curling tendrils of a Paris fog into a lambent reality of lights and music and wild laughter, when you snap out of the waking nightmare that has held you tossing and turning for decades, and you glance up from a desk cluttered with the reports of a dozen grisly unsolved murders, or from a losing game of chess, or from the still-breathing body of a young woman from which you have just siphoned several unbearably sweet mouthfuls of needed blood, and there it all is, the whole born world summed up in a single glimpse, shining and clear, a lightning-bolt clarity, more perfect an expression of what is than any painting in the Louvre could ever be,

everything looking so fresh and strange in its brightness that you might be a visitor just dropped in from
Atlantis or Mu or some mythic world of the ether, and
you understand once and for all that the truth you
have been searching for your entire life is no Mystery,
it is like every truth a simple brightness that will support no interpretation, no analysis, that is only itself,
and it might come to you in the guise of a pretty girl
in a checkered apron setting tables in front of the Café
Japonais just off the Bois de Bologne, it might reveal
itself to you in an arrangement of pears and cheese on
a plate in a hotel in Cannes; it might stream up at you
from the self-inflicted wounds of a dead boy who
painted azure wings around his eyes and spent each
morning posing naked in a mirror and pretending he
was a famous courtesan; it might announce itself in the
taste of a stale sandwich eaten late at night; it might
chill you in a dash of cold rain; it might terrify you in
the form of a rat darting from an alley under your foot;
it might arise like steam from the impassioned confession of a plump, tearful housewife stranded with you
in a train station who shows you the silver angel pin
given her as a farewell present by her lover, a vaca-
tioning schoolteacher who could not commit himself to
any woman because of the secret grief he carried that
annihilated his every happiness with guilt; it might be
anything, anywhere, but for now it glided from the
process of a kiss, and when you looked up this time,
you saw the face of the kissed woman still rapt from
the pressure of your lips, slivers of green irises showing beneath her lids, like beautiful gemmy green coins
placed on her eyes, her red lips still parted, dizzy and
dying from the truth of her own moment, and the
ranked pines bending all to one side in a strong gust
of wind, shaking their shaggy pelts, then straightening,

all with a slow, ponderous motion like a chorus line of dancing bears, and the puddled sunlight ebbing and flowing with their movement, and the trillion brown needles making infinite hexagrams in their decay, and lastly, mostly, chiefly, the ugly centerpiece of all this excellent clarity and serenity, a scarred iron shutter half-covered with dirt, and beneath it, up to its neck in cold water, in the damp, dust-thronged air, a living being, its blackened head like a bizarre seed from which the darkness of its prison is seeping, its breath wheezing, its mind empty of everything but pain, waiting, no longer hoping, only waiting for your moment to end, for you to remember what had happened and say, as Beheim said then, "I don't know what to do with him."

Alexandra sat up; she started tying the torn strips of her blouse together so that the material covered her breasts; her long hair fell like a veil over her face. "As far as the Patriarch is concerned," she said, "you may wait until dark and return him to the castle if you wish. Or you may end his life here and now. It's your choice."

"My choice." Beheim let the words drift away without resolution. He wanted someone to take this business off his hands, he had not bargained on being an executioner. Then, struck by an inconsistency, he looked over at Alexandra, who was examining her repairs with displeasure. "How can you know what the Patriarch requires?"

"He instructed me as to his requirements."

"But the fact that Agenor is the murderer . . . He can't have known. He might consider tempering his judgment."

"No, he would not." She put up a hand to forestall another question. "He is with me in some fashion.

How this is done, I do not know. But he is with me. He hears what I hear, he makes his wishes clear."

"Does he speak to you?" Beheim asked, his curiosity piqued. "Do you hear his voice in your mind?"

"It's not like that. I simply know his will." She spread her hands in a gesture of helplessness. "I can give you no clearer explanation."

Something else occurred to Beheim. "Was the Patriarch with you a moment ago?"

"That's difficult to say. Perhaps. I assume so."

"Then perhaps I should assume that was his wish, too. What you did."

"What *we* did," she said, a frown line etched in her brow. "No, it was my wish. Our wish."

The pines encircling the clearing shivered; the circle of light in their midst fluttered at the edges, making Beheim think of a peculiar glowing, agitated creature he had seen once through a microscope at the Sorbonne.

"You mustn't doubt everything," Alexandra said.

A hollow, muffled voice sounded from beneath the shutter, its tone one of complaint.

Beheim paid it only passing attention; he turned toward the castle, ragged slants of its dark gray matter visible through the branches. "Oh?"

She came up behind him, touched his waist. "You should take some things at face value. If I were your enemy, you would not have survived our kiss."

Agenor's voice again, louder, unintelligible.

"As I recall," Beheim said, "it was I who held the upper hand."

"You're strong for one so new," she said. "And you've grown stronger for all that has happened. Strength is to a degree a question of the will, and your will has matured a great deal during the past day and night. But I am stronger than you." A pause. "Shall I prove it?"

"No."

A pounding on the iron shutter preceded a slight dimming of the sun.

"Why . . ." he began; then said, "Never mind."

"Why do I fancy you? Is that what you want to know?" She moved away from him, stepping out toward the center of the clearing, and when she spoke again, there was an edge to her voice. "I believe that Agenor was right about you. Eventually you're going to be quite a powerful figure. That attracts me."

"Politics, eh? That's all it is?"

"You're the one asking difficult questions. Don't expect honeyed answers. Those I've already given you. If you're too deaf to have heard them, too blind to see what I am offering, it'll do no good for me to try to enlighten you further."

They stared defiantly at one another while Agenor's pounding grew louder and more sustained.

If he could not trust her, he thought, if he could not trust himself, what was the use in going on? Sooner or later he would have to put his faith in someone, risk everything, and she was the only one he had ever trusted, even for a moment. Agenor he had feared, revered, imitated. But never trusted. He stepped toward her, ready to start over, but she backed away.

"Not so fast," she said flatly. "It takes me a while."

"Look, I'm sorry, I . . ."

"No apologies," she said; she pushed the fall of her hair back behind her ears. "I don't need your apology. I understand how it is with you. Don't worry. Everything will be fine. It just takes me a while to make this kind of accommodation."

She turned away from him, gazing off into the woods.

Feeling half-rejected, Beheim discovered, was no more pleasant than straightforward rejection. The pounding on the shutter began to grate on his nerves, and finally he said, "Oh, hell! What do you want?" and heaved at the shutter so that a few inches of the water beneath were exposed. He heard a furious splashing— Agenor retreating to the far end of the pit—and was ashamed for having gotten angry.

"What is it?" he asked, unable to rid his voice of annoyance.

A feeble splash, a hoarse exhalation.

"Are you in pain?" Beheim asked, dropping to his knees.

"Yes," Agenor said. "But the darkness is healing."

The silence that followed seemed to be flowing up from the blackness of the pit, from the shadowy fathom beneath the shining strip of water.

Beheim felt unequal to the moment. "What shall I do?" he asked. "I can see nothing for you at the end of this but death."

A long pause, then a sloshing sound; as if Agenor were moving his arms in the water.

Beheim said, "Shall I take you back to the castle? After dark, I mean."

"After dark?"

Was there a hopeful note in Agenor's voice?

"In that instance I would, of course, send to the castle for an escort," said Beheim.

"Of course." Another pause. "And is there an alternative?"

"If returning to the castle is not to your liking, then we would . . . finish things here. Lady Alexandra is serving as the Patriarch's agent. She would witness all you might tell us."

"I see." More stirring and sloshing.

Beheim pictured Agenor making idle waves in the darkness, mulling things over.

"Michel," said Agenor, "will you come down to me. I would see you again before"—he let out a sodden chuckle—"before we finish things."

"No, lord, I will not."

"I understand, my boy. I understand completely."

"I'm sorry."

"Not at all. It was a foolish request."

There was a silence; then, to Beheim's astonishment, laughter came from the pit—slow, sly, private laughter such as might have been sounded by a man alone in his study, delighted by a secret joke. It unnerved him to hear it.

"What if I've been wrong?" said Agenor, and laughed again. "What if I have been wrong?"

"Lord?"

"You will put me to the question, Michel, will you not?"

"If you wish."

"I'm certain you know what questions to ask."

"I do."

"Then I don't suppose there's any reason to delay things," Agenor said; after the passage of a few seconds, he added, "I'm getting cold."

Beheim could find no words of comfort. There was a heaviness in his chest such as one feels prior to the onset of tears, but his eyes were dry, and he did not believe he would shed many tears for Agenor. He no longer was secure in his conception of the man; those things he thought he had known about him had all proved flimsy and untrustworthy.

Then there was the Golden.

Despite the permissiveness and violence of his new life, he was still enough of a man—a policeman, at any rate—to be revolted by this particular crime, to harbor a moral distaste for the incredible vulgarity of its license.

Yet he was not without emotion where Agenor was concerned. Some of his memories of the old man were proof against all that had happened; he could not believe that the moments they represented were every one of them empty, worthless, bereft of the good truths they had seemed at the time to embody.

Alexandra's hand fell to his shoulder, giving him a start. The weight consoled him, and he put his own hand over hers.

"Do you know," said Agenor with a trace of his old air of professorial good nature, "that you two will be the first of our Family ever to witness an Illumination? Previously those who oversaw the ritual were forced to stand in a dark place where they could hear the answers to their questions. But you . . . you will see everything. It's quite spectacular. At least so I've heard from servants who've borne witness."

A tremor in his voice belied the casual tenor of his words.

"Quite an opportunity," Agenor murmured. "You must be sure to . . ." The sentence ended in an exhausted sigh; apparently he had no more energy for self-delusion.

"Let this be a lesson to you, my friend," he said. This followed by a harsh noise—laughter or sob, Beheim could not be sure. Then in a firmer tone, as if he had recalled that he was speaking to a wider audience: "A lesson to you all. We need no great enemies, no bloody men with stakes and torches, so long as we have ourselves. So long as we have the strength to claw at our own hearts."

He stirred about for several seconds. The water at Beheim's end of the pit rippled and slapped against the bank of black soil.

"You must put the questions forcefully," Agenor said. "Shout them if necessary. I will be in great pain, and you will have to make me hear you. Once I do, I will fasten onto them as though they were ropes that might haul me up from the fire. That is how I've heard it proceeds. Felipe held the view that the questioning triggered some mental process, possibly one akin to those exercised by Hindu yogis, that made the pain more tolerable. An alteration of the brain chemistry, perhaps. I find myself hoping that his opinion was accurate."

Beheim, moved by a feeling of uneasiness, a product—he assumed—of his conflicting tempers, was tempted to heave the iron shutter aside and have done with it.

"One envies the Christians at moments like these," Agenor said. "To yearn toward heaven with one's dying breath, to strain for a glimpse of whiteness, for the perfumed fantasy of a loving god. Ignorance is a powerful consolation. It is no solace to know that the fall is endless. Ah, well!" He splashed about, muttering something that Beheim failed to catch. "Michel, I cannot ask that you think well of me, but I hope in the days to come you will remember the things I have tried to impress upon you and take them to heart. They may have been spoken by a fool, but there is nevertheless some virtue in the words."

"I will remember," Beheim said solemnly.

"Then"—another sigh, more, it seemed, a clearing

of the lungs, a preparation for the painful trial ahead, than an expression of despair—"then I am ready."

Beheim came up into a squat, gripping the edge of the shutter; his muscles bunched, but he could not bring himself to act.

Alexandra bent to his ear, whispered, "You are being cruel, not kind. Don't make him wait."

He nodded, he closed his eyes, he tightened his grip.

Her lips brushed his temple. "Do it now."

With a shout that seemed to release a fierce heat trapped inside him, Beheim flipped the shutter off to the side of the pit, coming to his feet as he did. He had a glimpse of Agenor in a corner of the pit, his scorched head, his fingers grasping the top of the pit, his heels dug into the soil just above the water level, bunched up, coiled like a man about to spring.

And spring he did.

Screaming, he threw himself at Beheim, striking him with his shoulder at the knees, knocking him to the ground. Beheim twisted as he fell, landing heavily on his side. He tried to roll away, but Agenor was on him, battering at his head with burning hands, then coming astraddle of him, grabbing him by the neck, squeezing. Framed incongruously by blue sky and pine boughs, the cracked and blackened oval of his face was nightmarish: the lips crusted with charred tissue, here and there a bloody split, like the rind of some vile fruit bursting with poisonous ripeness; nose reduced to flaps of charcoaled cartilage that flapped horribly with the passage of his breath; the brow so ravaged that through the scorched crackling skin could be seen thin sections of white bone. The teeth, too, were white, revealed in a grimace or a smile, but the gums were blistered and bleeding. Only the eyes were clear, and they were the eyes of a madman, bulging and wild and rimmed with red, making it appear as if someone hale were peering through a mask of hideous deformity. Beheim could not see the flames that were consuming Agenor against the bright sky, but the air around him rippled with heat, and he felt the skin of his neck blistering beneath the old man's hands. He thrashed about, trying to unseat him, but Agenor's strength was irresistible. The life was being choked from him. His field of vision was reddening, black wings trembling at the edges, odd tangles of opaque cells drifting, vanishing, the air going dark as if it, too, were being scorched.

Then, out of the corner of his eye, he saw Alexandra rush forward and jab at Agenor with a stick. The pine branch with the sharp end, the same with which he had threatened her. She slammed it into the side of Agenor's neck, and it pierced skin, muscle, and cartilage, penetrating deep with a horrid crunching noise, lodging there like a crudely feathered arrow. For a split second Beheim did not think it had had any effect, but then Agenor, without a cry, went sliding out of sight, his weight suddenly removed from Beheim's chest, the hands slipping from his neck. Gasping, coughing, Beheim crawled a few feet away. Alexandra caught his arm, helped him stand. He spun about, spotted Agenor staggering up, using the boulder for balance and tugging at the pine branch piercing his neck, his movements stunned and slow, like those of a sick animal. Beheim felt no pity for him now, only rage and the desire to inflict pain. He glanced about the clearing. Not far to his right was a pine tree whose lowermost branch was seven or eight feet long and had a forked end. He went over to it and, using the strength of his rage, wrenched at it, pulled, twisted it

free. Holding it like a spear, he crossed the clearing
to Agenor, and as the old man turned, still tugging at
the sharp stick, Beheim jammed the forked end of the
branch against his neck and pushed him back onto the
boulder, pinning him there as one might pin a serpent.
Agenor let out a sibilant cry and tried to wriggle free,
but Alexandra joined Beheim, helped him hold the
branch in place, and though Agenor's struggles grew
frantic, he could not escape. The pine needles close to
his face were burning; his clothes were burning, his
flesh, all enveloped in a pale, rippling envelope of
flame, but the process of immolation was slower than
would have been the case with normal flesh, the ero-
sion of meat and sinew from bone more gradual, and
thus, Beheim supposed, the pain was more brightly
particular and involving. Agenor's screams seemed evidence of that, going high, higher, until there was
nothing human about them and they seemed the out-
cries of a bird or the squeals of a rat. Slabs of shiny
black char split away from his cheek, from the pierced
side of his neck. A large notch had been eaten away
from his lower lip, the gum burned through, and the
bone beneath going brown. His shoe leather had been
seared to his feet, so that he appeared to be wearing
special footgear with separate toe sheaths and the
laces embedded in glazed, dark red skin.

"I have a question for you, Lord Agenor!" Beheim
shouted, ramming the forked end more tightly against
the old man's throat. "Do you hear?"

There was a slight diminution of the old man's
struggles.

"Listen to me! For the Family has need of your
witness! Our enemies beset us! We are sorely pressed!
What shall we do? Shall we remain in our old fast-

nesses, or shall we go into the East and make a new home there?"

Agenor ceased his struggling, shaking with the processes of the flames, his face now a black ruin, shattered textures and planes of carbonized tissue, some bits shining like fresh fractures of anthracite, others bearing traces of color from some baked fluid or another, some yield of vein or gristle. His eyes were gone, boiled away beneath hardened black crescents. The branch piercing his neck was aflame, as was the forked branch that held him.

And yet he spoke.

The first words were hopelessly garbled. Beheim, astounded, ordered him to repeat them.

"Soo . . . ooo," Agenor said, growling the syllables; he repeated them several times, then succeeded in pronouncing an entire word, sounding each syllable separately. "Su . . . ma . . . rin . . . da. A town . . . on the river Maha . . ." The end of that word, a name, was degraded by his torn throat into a guttural snarl; but after a pause he said, "Mahakam. You must . . . upriver. Six days." Smoke trickled from his mouth; a dark clot of blood welled forth and sizzled on his chin. After that he spoke with less effort and distortion. "Six days . . . by boat. Then three days' walk. Go south and east. To a hill. A high . . . hill. Mahogany trees. A stand of mahogany among . . . lesser trees. Facing a saddle . . . a saddleback mountain. Across a valley."

"Where is this place?" Alexandra asked, but so softly that Beheim was forced to repeat the question.

"Borneo," came the response.

"What then?" Beheim shouted. "What will happen?"

"Build there," Agenor rasped. "Build deep. Then there is peace for a thousand years."

Another gout of blood, thick as stew, spilled from his mouth and was instantly transformed into smoke and a sticky residue.

"What do you mean, 'build deep'?"

"A house... escape tunnels beneath. Rooms. Armories. Store ... houses. If trouble comes ... you will need ... these things."

"And Europe? What of the Family in Europe?"

From Agenor's tormented throat issued a terrible, hoarse, declining wail that seemed to Beheim an answer on its own. "A hundred years. Banat in ruins." He said more, a broken cascade of gravelly syllables, but it was incomprehensible.

"Ask him whether we—" Alexandra began, but Beheim cut in, saying, "Let him die."

"He is dead already," she said. "Use him. Ask him the question you must ask so that when we leave this place, we do so secure in our hearts as to the future the two of us must face."

Her expression was tense and worried; the ends of her hair lifted from her shoulders. Reflected fire danced in her eyes.

He nodded. "As you wish." He turned to Agenor, a charred mummy pinned by a black two-fingered hand, and said, "What of Alexandra and me? What lies ahead for us? What should we do?"

"Su ... marin ... da."

"Are you saying we must go there?"

"Your only hope," Agenor said. "There is danger everywhere. Do not linger at the castle. Go ... into the East. To Sumarinda."

"Now?" asked Beheim, incredulous.

"Now," said Agenor, making the word into a whispery howl. "You will have your triumph. Your day. Do not hes ... hesitate. Go now."

Beheim tossed the forked branch into the woods and stepped away, drawing Alexandra with him, as Agenor pitched onto his side and lay at the verge of the pit. One of his legs, utterly carbonized, had snapped, and he clawed at the dirt, trying to pull himself along, making very little progress. Smoke leaked from the splits in his skin. The needles upon which he was lying burst into flame.

"There's more to ask!" Alexandra said, clutching at Beheim as he moved away from the pit, searching for a stake with which to finish Agenor.

"What?" he said. "How long will we live? Will we win at love? I doubt he could tell us much. He only offers possibilities. Let's kill him and get on with supplying our own answers. It seems we have a great deal to talk about."

There was a splash; they glanced back to find that Agenor had fallen into the pit. A veil of steam was rising from the water, obscuring the trees behind it. Agenor was floating, half-submerged, become a figure of almost unrelieved black, his skin crispy and bubbled and ridged, his arms beating ineffectually. An ugly black one-legged doll nearly the size of a man. Thin smoke was lifting from him, the inner meat still burning. Bubbling noises came from his lipless scar of a mouth.

"Damn!" said Beheim, realizing that he would have to go down into the water in order to finish him, and not at all sure that he wanted to do that.

Agenor was spinning slowly, as if taken by an idle current, and this bewildered Beheim, seeming contrary to physical laws.

Then something happened still more contrary to the expected.

The water immediately surrounding Agenor be-

gan to gleam—he might have been leaking some spectacular silver fluid—forming an outline around his
body, and from the splits in his skin, a fine radiance
began to shine forth, a pale silvery effusion that grew
brighter and brighter, the separate beams growing
distinct in the gloom of the pit, until it appeared
that a hellish core had been exposed deep within that
charred shell. The water lapped with increasing force
at the walls of the pit, slopping higher, bringing down
clods of dirt. The light waxed more brilliant yet. It
looked as if stars were being born in the moribund
flesh, and soon the flesh started to flake away, in peels,
in slices, as if Agenor were being filleted. Not long
thereafter the organs and intestines became visible,
steeped in light, packed neatly in their cavities, all the
intimate horrors of an ordinary life. The light inspired
them to a kind of excellent decay; they lost shape,
pulped, their substance flowed into a greenish sludge
that mingled with the water, and at last the skeleton
was left enveloped in a lozenge of shadow, rather like
the shadow of a coffin. No common rack of bones,
this—a construct of silvery wires set with nine points
of incandescent brilliance, resembling the map of a
constellation that one might find in a guide to the
heavens, though the quadrant of the sky in which this
constellation ruled was unknown to Beheim.

The water seethed and lashed about, and the
bones of the skeleton began to drift apart, as if the last
of the cartilage were dissolving, the joints losing their
hold, making of it a silver puzzle of stars and bones
that whirled about in the troubled water, moving to its
own rhythms, its own turbulence, and then even these
fragments experienced a dissolution, the silvery stuff
of their essence blurring and conjoining with the less
lambent fluid of the water, until at the last there was

a tossing pewter-colored sea within the pit, like an element of a miniature storm.

Beheim thought it was over, but then a bassy humming vibration issued from the pit, trembling the ground beneath his feet. Alarmed, he yanked Alexandra back from the edge and they moved timorously upslope toward the shelter of the pines. The humming grew louder, its dark note seeming to dim the sun, to spread new depths of shadow from the boughs that overhung the clearing, and with an explosiveness like that of a volcano breaching the earth, the force of it knocking Beheim and Alexandra onto their backs, whatever remained in the pit flew upward in a beam of gleaming stuff . . . not fluid, not solid, but having the qualities of both, a wide flood of Agenor's essential things streaming into the heavens, becoming paler and paler against the light, and as the humming died, contriving a curious shape in the upper reaches of the sky, a vague shadowy figure, an emblem of some sort—or so Beheim thought of it—a sigil, the imprint of some cryptic meaning too intricate to hold in the mind except as symbol, very like the symbol he recalled seeing in his mind's eye upon hearing the song of his blood, and he wondered now if the grand design that particular shape had seemed to signify had only been the promise of this terrible death. It hung motionless for several seconds, maintaining its smoky form against the tuggings of the wind, and then, with no further ado, it faded utterly from the earth.

Chapter SIXTEEN

They had expected to find nothing in the pit, but when they looked, they discovered that the dirt walls were flecked with bits of tissue, nuggets of bone, sticky lumps that might have been congealed blood, and this caused them to wonder even more at what they had witnessed, to doubt its reality, though to what degree they should doubt it was yet another problematic matter; it also caused them to shy away from each other for a time—to have seen what they had made them painfully aware of their natures, and the idea that they each had such a death inside them, such a pyrotechnic and unwholesome potential, did nothing to encourage intimacy. Beheim was particularly unsettled by the experience. He kept staring at his hands and expecting to see silver bones and phosphorescent stars, wondering what more he would come to learn about this unfathomable life within him, and when he turned his eyes to Alexandra, instead of finding consolation in her beauty, he thought of what Agenor must have seen, his very mind on fire, staring out through the flesh of his tormentors into a spiraling future of jungle rivers and small brown men and steamy tropical towns, and how

283

he must have felt knowing that his vision, the key, perhaps, to their eternities, was the agonizing engine of his oblivion.

They idled about for quite some time, speaking infrequently, and as the sun dropped below the pine tops—four o'clock or a little later, Beheim reckoned—they sat down facing one another beneath a tall pine at the edge of the woods, a few hundred yards from the castle walls. A wind lifted the boughs, and that wind was the only sound, a silky rush that infused his agitated thought with a cool trickle of calmness.

"There's no reason we have to go back at all," Alexandra said. "We've enough of the drug to last a good while. I have Felipe's journal. There'll be no difficulty in making more."

"What of the Patriarch?" he asked.

"It's not him we have to fear. He may well have forgotten about us by now. For the time being, anyway. It's the Agenors and the Valeas. Roland's friends. And Felipe's. They won't act at once. Chances are they won't find out what's happened until everyone's gone home. But sooner or later they'll decide to do something."

"Then you're right," he said. "We shouldn't go back."

She made a delicate noise, one he took to signal uncertainty.

"What's wrong?"

"Nothing," she said. "Everything. I don't know." She picked up a pine needle, poked it against the back of her hand, snapping it. "I'm just not sure about any of this."

"About me?"

"You, yes. And me. And everything else."

"Do you doubt the credibility of Agenor's Illumination?"

"I'd give anything to be able to deny its credibility. But how can I? The fact is, I understand it all too well."

"What do you mean?"

Alexandra shifted, sat cross-legged, smoothed her skirt down over her legs. "We're to go to this place halfway round the world, this . . . What was the name?"

"Sumarinda."

"Yes, Sumarinda. And we're to proceed into the jungle, build there, make a life there. Protected. Distant from everything."

"So it appears."

"Can you imagine anyone else you've met in the Family picking up and going off to Borneo? Even if they knew it was because of knowledge gained during an Illumination, knowledge that would save them?"

He considered this. "A handful, perhaps."

"But we *have* to go," she said. "And we'll be alone. Eventually others may come. Perhaps others yet will come hunting us. But we'll be alone for a long time. Most of the Family will never leave the old ground. They'd rather die . . . and they will."

"You're frightened of being isolated?"

"Aren't you?"

"It's different for me. I've never felt secure within the Family. I've always had a feeling of isolation."

For a few seconds she concentrated on tracing a design in the dirt with her forefinger, then rubbing it out. "You know," she said, "if he had worked it all out in advance, Agenor couldn't have engineered a better result. This is the best he could hope for—to seed a new colony."

"Perhaps that's exactly what he did."

"Can you believe that, having gone through what we just have?"

"The old bastard was lucky, I suppose. But you never know. Perhaps he merely weakened at the end. It might be that his scheme had gained too much momentum for any personal failure to affect it. At any rate, you're right. He achieved everything he ever wanted. He succeeded in becoming a martyr, and his dream came true."

"It might come true," she said. "Then again, it might not."

She lowered her head, and a slant of sunlight fell across her hair, bringing up the reddish highlights. He studied the long white curve of her neck, how it glided up to form her chin, down to the slope of her breast. There was, he thought, no end to that line. It was all through her, a single gliding, graceful premise. It would be easy to forget everything else except that line. And that, he realized, was as close as he would come this day to a decision. He pushed up to his feet, dusted off his trousers.

"Let's take a walk, shall we?"

She glanced up at him, weary looking around the eyes. "Where?"

"Up the Mahakam River, eventually." He extended a hand. "To the village down in the valley for starters. I can't see any reason to go back, can you?"

She lowered her head again. "It's too dangerous."

"Then what's the point in waiting here any longer? As I recall, the evening coach passes through the village shortly before midnight. We can stop at an inn and wash up. We'll sleep on the coach. Have you fed recently?"

She nodded.

"Good," he said. "I'd prefer not to risk anything in the village. Now come along."

He helped her up, and after Alexandra had retrieved her shawl and draped it so as to hide the damage done to her blouse, they started off down the slope, following the stream that cut across the lower portion of the hill. When they reached a notch between hills, they left the stream and headed off along a dusty coach road that wound through a birch forest. Twilight was settling, and the white trunks gleamed pale as ghosts in the accumulating dark. Now and then they passed a cottage with whitewashed walls and a neatly thatched roof and a lantern glowing orange in the window. Beheim felt disconnected from the scene. Like a monster prowling the streets of a sleeping city. Now that he knew who he was, it was strange to walk among men. It seemed he had been a long time absent from them. Yet he also felt that his disconnection was unimportant, irrelevant, and that other, more radical recognitions would come to overwhelm it.

"Do you have any money?" Alexandra asked as they approached the outskirts of the village; a church steeple was standing up above the trees, its bell tower almost touching the evening star, like a benediction upon the peace and sweetness of the place.

"Enough for the moment," he said. "Money won't be a problem. We can always get money."

"I know," she said. "I just wondered if we'd have to get some now."

She stopped walking and stood gazing off into the village. Snatches of music came on the wind, and then, behind them, they heard the creaks and clopping of a horse-drawn cart.

"What is it?" he asked.

"Mystery," she said.

He looked toward the cozy houses nestled in among the trees, the pretty lights and proven shadows, the quick, uncertain lives, and he had a flaring up of a wild, plunderous feeling. Yet the feeling did not stay, did not nourish, and when it had fled, the sight of the town seemed for a moment as fabulous and impossible to interpret as had that last fleeting glimpse of Agenor's being, dissolving against an empty sky.

The cart was lurching nearer, rattling along. Beheim saw the crooked black silhouette of the driver raised above the plodding bulk of a dark horse.

"I don't know what any of it's going to be like anymore," Alexandra said. "I can't imagine why it should be different, but I . . ." As she turned to Beheim a glint of reflected light streaked her left eye like a meteor crossing a tiny sky. "I know it will be."

The driver of the cart grunted a command to his horse and pulled up beside them. He was an old man, older than Agenor and far more frail, with a rag tied around his head, muffling his ears, and fingerless gloves, and a frayed woolen coat. "Can I offer you a ride into town?" he asked. "It's a bumpy patch ahead. Be hard walking for the lady."

Beheim, hearing the flabby rhythm of the driver's heart, felt a twinge of disgust, a desire to leap aboard the cart and end his sour little life. But he only said, "Thank you, no." Then, with a forced smile, not wanting to become a story told at an inn about the unfriendly stranger and his tall, silent woman, he added, "We're going a lot farther than that, so we might as well get used to walking."

The driver sucked on a tooth, spat. "So are we all," he said with bad grace. "Doesn't mean you can't be a gentleman and give the lady here a bit of a rest."

He gave the reins a twitch, starting the horse off again into its plodding gait.

Alexandra laughed. "Serves you right for trying to be one of the country folk."

"I hope you're better at it than I," he said. "Because in a few minutes we're going to be sitting down to supper with them."

"Oh, I'll be in my element." She danced off a ways along the road. "I just shows 'em a few fancy steps, I whispers in their ears, and next you know, they're begging to be my footstool."

He laughed, too, following her. "I'll wager they're aiming a bit higher than your feet for their reward."

She pretended to aim a slap at him. "You've a dirty mouth for such a fine gentleman!"

He caught her arm, pulled her close, and for a few seconds they went waltzing along the road, teasing one another, their voices happy; but once they disengaged, their mood dimmed.

"It's different already," she said as they stood with their arms about one another. "It's as if I've . . ." She seemed to be searching for the right words. "As if I've shed a skin. That's it, that's what it's like. It's all so fresh. The smells, the colors. Everything. It's as if I've shed an old skin, and the new skin is more sensitive, but not as strong. Don't you feel it? You must."

He told her yes, he felt much the same. But that was a lie to comfort her. All he truly felt was the absence of an oppressive weight, the freedom of being his own master again after two years of hallucinatory servitude. Changed as he was, new as he was, the world he saw before him was the known world, the familiar, a world he neither feared nor despised, but one toward which he now directed an almost childlike enthusiasm and curiosity.

The wind picked up, spinning the birch leaves, conjuring a liquid rustling that swelled into a river of breath, singing in a long-voweled rush, pouring along the curved throat of the old coach road; through the fluttering leaves, the lantern-lit windows of the village were fragmented into a fiery orange glitter, like the facets of a jeweled sun showing among the tatters of night; the white trunks of saplings deeper in the forest swayed like drugged dancers; and from somewhere close by, all but overwhelmed by the coursing of the wind, sounded the tinkling of a bell, a crystalline voice that spoke to Beheim in syllables of ice, telling him of something mystical and lost that he could know and be empowered by if he would only go forward now. Then the whole, wild tearing substance of that moment came into him with the abruptness of a revelation, and he wanted to throw back his head and howl, adding the windy noise of his soul to the great movement of time and fate that was carrying him off into heat and decay of the solitudes.

Alexandra murmured something. He heard only the words, "I wish . . ." but knew from the tightness of her waist, the hammering of her pulse, that she was still afraid.

He cupped her face in his hands, kissed her brow, stroked the cool, massy flow of her hair. The tension left her, and she relaxed against him. Over her shoulder he watched a squirrel hop out onto the road, its gray coat almost blending with the grayed surface of the dust. It stood on its hind legs, sniffing the air, then scampered closer, stood erect again. It showed no sign of fear, apparently undisturbed by their unnatural scent, and Beheim wondered if Alexandra's image had been apt, if indeed they had shed some dry scaly garment, some burdensome physicality that had prevented them from themselves blending in with the drab colors of the ordinary.

"Love," he said, using the word lightly, as a name rather than a pledge.

She pulled back from him, startled.

"Time to go," he said. "They might wonder in the village why we're not afraid of walking about in the dark."

He kissed her on the mouth, let the kiss develop slowly, flirting with her tongue, and when they broke apart, she caught his head and held it still, held his eyes, not searching, not trying to impress her will, but—it seemed—opening to him, allowing him to penetrate her with his own will, to give her his confidence. Something began to show in her face that he had never seen before, a kind of clean expectancy that had nothing to do with want or need.

"Well," she said at last, taking his hand. "I'm ready."

Night was closing down over the valley, wild stars showing bright as pain over Castle Banat, and as they walked with their heads bowed their hearts were racing, their minds heavy with thoughts of the future, of how they would pass the evening in the village of their weak and multitudinous enemy, and then travel out along the road of the willful blood, toward the end of an old romantic darkness and the secret splendor of the dead, toward the Light of the East and the hill of Mahogany, toward the crimes and sacred central moments of a new Mystery and the beginning of a strange green time.

Great contemporary literature from Bantam Books

Flicker

Theodore Roszak

A novel of superlative suspense in which innocence and evil flicker across the page like the play of light and dark on the silver screen...

"The book's heart of darkness—the terror of the unseen, the shock of sudden silence, the teeming world of monsters lying just out of sight—is almost perfect.""—San Jose Mercury-News

❏ 29792-9 $5.99/$6.99 in Canada

Outside the Dog Museum

Jonathan Carroll

Jonathan Carroll infuses all of the shimmering power of magical realism into this novel of Harry Radcliffe, a genius commissioned to design an architecural wonder that soon begins to reflect the architecture of the human spirit.

"I envy anyone who has yet to enjoy the sexy, eerie, addictive novels of Jonathan Carroll."—The Washington Post Book World

❏ 56164-2 $5.99/$6.99 in Canada

Under the Gypsy Moon

Lawrence Thornton

In the midst of the Spanish Civil War, novelist Joaquin Wolf learns what must be fought against, even to the death, as well as what is worth fighting—and living—for.

"Beautifully lyric...[Thornton's] prose is finely honed and his touch sure."—Chicago Tribune

❏ 55001-2 $6.99/$8.99 in Canada

Available at your local bookstore or use this page to order.

Send to: Bantam Books, Dept. FB 7
          2451 S. Wolf Road
          Des Plaines, IL 60018

Please send me the items I have checked above. I am enclosing $_____ (please add $2.50 to cover postage and handling). Send check or money order, no cash or C.O.D.'s, please.

Mr./Ms._____

Address_____

City/State_____Zip_____

Please allow four to six weeks for delivery.

Prices and availability subject to change without notice.   FB 7 8/93

DON'T MISS
THESE CURRENT
BANTAM BESTSELLERS